Praise for *Home Fires*

'Elizabeth Day writes with unflinching, responsible honesty'
Sadie Jones

'It's to Elizabeth Day's credit that she turns her back on the
conventional narrative to explore the realistic consequences
of war and violence on the women who, to cite the song to
which the novel's title alludes, keep the home fires burning.
Day chooses the tough option at every turn, with the result
that the novel becomes a powerful and, at times, heartbreak-
ing account of Caroline and Elsa's inability to deal with their
crises. The prose is crisp and forthright, particularly when
Day is describing the variations of violence, although she has
a piercing eye for a telling phrase or a poetic flourish' *Irish
Examiner*

'Brilliant' Viv Groskop, *Red*

'Day is an empathetic observer. She is meticulous in teach-
ing and dissecting each sentence her characters experience
... *Home Fires* conveys a broader version of life with the
claustrophobia of emotional repression' Eileen Battersby,
Irish Times

'Day has created a compelling study of grief, not least the
conflicting ways in which the bereaved may wish to remember the dead ... A bold novel, shocking in what it confronts
and also in its suggestion that love will, ultimately, survive
trauma' *Daily Telegraph*

BY THE SAME AUTHOR

Scissors, Paper, Stone

A NOTE ON THE AUTHOR

ELIZABETH DAY is the author of *Scissors, Paper, Stone*, which won a Betty Trask Award. She is an award-winning journalist who has worked for the *Evening Standard*, the *Sunday Telegraph* and the *Mail on Sunday*, and who is now a feature writer for the *Observer*. She grew up in Northern Ireland, and lives in Putney, London, with her husband.

Home Fires

ELIZABETH DAY

BLOOMSBURY
LONDON · NEW DELHI · NEW YORK · SYDNEY

First published in Great Britain 2013
This paperback edition published 2014

Copyright © 2013 by Elizabeth Day

The moral right of the author has been asserted

Bloomsbury Publishing, London, New Delhi, New York and Sydney

50 Bedford Square, London WC1B 3DP

A CIP catalogue record for this book is available from the British Library

ISBN 978 1 4088 4355 0

10 9 8 7 6 5 4 3 2 1

Typeset by Hewer Text UK Ltd, Edinburgh

Printed and bound in Great Britain by CPI Group (UK) Ltd, Croydon CR0 4YY

MIX
Paper from
responsible sources
FSC® C020471

www.bloomsbury.com/elizabethday

For my grandparents, who wanted me to write stories.
And, as ever, for Kamal.

Prologue

THE WATER IS CLOSING in.
Her limbs are heavy. Waterlogged like wool left to soak.
Slipping, sliding, she feels herself go.
She smiles.
Nothing to stop her from falling.
Not now. Not any more.

PART I

Elsa, 1920

THEY HAVE COME TO see the marching men.

She is holding her mother's hand, her fingers clasped around the familiar firmness of palm, knuckle, skin. She clings to it, tightly.

Her mother has told her that she must not, for any reason, let go in case they lose each other in the crowd. On either side of her, people jostle for space. She can hear the swish of ladies' dresses, the dry coughs and small exhalations. All around, there are legs and waists and shoes. She fixes her gaze on the back of a pale blue skirt directly in front of her, the heavy material gathered up in an old-fashioned bustle that sticks out as if it is a face, as though the skirt is talking to her.

If she cranes her head round, still holding on to her mother's hand, she can just about make out the street, appearing here and there in between the gaps left by shifting adult limbs. She wishes she could see better. She is always wishing for more than she has. When her father came back from the war, it was one of the first things he noticed about her: that she was too impatient, that she should be quiet and meek and talk only when spoken to.

'Bite your tongue, child,' he would say, even though he had been away for years and was a stranger to her.

She stares through the crowd, trying to focus on the procession. Her mother has told her this is a solemn occasion.

Solemn.

She likes the sound of the word, dense and slippery on the tongue.

There is a quick movement to one side of the blue skirt, a shifting swirl of something that Elsa takes several seconds to make out. Squinting hard, she sees it is the brown-beige lacquer of a horse's hoof. From her vantage point, she can make out the silvery glimmer of its shoe, a crescent shape nailed neatly into the curve of its foot. The horse walks forward. The road is coated with sand and when the horse's hoof makes contact with the ground, it thuds gently, the impact blotted by the granular surface.

The pale blue skirt with the bustle moves to one side so that Elsa now has an uninterrupted view of a broad sweep of street. A black gun carriage, pulled by six dark horses, draws in front of her. One of the horses is more jittery than the others, bucking its head against the bridle, nostrils flaring and shrivelling as it walks past. The crowd is quiet and then there is a rustling and when Elsa looks up she realises that it is the noise of everyone simultaneously removing their hats.

Behind the horse-drawn carriage, several hundred men are marching. Their feet thump with simultaneous regularity on the ground and behind that noise, there is another, less definable sound of the clatter and jangle of metal. Thump, clatter. Thump, clatter. As they pass, she sees the colour of their uniforms changing like a spreading bruise: blue into green into gunmetal grey, the shade of a thundercloud.

The silence of the crowd presses down on her. She turns back, tilting up her head to reassure herself her mother is still there. When she sees her, Elsa notices that her mother's eyes are glinting, that the tip of her nose has reddened. She is still holding Elsa's hand but her fingers have loosened. She seems distant, swallowed up by the men and women to her left and right, as if she is no longer Elsa's mother but simply a person among many others.

'Mama?' Elsa whispers.

Her mother bends down, leaning on the handle of her umbrella, bringing her lips level to Elsa's ears. 'Yes?' Her voice is distant, unspooling.

'Why are all the men wearing different colours?'

Her mother looks at her strangely. 'The soldiers wear different uniforms,' she says. 'Some are in the army, as Papa was, but some are in the navy or the air force.'

Elsa nods. She recites the names in her head like a poem: army, navy, air force, army, navy, air force.

The men file on by.

It was their next-door neighbour Mrs Farrow who had suggested the trip to London.

'They are bringing home an unknown soldier to bury,' she said one afternoon, sitting by the bay window of the drawing room, backlit by the fading sunlight so that Elsa could make out the fuzzy outline of downy hairs across Mrs Farrow's cheek. Elsa's mother seemed distracted but before she could say anything, Clara the maid brought the tea tray in, tripping over the edge of the woven silk rug and almost sending the crockery spinning to the ground. She managed to right herself just in time but her cap slipped down her forehead, giving her the appearance of a skittish, one-eyed shire horse. She looked flustered, embarrassed. Elsa felt sorry for her.

Her mother sighed and raised her eyebrows. Mrs Farrow glanced away, politely.

'Thank you, Clara,' her mother said. 'That will be all.'

Clara bobbed her head and mumbled something under her breath. She had often overheard her mother saying the war made it difficult to get good domestic staff. Perhaps, now it was over, Clara would go. She hoped not. She liked Clara.

Her mother did not immediately respond to what Mrs Farrow had said, but instead busied herself with the tea. Elsa watched as she poured the milk, a growing pool of white leaking to the edges of the cup.

Eventually, her mother spoke. 'Does it not strike you as being –' she seemed to be searching for the right word, 'a little morbid?'

Mrs Farrow laughed. 'Alice, the whole war was morbid. I think the burial is intended as a symbol.'

'A symbol?' She passed the cup of tea across. There was a plate of cucumber sandwiches on the tray, the bread springy and thinly sliced, the translucent green discs slipping out like wet tongues. Elsa looked at them longingly. She was always hungry and hated herself for it. Her father said it was unladylike to display one's appetite so nakedly.

'Yes,' Mrs Farrow continued, placing her cup and saucer on the lacquered side table. 'All those poor people who were denied a funeral, who did not have a chance to grieve for their fathers or brothers or sons.' She dipped her head. There was a small pause. 'Or their husbands,' she said, quietly.

The thought seemed to float between the two women, a leaden shadow that redistributed the weighted atmosphere of the room.

'But of course, Alice, it is entirely up to you,' Mrs Farrow said. 'I merely thought that, as I intended to go and take Bobby with me, you and Elsa might wish to come along too.' She stopped, before adding rapidly, 'and Horace of course.'

The mention of her father's name caused Elsa to breathe in sharply and to hold the air there, deep down in the pit of her stomach, where it would not make a sound. It made her feel small to do this, unnoticeable, a crumpled-up ball of paper that could be flicked to one side.

She sat on the chair by the fireplace not moving, straining to understand what was being said without appearing to eavesdrop, without drawing attention to herself. Through the corner of her eye, she could see her mother smiling her blank, colourless smile. Elsa had never met anyone else who could smile in quite the same way, so that whoever was on the receiving end of it could read whatever they wanted into the shape of her lips. It made her shiver to see it. The smile seemed to belong to another person; a borrowed piece of clothing.

She suspected that Mrs Farrow knew her father would not come, but the truth of it would not be spoken out loud. She glanced across at her mother. The smile was still there, fixed in place like glass in a window.

Her father didn't want anything to do with the war, not any more. He couldn't even touch the newspaper if there was a mention of the war on the front page. He would go out of his way to avoid the engraved plaque of names that had recently been erected at the bottom of their street. 'Our Glorious Dead' was the inscription across the top. Elsa thought that was an odd phrase. She couldn't imagine a glorious way of dying. Even Our Lord Jesus who died on the cross – how could you call it glorious when he had nails hammered through his palms and feet?

But that was the phrase they had carved smooth and clear into the stone, the lettering cut so deep that Elsa could fit the tip of her little finger in the shallow grooves of the curving G. The stone felt cold to the touch.

On the morning they went to Westminster Abbey with Mrs Farrow, Elsa's father was locked in his study working on his papers. They left him behind, even though he was the only one of them who had experienced the war first-hand.

Now here she is, holding her mother's hand and standing amidst rows and rows of silent strangers. Above her, the russet-brown leaves of the sycamore trees quiver and twist in the sunlight. Mrs Farrow says it is 'unseasonably warm' for the time of year and Elsa thinks the men in uniforms must be hot, the collars of their tunics scratching against their neck as they walk. Hundreds upon hundreds of them seem to march past her and she imagines that each one of them has a family akin to hers that stretches all the way back from children to parents to aunts and uncles and grandparents and nieces and nephews and cousins and wives.

At school, the teacher had once drawn the family tree of Queen Victoria in chalk on the board. It had branches like a real tree, but made straight and long, and where you might have expected there to be a leaf, there was instead a name, a date of birth, of marriage and of death. She had been intrigued by that family tree, by the simple beauty of it, by the way everything could be connected. She had found the idea of it comforting.

She recalls it now, mapping out a family tree for each of these soldiers in her mind's eye, the lines unravelling and criss-crossing through the generations, each interlinked branch expanding until she imagines the chalked-out marks covering the ground and the sky and the faces of the people who stood around her.

She begins to feel faint and her vision blurs around the edges. She blinks twice in quick succession to clear her sightline, dropping her head so that the muscles in her neck relax. When she looks up again, the procession is retreating into the distance, on its way to the Abbey. Someone has put a dented steel helmet on top of the coffin and Elsa finds herself wondering if it had been the unknown soldier's helmet or not. How would they have worked it out? And if it wasn't his helmet, whose was it? She does not like the thought of a soldier lying on his own, his head uncovered and defenceless. Would he be missing his helmet now, wherever he was? Wouldn't his family want it back?

Her arm is aching. She wishes she could shake herself loose and let go of her mother's hand. She twists back to look at her and sees that her mother is crying. She is embarrassed for her and shocked that she is showing such visible emotion in public.

But then Elsa realises that someone else is crying too. There is a tall woman in a pale pink cloche hat and threadbare gloves standing next to her. The woman has not made eye contact with anyone since she arrived a few minutes before the horse-drawn carriage came past. She had been flustered because she was late and her face had been covered in a light sheen of sweat. She had jostled her way to the front, bumping into Elsa as she did so but offering no apology. Instead, the woman had stood impassively to one side, her shoulders sloping. Her demeanour had not altered as she saw the coffin but now Elsa sees that tears are slipping down the woman's cheeks, making her face appear misshapen. The woman is sobbing openly, oblivious to anyone else around her. The sobs are dry little hiccups and they catch in the woman's throat as though she does not want to let go of them completely, as though she is frightened about what might happen if she forgets to control herself.

For a second, Elsa is ashamed for the woman and for her mother, but then her ears seem to pop, as if they had been filled with wax until that moment, and she hears the same scratchy sobbing sound replicated a dozen times over from all different directions. The whole crowd seems to be crying as one, their breaths heaving and creaking like a swinging rope.

She is unsettled by the strangeness of what is happening and, in search of reassurance, turns to find Mrs Farrow but her neighbour's eyes are shaded by the tree leaves and Elsa cannot make out the expression on her face. Mrs Farrow's son Bobby, who has been unusually quiet throughout the procession, is looking intently at his feet, scuffing the toe of his boot into the sand until his mother tells him to stop fidgeting. After several minutes, the woman in the pale pink cloche hat wipes her eyes with her gloved fingertips and turns to go. Slowly, the crowd thins out and disperses. Her mother lets Elsa's hand drop and Mrs Farrow suggests they should start making their way home.

On the train back to Richmond, the four of them sit in a carriage, empty apart from an elderly gentleman in one corner, his left eye obscured by a glinting monocle. For a while no one speaks.

'Alice, my dear, are you quite well?' Mrs Farrow asks. The train judders forwards, hissing and spitting as it does so. Her mother nods, listless. Mrs Farrow leans across to pat the back of her hand. 'That's the spirit.' She turns to look at Elsa and cocks her head to one side.

'What a day,' she says.

She has dark brown eyes that are almost black and Elsa finds that she cannot look away. She gazes back at Mrs Farrow without speaking. Bobby is swinging his legs against the train seat, his feet beating out an irregular rhythm.

'Quiet now,' Mrs Farrow says, resting a cautionary hand on his arm. He stops immediately and Mrs Farrow smiles, gently. She is a kind woman, Elsa thinks. Kind but firm.

She wishes she could say something to her, something that would explain how she feels. She wishes she could tell Mrs Farrow that she is scared to go home, that she does not like her father, that his return has changed everything for the worse, that her mother no longer loves her as much as she used to, that she does not know what to do about any of it, any of it at all. She wishes she could find the words, that she was old enough to know how.

Instead, Elsa breaks away from Mrs Farrow's gaze and rests her head against the leather-lined upholstery. She does not want to have to think. After a while, she falls asleep. The war fades away in her mind: a bubble pricked before it reaches the ground. For the remainder of the train journey, her thoughts sink under a shroud of blankness, the flakes of its quietness falling like silent snow.

Back at the house, her father is nowhere to be seen.

'I expect he's still in the study,' says Elsa's mother, removing her gloves finger by finger. She leaves them on the hall table in a careless heap. Elsa stands by the doorway, not wishing to make a noise. Her mother looks at her and something about the way she is hanging back, wordlessly, seems to aggravate her.

'What are you doing, dear?' she says. 'Close the door properly behind you and then . . .' The sentence hangs between them, incomplete. A single strand of hair sticks to her mother's forehead. Elsa wonders if she has noticed it there, the gentle itch of it against her skin. 'Why don't you go up and see if your Papa would like some tea?' says her mother, walking into the drawing room.

She watches her go and whereas, in the past, Elsa might have felt a lurch of disappointment at her mother's absence, she realises that her feelings have changed. She does not allow herself to need her, not like she used to. She thinks: I am no longer a baby.

Elsa, still in her coat, makes her way towards the staircase. She walks slowly, so as to eke out each second before she has to confront her father, before the shape of the day will be changed by his mood. She holds out her hands. The right one is shaking and she is irritated by this, annoyed with herself for not being able to steady her nerves.

Upstairs, she creeps down the corridor to her father's study. The door is ajar, a glimpse of sunlight streaming through in a narrow beam across the carpet. For a moment, she is dazzled by the whiteness of the light. Then, she can see her father, at his desk. He is sitting upright in the oak chair, his arms resting on the blotting pad. There is no evidence that he has been working on any papers. He is staring straight ahead, not moving, barely even breathing, and facing a blank wall that used to have a picture on it. There is a faint, discoloured triangle on the picture rail where once it had hung. It had been a faded reproduction of a country scene: a silty river, a hay cart, a pale blue sky, a man in a bright red coat. Elsa wonders where it has gone.

She knocks on the door. Horace starts at the noise. He shakes his head, as though to rid it of something and then takes out a pile of loose paper from a drawer, setting it in front of him.

'Yes,' he says. His voice is tired.

Elsa walks in. 'Good afternoon, Papa. Mama has sent me up to ask whether you would like any tea.' The words tumble out quickly. She dislikes how childish she sounds.

He shifts the chair round so that he is looking directly at her. She takes a step backwards, pressing herself as close to the wall as she can. His eyes seem unfocused, glittery.

'Tell me,' he says, leaning forwards, his expression intent. 'How was it?'

Briefly, she is not sure what he is asking about. And then she thinks: of course, the procession. He is interested after all.

'It was . . .'

'Well, speak up, child, speak up.'

Elsa clears her throat. 'It was . . .' she cannot think what to say. What does he want her to say? What is the right way to answer? 'It was busy.'

'Busy?' He repeats, eyebrows raised. Then he chuckles, a quiet sound that makes her nervous. 'What else?'

'It was impressive, sir.'

He nods his head. 'Good, good.' He stands up, without warning, the movement so quick that Elsa is startled. He comes towards her, arms behind his back. When he gets to within a foot of his daughter, he stops. He seems to be considering something, the thoughts scudding across his brow. And then he brings his right arm round to his chest and she notices that his hand is clenched tightly in a fist.

Elsa flinches.

He looks at her, surprised, then shakes his head again: quickly, in a succession of jerky movements.

'Did you think ...?' he starts. Then again: 'Did you . . .' He does not complete the question but goes to the desk and sits down so that his back, once again, is turned towards her. 'Go,' he says, the words sharp, unkind.

She stands there for a second too long. 'For God's sake, go!' he shouts and as she is running out of the study, she hears a crash and then a falling sound.

It is only later that she realises he must have thrown something at the wall.

Caroline, 2010

'CAROLINE?'

She can hear Andrew calling her from downstairs but she can't bring herself to answer. She lies on their bed, drifting in and out of consciousness, her thoughts half-disappearing into a grey sludginess that teeters perpetually on the brink of sleep. The curtains are drawn and fluttering gently as draughts filter through the gaps in the window frame.

They had been meaning to get the whole house double-glazed for months. Now, it seemed unlikely she would ever care enough to make it happen. Bricks and mortar did not seem to mean very much any more. The house had become a void; an unconvincing imitation of the home it had once been.

It seems almost funny to think of how concerned she used to be with how it looked, of how she had spent hours leafing through interminable sofa catalogues and pale, tasteful paint samples until she found the perfect combination of style and homeliness. She had liked the act of redecoration, of papering over something that she did not want to see. The smell of fresh paint, of clean, glossy newness, was soothing to her.

She had spent years refurbishing the house, stripping back the damp, acrid-smelling carpets, sanding the floorboards and covering them artfully with thick, woven rugs. She had painted every single wall and skirting board herself, from the duck-egg blue of the downstairs bathroom to the delicate ivory hues of their bedroom, offset by the wrought-iron bed frame and the dark, almost blackened wood of the wardrobe. She had discovered that you can learn taste quite easily. The home she had created for her family bore little relation to the Artex tiles and pebble dash of her youth.

There was one room she left untouched so that, now, still, after everything that has happened, the walls are magnolia, the floor is carpeted in a brownish-grey that does not show up the dirt. There are two stripped-pine bookcases on either side of the fireplace, the shelves devoid of books so that they stand empty as a toothless mouth. The wardrobe door bears the pitted marks of blu-tack and the shallow black dots of drawing pins withdrawn. The sheetless single bed, covered by a thin, tartan blanket, looks hollow. In this room, it is only the spaces that have been left behind.

Sometimes, when she passes the door, she thinks she sees him there in a lump beneath the blankets, sleeping in, wasting half the day, snoring gently. But it is always a trick of the light, or of the mind. And then she is forced to remember, all over again.

'Caroline!' Andrew's voice resurfaces, this time more impatient. She knows she should answer but she thinks hazily that if it is important, he will come upstairs to find her. She stays sheltered underneath the duvet, numbed against any sense of time by those oblong white pills the doctor has given her to blot out the sharpest edges of her grief. Xanax, they are called, and the name makes her think of a creature from science fiction, an alien being burrowing away inside her, reshaping her internal moonscape.

'These should make you feel a bit better,' the doctor had said, in an attempt to be reassuring. But they do not make her feel better so much as remove the need to feel in the first place, so that her distress becomes strangely separated from her sense of self. The pain is still there but it begins to exist almost as a curiosity, a thing to be looked at and acknowledged rather than the awfulness that envelops her, that makes existing on any sort of practical level seem impossible.

Most of the time these days, she finds that the best way of dispersing the encroaching shadow, the slow puddle that spreads across her consciousness like spilt ink, is to take another pill. She is aware that she is ignoring the doctor's advice. The printed label on the front of the brown plastic bottle tells her she is allowed a maximum of four over a period of twenty-four hours. Yesterday,

Caroline took six, convincing herself that she needed them, craving the consolation. Also, if she is truly honest, part of her likes the thought that she is deliberately causing herself harm. There is something so comforting in the thought of self-destruction, in the thought of painting herself out altogether.

'Caroline! Where are you?'

But there is Andrew to think about, of course. There is always him. Always, always Andrew . . . She hears him bounding up the stairs, taking them two at a time and the mere thought of this makes her feel exhausted. She is mystified that he can still possess so much energy. There is something unseemly about it, she thinks, something untrustworthy about his absurd good health. His hair has turned grey in the last twelve weeks but oddly this change appears to suit him, emphasising the prominent incline of his cheekbones and the dark hazel of his wide-set eyes. He has grown into his looks, the weathering of his flesh lending him an air of self-contained purpose.

By contrast, Caroline's looks have been slipping away from her, as though her physical appearance is no longer under her control. Her skin, once fair and smooth, has turned sallow. She has dark circles under her eyes and a delicate web of faint wrinkles at each corner, radiating outwards. Her lips have narrowed and dried so that she finds herself licking them without thinking, running the tip of her tongue across the surface, feeling the sticky bits of skin dislodge as she does so. She has lost weight and although she has always disliked being plump in the past, has always tried to shift the extra heaviness around her belly and thighs, this new thinness does not suit her: her arms poke out of T-shirts and her hair has got thinner at the ends, sparse as straw.

She is not yet so far gone that she does not care about these changes. She has never been enamoured by her own appearance but these days it makes her sad to look at herself in the mirror. She sees an image of a face reflected but it does not seem to be her. There is no recognition at the image in the glass. There is nothing there, just emptiness, a lack of expression.

She feels defeated.

* * *

16

She senses Andrew sitting down on the edge of the bed, his weight causing her to roll slightly towards him. She thinks: why can't he just leave me alone?

'How long have you been in bed for?' he asks and she hears in his voice the tone of disapproval. In fact, she does not know the answer. Her sense of time has become rather elastic but she knows she must offer him something concrete, so she lies.

'About forty minutes or so,' she says, choosing a number that is long enough to convince him she is telling the truth and yet short enough still to be within the realms of respectability.

He nods his head once, satisfied, and then he reaches out and strokes her hair softly. She has not had a shower for days and for a brief moment she worries that Andrew will notice the grease, coating the palm of his hand.

'Darling, you must try and keep going,' he says.

He is a good man, her husband. She knows this. He is good in spite of her badness, in spite of her being unable to pull herself together. He loves her still, even though he knows her love has gone somewhere else, has been lost and cannot find its way back.

'There's something I need to talk to you about,' Andrew continues and she notices there is a small note of hesitation in his voice. She can still read him so precisely, so intimately. This knowledge, which used to provide her with such a sense of security, now seems only to frustrate her. She hates the thought that they have become so dependent on each other, moulding their shapes and their silences around the solidifying shadows cast by the other person.

'It's about my mother.' Andrew's voice drifts back. 'She's taken a turn for the worse. Mrs Carswell called up this morning and said she'd found her in her nightdress, lying in a heap at the bottom of the stairs. We don't know how long she'd been there but she wasn't making much sense, apparently.' Andrew breaks off, waiting for a response. She opens her eyes lazily and meets his gaze. He looks sad and confused: a small boy. 'It was already hard enough understanding her on the phone so goodness knows what state she's in now.' He shakes his head. Caroline sits up, propping the pillow against the curved bars of the bed frame so that the coldness of the iron does not press through her cotton nightdress. The effort of this single movement leaves her momentarily dizzy and unable to speak. She touches Andrew's wrist lightly. He grabs hold of her hand too eagerly and lifts it up to his lips, brushing a kiss against her knuckles. She lets him hold her hand for a few moments longer and then slips it back down to the mattress.

'Poor Elsa,' she says and she can hear that the words are slurred. She tries to remember how many pills she's taken today but she can't. Not a good sign.

Andrew looks at her quizzically. 'How are you feeling?'

'Oh . . . fine.' Caroline turns away. She glances at the rosy wash of the linen curtains held up against the fading evening light. There is a tap-tap-tapping sound against the window like pebbles scattering across glass. 'Is it raining?'

'Yes, I think so,' Andrew replies. 'It might even be hail by the sounds of it.' He clears his throat. 'Anyway, Mrs Carswell said that she's not sure how much longer the current arrangement will be . . .' he pauses, searching for the right word, 'viable.'

'Oh?'

'She was very nice about it but she doesn't think she can offer Mummy the necessary level of care. She seemed to think that Mummy might need someone with her on a more permanent basis and she suggested . . .'

Too late, Caroline can see where this was going. A scratchy panic rises up her gullet and lodges itself there.

'Well, she suggested that maybe Mummy could come and live here,' Andrew finishes, speaking the words quickly so that the damage is done as quickly as possible. 'After all, we've got the room.'

She doesn't say anything but the thought of looking after anyone else, of having to plan what to make for dinner, of having to exist on a day-to-day basis, of continuing normal life, of picking it up where they had left off as if she were picking up a fallen stitch in a piece of knitting . . . the thought of it overcomes her and seems to press the breath out of her lungs.

'I know that the timing isn't ideal,' says Andrew. 'But she is my mother, after all, and I feel I owe this to her.'

His voice is firmer now, less apologetic. He has a streak of steeled strength buried underneath all those layers of politeness and good-humoured kindness and a strong sense of right and wrong. It is part of the reason she used to love him so much.

'Andrew, I don't know if I can . . .'

'Darling, I know you feel very weak at the moment –' She looks at him, disbelieving. Does he honestly believe that is all it is? Weakness? 'But maybe, just maybe, having someone else in the house might alleviate the pressure a bit.'

'You think I'm wallowing, that I'm being self-indulgent.'

'No, no,' he insists. 'I think you are having a terrible time, of course you are, but you can't go on like this. At some point, you, we, both of us, we'll have to get on with our lives . . .'

'And forget Max ever existed?'

Andrew looks taken aback. 'Neither of us will ever, ever do that,' he says quietly. 'But it's been four months now –'

'Three-and-a-half.'

'OK, three-and-a-half months and I'm worried about you. I'm worried about these things –' he takes the bottle of pills that is on the bedside table and rattles it in his hand. 'You need to start living again. And part of that is being able to look outwards, to think about other people.'

She doesn't say anything. She knows that this is Andrew's way of coping: always doing things, thinking about the next thing, losing himself in involvement.

'I'm not suggesting we move Mummy in immediately, but I do want her to come and stay with us. I know it's an awful lot to ask but she's old and fragile and she needs our help.' He looks at her cautiously.

Caroline closes her eyes. After a while, she feels Andrew stand up and hears him walk out of the room, his footsteps going down the stairs. There is the sound of plates clashing as he loads the dishwasher. She is angry at that, at the resumption of normal service in the kitchen below, and she reaches, without thinking, for the pills, pressing down on the white lid of the bottle so that the catch releases as she twists. Caroline puts one in her mouth and swallows it with a sip of water from the glass on the bedside table. Within seconds, she eases into the familiar fog. Her thoughts relax. Her mind unclenches and fills slowly with the whiteness of space.

The image of Andrew, washing plates, dissipates and his face is rubbed out, slowly, bit by bit, until there is nothing of him left and she falls into a state of numbness that is not quite sleep but near enough.

If she casts her mind back, she can remember the first time she met Elsa. The image comes to her completely intact: she is in the passenger seat of Andrew's car, feeling the sticky rub of leather against her bare legs, and they have turned into a short gravel driveway and parked underneath the bending branches of a yellow-green willow. She has to be careful opening the door so that it does not scratch against the tree trunk and then she must squeeze herself out, shimmying through the narrow space, making sure her skirt doesn't ride up her thighs as she manoeuvres herself upright and out of the car.

The house is medium-sized with latticed windows and a rambling rose climbing up the façade towards the tiled roof. The walls are painted the pink of iced cakes and there is a double garage with wooden doors to one side. Caroline has never seen a double garage.

'Do they have two cars, your parents?' she asks.

'What?' he says and then he notices her looking at the garage. 'Oh, I see, no, only the one. They use the garage for storage mostly. Actually, there's still some of my stuff in there.'

'What kind of stuff?'

'University stuff, old boxes of clothes, you know,' he says. She nods her head as if the idea of university is unremarkable but inside she is impressed. She likes the fact that he is clever and more educated than she is. Caroline had never done well at school. Her father had always said she'd never amount to anything and, after a while, she began to think he was right and stopped making the effort. If her Dad could see her now, she thinks to herself, about to go for lunch with her boyfriend in a house with a double garage. That would make him stop and think.

She is nervous as she walks to the front door, her arm linked through Andrew's. Sensing her unease, he smiles at her and pats her hand.

'It'll be fine,' he says and a lock of hair falls forward over his left eyebrow. Caroline likes the way his hair does this. It was one of the first things she had noticed about him.

'You'll be wonderful,' Andrew is saying.

She does not believe his reassurance, but she knows the appearance of confidence is important. She feels so lucky to be Andrew's girlfriend, so surprised and flattered that he would choose to be with her that she is constantly on guard in case she does something wrong, in case she says something that will make him see who she really is.

The front door opens and a woman emerges, arms crossed over the front of her oatmeal-coloured cardigan, a small, precise smile on her face.

'Andrew,' the woman says and she leans forward, bending from her waist so that she does not step out beyond the doorframe, and then she brushes Andrew's cheek against hers and kisses him but the kiss does not make contact so that all that is left is the suggestion of it.

Andrew's mother is slender and elegant and taller than Caroline expected. She is wearing a tweed skirt that stops just above the calf, belted tightly around her small waist. Her hair is grey but she does not look old, even though Caroline knows that she is in her sixties.

She glances down at Elsa's shoes. She has found that you can learn a lot about someone from their shoes. Elsa's are made from expensive leather, buffed to a gleaming black patency, and Caroline is surprised to notice they are high-heeled, with a flat gold circular button on each toe. The shoes are beautiful but impractical, especially in the middle of the Cambridgeshire countryside. Caroline finds herself wondering whether Elsa has different, outdoors shoes that she keeps by the front porch or whether she has put these heels on because she feels the need to dress for the occasion. She makes a mental note of this, storing it for later.

'And this must be –' Elsa says.

'Yes, Mummy, this is Caroline.' He places the flat of his hand on Caroline's back and she takes a step forward, leaning in at exactly the same angle as Andrew did for a perfunctory brush of the cheek, but Elsa puts out her arm and, slightly too late, Caroline realises she is meant to shake hands.

'Oh,' she stumbles. 'Pleased to meet you, Mrs Weston.'

'Do call me Elsa,' says Andrew's mother. 'Mrs Weston makes me feel far too old.' And then she takes her hand back a touch too quickly, moving it up to the silver chain necklace lying delicately across her collarbone as if checking it is still in place. For a few seconds, Elsa leaves her hand resting there, her long fingers static but tense, like a lizard on a rock.

'The pink walls are very pretty,' says Caroline and the words are out before she can stop them and when she hears them she feels stupid and wishes she hadn't said anything.

Elsa gives a mock shudder. 'Oh don't! We've been wanting to get them painted ever since we moved in.' She stands to one side, beckoning them indoors. 'Come in, come in,' and she leads them through a dark, windowless hallway into a room with mismatched armchairs and a cream sofa running the length of one wall. A large tabby cat is dozing in a basket by the fireplace and the sound of its purring mingles with the tick-tock of a grandfather clock. Andrew squeezes Caroline's hand, then lets go and, instead of sitting down with her, walks across to the bookcase, where he stares intently at the orange paperback spines.

She stays standing, shifting her feet.

'Where's Father?' he asks and Caroline thinks the word seems formal, stilted. She calls her own parents Mum and Dad. Or she did, before she left home. She pushes the idea of them away. She does not want to think of them, not now.

'Oh, he got held up with some paperwork,' Elsa says. 'Lecture notes or something, you know what he's like. Please, Caroline –' She gestures to one of the armchairs and Caroline sits down, perched on the very edge of the seat because she is aware, all at once, that her skirt is too short. She presses her knees together, feeling the flesh between them get clammy and hot, and then she searches for something to say. She is so desperate to impress Elsa, so keen that she should not make a fool of herself or say something wrong. She wants, more than anything, to fit in.

Her nose starts to run but she has no handkerchief so tries to sniff discreetly.

Elsa is bending down to the gramophone player, putting on a record and placing the needle carefully on the vinyl. A piece of classical music starts up, hesitant and stuttering. Caroline can make out a piano and some strings. It is soothing, she thinks to herself, relaxing. Perhaps she can ask about the music. She clears her throat.

'This is lovely,' she starts, but even those words sound wrong – her accent too nasal, her vowels too flat. 'What is it?'

Elsa walks across to the sofa, her heels click-clacking against the parquet floor. She balances herself on one of the arms, crossing her legs so that Caroline can hear the smoothness of her sheer stockings as they slide against each other.

'Chopin,' Elsa says. And then she smiles, brightly. 'It *is* nice, isn't it? The sonatas have always been a favourite of mine. What kind of music do you prefer, Caroline?'

Caroline feels her cheeks go hot. She does not know how to answer. She looks at Andrew for help but he still has his back to them, still examining something of interest in the bookcase.

'I – I – don't listen to much music,' Caroline says. 'But I like this very much.' There is a pause, so she continues. 'It's so –' she searches for the right word. 'So delicate.'

Elsa nods her head, slowly, obviously, as though she is making an effort to be encouraging. 'I agree,' she says in a way that suggests exactly the opposite. 'Nothing quite so elegant as the tinkling of the ivories, is there?' She glances at Andrew. 'What do you think, darling?'

He turns around, hands in his pockets. 'What would I know, Mummy?' He smiles, affectionate, joshing. 'I only listen to young people's music these days.'

Elsa laughs. She throws her head back as she does so, revealing the soft pallor of her throat.

'Oh darling, I hope that's not true,' Elsa says. 'You're not getting all rebellious on me now, are you? Do you know, Caroline, he was always such a serious little child. He used to look at me exactly the way he is now, even as a baby. The Steady Gaze, we used to call it.' She cocks her head to one side. 'Does he do that to you?'

Caroline shakes her head, unsure of how to reply. She stares down at the hem of her skirt, wishing she had chosen to wear something different. Before coming, Andrew had told her his mother was fashionable, that she liked clothes, and Caroline had taken this literally. She had worn the most up-to-date items in her wardrobe: a bright yellow miniskirt and a chiffon blouse with swirly patterns, tied at the neck with a bow. But now she saw that had been a mistake. Andrew did not mean fashionable – he meant classic, refined; he meant his mother had taste and wealth and breeding. He meant his mother was posh, but, like all posh people, he would never have seen the need to say it.

She feels acutely uncomfortable sitting here, in her out-of-place clothes and her overly styled hair. Elsa seems to have no make-up on other than a small circle of blush on each cheek. Caroline's lashes are caked in mascara. Her lids feel heavy as she blinks. She is worried that her eyeliner has smudged, that there are dark, unbecoming patches of black on her skin that everyone is too polite to mention. She has lost the thread of the conversation and it is only when she hears her name again that she resurfaces.

'So,' Elsa is saying, 'Andrew tells me he found you on a door-step?' She smiles as she asks the question but Caroline can sense the implied disapproval, the deliberate intimation that the idea of this is somehow ridiculous, to be made fun of.

'Yes,' Caroline says. 'I was locked out.'

In fact, she had been crying. A few weeks earlier, she had run away from home with £20 in her pocket. She had caught the train to London, found a room to rent in a dingy flat in Notting Hill and, after a few days, got a job as a cinema usherette in the Coronet. She spent the evening of her nineteenth birthday handing out mini-pots of Italian ice-cream and a middle-aged man had cornered her by the Ladies' and tried to stick his tongue down her throat before she kneed him in the groin, letting the ice-cream tray fall to the ground. She lost her job after that. She had soon realised that city life was not as liberating as she had expected it to be. She was glad to be away from her parents but she found she missed the familiarity of her childhood home, the dreary pebble-dash bunga-low beneath the flight path in Sunbury-on-Thames. She had been so unhappy there, had hated it so much and yet now, when she was finally free of it, paradoxically, she found she missed it. Still she kept trudging on, attempting to forge a new life for herself, eating unheated soup out of cans, buying clothes in second-hand shops, trying not to speak to anyone, not wanting to be discovered. She felt as though she could have slipped through the seams of life altogether and no one would notice she had gone. She became small, unobtrusive, silent. She left no trace. And then, one day, she had lost her keys, sat on her doorstep and started to cry. And that was how she had met Andrew.

'She was in tears,' Andrew is saying now. He is crouching down by the basket, tickling the cat's chin with the tips of his fingers and grinning at Caroline as he talks. 'I could never resist a beautiful damsel in distress so I did what any decent man would do and took her for a coffee to warm her up.' He stops and Caroline is flushed by the compliment. She has never thought of herself as beautiful before. Her shame dissipates, replaced by pride that Andrew wants to talk about her, wants to prove how much he cares in spite of his mother's unconcealed belief that he could do better. 'I'm incredibly grateful that she said yes.' He winks at her and she is flooded with happiness. 'So, here we are.'

Elsa smiles, her lips stretched like a rubber band on the brink of snapping. 'Well, that's a charming story,' she says, getting up in one swift, fluid movement. 'Do please excuse me. I must go and check on the chicken.'

After his mother has gone, Andrew gets up and comes across to Caroline, bending down to murmur in her ear. 'She likes you,' he says and Caroline is so surprised by this obvious lie that she laughs.

'She thinks I'm common.'

He shakes his head, bringing his face close to hers so that the tips of their noses almost touch.

'No, she doesn't.'

'She thinks I look cheap.'

'You look gorgeous. That's what I think.'

Caroline giggles, feeling the knot in her stomach relax.

'She just takes a while to warm up,' Andrew says. 'That's the way she is. Don't worry so much.'

He traces the curve of her cheek with his fingers. She thinks, not for the first time, that he must have had practice at this. He is ten years older than her, so it stands to reason he would have had other girlfriends; girls who were prettier, classier, cleverer than her; girls from good families who knew what a Chopin sonata was. But instead of feeling downcast by this, it makes her even more determined to please him, to keep his attention. She wants to be better than the lot of them. She wants to prove his mother wrong. She wants to love him more than he has ever been loved before. And she can do it. She knows she can. She just has to keep trying.

Elsa, 2010

ELSA HAS BEEN TOLD by Mrs Carswell that she is going somewhere. She knows that she has been told this many, many
times but still she cannot quite remember where it is she is meant
to be going. If she could just reach out that little bit further, she
thinks, if she could only stretch the thread of memory that tiny bit
more, she would be able to grab hold of the elusive fact.

She looks around her for clues and finds she is sitting in her
customary armchair and there is a battered leather suitcase in the
corner of the room, staring at her accusingly.

Where am I going? she asks herself.

Will the journey be long?

What will happen when I get there?

Much of Elsa's life nowadays seems to be taken up with the
thankless task of trying to remember things. It is as if she is trying
to see something clearly through a frosted window – the outline is
visible but the detail, the crucial sense of it, remains cloudily lost.

She blames Mrs Carswell for this. Elsa is waging a secret war
against her daily. She still calls her 'the daily', at least in her own
mind, even though, for the last few months, she has been doing
considerably more than simply cleaning the house. Mrs Carswell is
a fat, red-cheeked publican's wife wreathed in purposeful cheerfulness that Elsa finds especially irritating. It is Mrs Carswell's
briskness, tinged with condescension, that is so galling. It is always
'How are we today?' and 'Shall we tuck this blanket in a bit? We
don't want to catch cold do we?', always delivered with an inane
grin, always accompanied by the rapid, forceful movements that

make Mrs Carswell's flesh rise and wobble like a baking cake. Elsa will sit there, the blanket now tucked in so uncomfortably tight it seems to cut off the circulation in her legs, and the resentment will rise silently within her until she becomes more and more furious and determined to say something.

But she is never able to find the right words. Ever since she'd had that fall a while back, she has not been feeling herself. And then there had been a stroke – at least, that's what she has been told; all she can remember is waking up one morning with a burning sensation in her head, unable to move – which leaves her frustratingly incapable of expressing herself. She knows exactly what it is she wants to say and yet she can never quite remember the way to say it. When she does try, her tongue lolls loosely in her mouth and her voice comes out as an embarrassing groan. It is mortifying. She used to be so eloquent, so fluent in her speech, so intolerant of other people's grammatical errors and sloppy vocabulary and now here she is, an old saliva-drooling nuisance pushed around and patronised by her former cleaner.

When she tries to describe it to herself, the metaphor she comes up with is a crack in the pavement. There is a crack, a fatal gap, between Elsa's thoughts and the capacity to act on them and in this crack grows a thick weed of festering anger, almost entirely directed at Mrs Carswell, who knows nothing about Elsa's blackly murderous thoughts.

Sometimes Elsa entertains herself by imagining a giant speech bubble magically appearing above her head containing all the vicious insults passing through her mind at any given time. She envisages Mrs Carswell turning round from the washing or the cooking or the lighting of the gas fire or whatever menial task she was engaged in and being confronted by the brutal reality of what was going on in Elsa's head. Elsa can while away several happy hours imagining her reaction: Mrs Carswell's mouth would slip open slackly, the expression one of horror compounded by the sudden, inescapable knowledge of how much she was hated. She would scream, perhaps, or whimper in distress. Then Mrs Carswell would run out of the house, shrieking, never to return.

Well, thinks Elsa grimly, one can but dream.

For the last couple of weeks, Elsa had been taking her revenge in small but deadly ways. A few nights ago, she had unscrewed the hot water bottle cap and let the tepid dampness seep all over her sheets. It had taken her the best part of an hour to get her arthritic fingers to do what she wanted them to, but she had managed it eventually and when Mrs Carswell came in the morning to get her out of bed, there was a delicious moment where Elsa noticed the glimpse of panic on her face when she thought her increasingly infirm charge had wet herself. Ha! Elsa thought. That'll teach her.

'Dear me, what have we here?' Mrs Carswell said, roughly pushing Elsa over on to her side so that she could inspect the cotton nightdress clinging wetly to her withered thighs. 'What have you done to yourself, eh?' She tutted gently under her breath before spotting the hot water bottle, lying flaccid and shrunken at the foot of the bed. 'Oh my stars,' said Mrs Carswell, picking up the offending object and examining it closely. 'How on earth did that happen? I thought I screwed it on ever so tightly.' She looked at Elsa levelly, her piggy little eyes flashing with something like distaste. 'Well. It's a mystery.' But Mrs Carswell was no fool. She knew what this meant. Still, she wasn't about to let on. 'Let's get you up, shall we?' she said with exaggerated brightness and she started dressing Elsa in dry clothes, managing to strip and remake the bed with such efficiency that within half an hour, the episode seemed barely to have happened. 'There,' said Mrs Carswell, clapping her hands together once the task was completed. 'All done. Let's get you some breakfast, shall we?'

Today, Elsa is taking a different approach. She has been left in the usual armchair by the single-bar gas fire in what Elsa calls the sitting room and what Mrs Carswell insists on calling the lounge. From here, Elsa can hear the tell-tale ping of the microwave that signifies Mrs Carswell is making lunch. A wheeled table, of the sort they have in hospital wards, has been moved over to the side of the chair, the white metal tray lifted several centimetres over her knees. On the tray is a single spoon with which Elsa is expected to eat her food. The indignity of that spoon enrages her. She is perfectly capable of using a knife and fork, even if it takes her longer and the results are rather messier than she would like. But to be reduced to a spoon – such a babyish piece of cutlery! – makes her feel so powerless, so demeaned that she can barely look at it without feeling her eyes fill with unintentional tears. After staring at it for a while, she tells herself firmly to lift her right arm (it is almost impossible to get her left side to do what she wants) and slowly, she feels her shoulder socket click into action. She lifts her arm, heavy as a flooded sandbag, and feels a shooting pain across her chest as she does so. Elsa winces and pauses for a second to gather her strength. Finally, she manages to get her hand on to the table, to close her knotted fingers around the spoon handle and to hide it, as quickly as she can, under the chair cushion.

She can feel her heart beating lightly against her chest in a breathless tap-tap-tap. A flash of memory comes to her of when she was a small girl, lifting up a dying sparrow from the patch of garden behind the house. The bird lay in her cupped hands, its beady eyes swivelling frantically and Elsa had wanted more than anything to help it, to soothe its panic with a friendly touch, but she found she was unable to. The bird twisted uncomfortably but had no strength to escape. She noticed its chest twitching and realised after a moment that this was the sparrow's heart, twitching frail and fast against its feathers, pressing so forcefully against the bird's delicate flesh that it looked as though something were trying to escape and burrow its way out. The thought disgusted her. She dropped the bird on to the ground and ran back into the house.

And then, another memory: this time, she is wearing a cotton nightdress that is too thin to keep her warm even in summer. She is walking noiselessly down the hallway, being careful to avoid the creaking floorboards and it is night-time, the heavy sort of darkness that envelops the first hours after midnight. She is pushing open the door to her mother's room, reaching up with one arm to turn the handle, the brass cool and dry against the palm of her hand. She stops in the doorway, until she can make out the recognisable outlines of the chest of drawers, the heavy oak wardrobe and the bedstead. She starts to walk on tiptoe towards the bed, inhaling her mother's familiar sleep smell – clean linen mixed with the faintest traces of her hair and the sweetness of her sweat. She can hear the rise and fall of her slow breathing, calmer than it is in the daytime. And then she can hear another, unfamiliar sound, a throaty, deeper noise that she cannot place. But before she has time to work out what it is, the bed jolts and a large, dense shape rises up from the mattress. She hears the shape take three strides across the floor and she feels herself being lifted up, her chest squeezed with the force of two hands pressing against her skin. 'This is no place for little girls,' says a male voice and then she finds herself in the hallway, her mother's bedroom door slammed shut behind her. She stares down at her bare feet, her toes turning white-blue with the cold, and she tries for a while to make sense of what has happened but she can't and so she walks quietly back to her room, feeling scared and alone. She thinks: I wish my father had never come back.

Elsa starts at the thought, as though she has woken, quickly, from a desperate dream. The cushion she has been leaning against slips to one side and she cannot get comfortable again. She sees the brown suitcase, lurking in the corner like a shadow, and grimaces. It is strange how these glistening shards of the remembered past come to her, strong and clear as though they were more real than what is happening to her in the present. They are never the memories she expects to have – first days at school, weddings, family Christmases – those regular friends that become little more than well-thumbed photographs the more they are leafed through. They are, instead, memories that she had forgotten she possessed, memories that had been buried deep beneath the seabed for years before rising: a gleaming piece of driftwood, the bark stripped back to reveal an untouched whiteness glimmering in the bleakness of daylight.

She calms down after a while and can feel the reassuring lump of the spoon's outline underneath her thigh. She hears Mrs Carswell opening the fridge door, humming off-key as she does so. The radio is tuned to a station that plays unchallenging popular music for older people and Elsa can make out the occasional tinny chord of easy jazz, her irritation rising with each syncopated beat. When Elsa had been herself, the radio had two settings – Radio 3 for classical music in the morning and evenings and Radio 4 for the news and *The Archers* in between. The wireless dial never wavered from this strict routine: if Mrs Carswell had ever listened to her commercial rubbish when she came to clean, she was always scrupulously careful to retune it at the end of her two-hour session. Now, Elsa noticed, she doesn't bother. Dear God, it is boring waiting for a lunch that she knows will taste exactly the same as her lunch yesterday and the day before that. She tries to entertain herself by taking flights of fancy in her mind but after a while, even her own thoughts bore her. She remembers a book she once read when her eyesight was still workable about a man who had suffered a brain haemorrhage and who had woken up with his mind perfectly intact but unable to move. The only way he could communicate was by blinking a single eyelid. It had struck Elsa at the time as a peculiarly nightmarish existence but now, horribly, she feels she is stuck in a similar limbo. Of course, she is still able to speak after a fashion but it takes so much effort to form the words and she is aware that her periods of complete clarity are becoming more and more irregular. She can shuffle around on her own but her movements have to be self-consciously slow and considered and planned some time in advance of being executed. It is the helplessness she couldn't stand: the enforced dependence on other people.

It embarrasses her to be so reliant on Mrs Carswell, a woman she had always looked down upon and poked fun at in the past. She had not meant to be cruel or supercilious, but it was rather that her relationship with Mrs Carswell was marked by the benign exercise of an employer's power over her employee. Mrs Carswell had understood this perfectly well. She was staff. Elsa was a lady. They belonged to different classes, different backgrounds, different life experiences. They were fond of each other but only in a distant, careful sort of way. At Christmastime, Elsa would give Mrs Carswell an envelope with two crisp £20 notes and a box of chocolate-covered Brazil nuts that she knew were a particular favourite. Mrs Carswell would be genuinely grateful, her face flushed with pleasure. Every year, Elsa received a card in return, always festively emblazoned with a garish snowman or a winter skating scene, always written with economy in Mrs Carswell's roundly looped handwriting. 'To Mrs Weston,' it would say and then there would be the printed line – Happy Christmas or Season's Greetings (which Elsa sniffed at for being politically correct) – and then Mrs Carswell always added the words 'with best wishes from Barbara and Doug' even though Elsa had never spoken more than two sentences to Doug and never once referred to Mrs Carswell by her Christian name.

But Elsa's increasing decrepitude has changed all that. Now Mrs Carswell is in control and although she remains polite and respectful, there is part of Elsa that suspects she rather enjoys the shift in circumstance. Mrs Carswell is no longer intimidated by her employer, by her big house or her clever words, and she no longer exercises that quiet, particular deference that Elsa had always believed was her due. The balance of power has tipped in Mrs Carswell's favour but Elsa is not surrendering without a fight.

She can hear Mrs Carswell dimming the radio's volume in the kitchen – this is another thing that drives Elsa mad: why does she not turn the blasted thing off when she is leaving the room? It's a terrible waste of electricity, she thinks to herself, but people never seem to care nowadays about things running out.

Mrs Carswell's footsteps squeak on the linoleum as she walks down the corridor towards the sitting room. Elsa holds her breath in anticipation. She shifts in her seat.

'Here we are then,' Mrs Carswell says, carrying a tray through the doorway. She places it on the table with an unnecessary flourish. There is a plastic cup of water, a small glass bowl of tinned fruit salad and a plate of glutinous-looking pasta shells covered in a virulent red sauce that had obviously come straight from a packet. 'Let's just get this serviette in place,' she says, apparently oblivious that the word 'serviette' causes Elsa to wince in pain. She unfolds a cheap blue paper napkin and tucks it into Elsa's collar, rough knuckles grazing the stringy veins in her neck. 'There we are.' Mrs Carswell straightens up, casting her eye approvingly over the scene in front of her. There is, Elsa thought, something so *self-satisfied* about her. Then Mrs Carswell notices there is no spoon. Elsa can see it happen: the trace of a smile fading gradually from her face, the brow becoming furrowed, her expression clouding over with uncertainty.

'What the . . .' Mrs Carswell shakes her head, causing her helmet-shaped hair to quiver like a set jelly. 'Well, I'll be jiggered. I could have sworn I brought that spoon out here.' She stands for a second with her fleshy pink arms crossed in front of her ample chest, assessing the situation, a vague crinkle appearing between her eyes.

Elsa is delighted. She couldn't have hoped for a better reaction. It's the confusion she relishes the most: Mrs Carswell, who was always so sure of herself, always so practical and efficient, is now reduced to second-guessing and hesitation. Let her feel what it's like to be confronted with one's own forgetfulness! Let her be filled with doubt, with the encroaching sense of paranoia that her faculties are not what they once were!

Elsa feels her insides contract with joy at the point she has scored and, before she can stop herself, her lips curve themselves into a crooked little smile. She notices too late that Mrs Carswell is looking at her curiously, her head tilted appraisingly to one side. 'I don't suppose *you'd* know where that spoon went, would you?' she says, her voice light and good-humoured. She throws her head back and laughs, a full-throttled sound. 'Well I never,' she says, bubbling with jollity. 'You little minx. You'll be the death of me, you will.' Mrs Carswell wags her finger vigorously, as though remonstrating with an endearing toddler. She makes a great show of searching for the missing spoon as if it were a game Elsa had devised purely for her enjoyment. 'Is it here then?' she asks gaily, bending down and looking underneath the piano pedals and then when she sees that is not the hiding place, she potters brightly around the room, examining increasingly ludicrous objects in order to make the joke last even longer. 'Ooh, I know,' she says, picking up one of Elsa's precious enamel pill boxes, 'it's in here, isn't it?' Mrs Carswell opens the delicate lid with her thick fingers and Elsa holds her breath. The worst of it is that Mrs Carswell thinks she is being a terribly good sport. She thinks that Elsa *wants* her to make light of it, to include her in the pretence when, in actual fact, it makes the whole episode gruesome and painful because Elsa is powerless to put her sharply in her place and tell her to stop being so silly. She tries to form a suitably icy put-down but her mouth feels too thick and slow. When she does finally ask Mrs Carswell to stop, the sound comes out as 'shop' which triggers a whole new comic monologue. 'Oh I see, you want me to go to the shop and buy a new one, do you?' Mrs Carswell giggles, her cheeks pink with exertion. 'Well, I'm afraid I'm not made of money. I can't very well go and do that when you've hidden it, can I? Ooh, you little tinker! I shall just have to get another spoon from the kitchen until you tell me where it is.' And off she bustles, repeating, 'Well I never, well I never' under her breath.

Elsa watches her go. She is crushed by exhaustion. How could it have gone so awry? She can feel the tears starting again. Since the stroke, she seems to be unable to regulate her feelings in the way she had been able to in the past. Everything appears heightened: the most trivial thing can make her weep while the mere sound of her son's voice at the end of a telephone line is often enough to give her a surge of love. She has become emotionally incontinent. Now here she is with tears streaming down her cheeks, their wetness serving only to underline the dryness of her skin. She wipes her face with the back of her hand. She would have liked a handkerchief but there is never enough time to get it out from the sleeve of her blouse. Lately Mrs Carswell has got a bit slapdash about dressing her and today Elsa is wearing an over-the-top cardigan with an extravagant feathered collar over a plain, checked shirt. Looking at these mismatched garments somehow makes everything seem worse and the tears start dropping on to her blue serge skirt, leaving damp dot-to-dot circles in the fabric. And still she cannot remember where it is she is meant to be going.

She must pull herself together. She does not want Mrs Carswell to see her like this. It would be too undignified. But she can hear Mrs Carswell's footsteps and then it is too late because she is in the room, crouching down next to Elsa, her fat, kindly arms around her, saying 'There, there. No harm done' and being so nice and so sincere in her comfort that Elsa feels even worse. Why had she been so mean to Mrs Carswell? What had prompted her spitefulness? She cannot remember. She is suddenly awash with gratitude and wants simply to snuggle into Mrs Carswell's chest and be protected from the harshness of the world around her. More than anything, she wants to be looked after; she wants not to have to fight this constant battle to defend herself, to pretend her mind is intact. She wants finally to surrender, to snap the worn rope that connects her to the rational present and to allow her thoughts to dissolve like melting granules of sugar in a mug of hot, hot tea.

'It's because you're leaving, isn't it?' Mrs Carswell is saying, patting Elsa's hair softly with the palm of her hand. 'Oh you poor darling, there's nothing to be upset about now, is there? Andrew will take good care of you, of course he will. Yes, of course he will.'

And then Elsa remembers: she is going to live with her son and his wife in Malvern. Her son is called Andrew and his wife is called . . . what is her name? She can picture his wife so vividly – peaky face, too much make-up, a skirt that is too short, hair all puffed up like she had something to prove – and yet she cannot put a name to her.

And there was a child too, wasn't there? A son, blond and broad and beautiful. A son called Max. Yes, she thinks, Max, that was it, and she can remember him also, sitting by the fire, his breath smelling of coffee walnut cake, the crumbs of a just-eaten slice falling on to the rug, a shame-faced smile when he realised he was making a mess.

It is all coming back to her, she thinks in a spasm of clear-sightedness, but Max . . . something had happened, something bad. What was it? Why couldn't she put her finger on it?

And as she is thinking these thoughts, the questions chasing round her mind, a half-recalled memory comes back to her, the edges of it gleaming like the planes of a cut diamond catching the light.

It is a memory of a christening.

Andrew, 1989

H E   H A S   N O T   B E E N   particularly involved with the preparations for Max's christening. In truth, he is not even sure that
he wants his child blessed by a God he doesn't believe in, but Caroline has been quietly determined that it is 'the right thing' to do
and so he has gone ahead with it. These kinds of things are important to her.

In the end, the service goes without a hitch. Max is extremely
well behaved until the moment Caroline hands him over to the
vicar, at which point his face screws up tightly and there is a dangerous semi-quaver of absolute silence while he breathes in,
ominously gathering his strength before emitting the most gargan-
tuan howl. The baby looks at them all, clenching his fists together
and punching the air, simultaneously bewildered and disgusted
that he should have been placed in such an undignified situation.

Andrew finds it rather gratifying to witness this unexpected
streak of stubbornness developing in his son's character. But Caroline, her face pale, immediately lurches forward from the pew,
hand outstretched as though she fully intends to take her child
back. Andrew grips her arm to stop her. 'It's fine,' he murmurs in
her ear. There is a silvery thread of sweat in the dimple of her chin.
She has been panicky since Max's birth, more than usually anxious. 'He's fine. Leave him be.'

Caroline does not acknowledge him, but shifts away to one side,
releasing her arm from Andrew's grasp. She sits perfectly still and
Andrew is left feeling that he has done something wrong, that he is
being reproached by her, silently. But then, when they stand to

sing the next hymn, she turns and smiles at him and mouths 'Thank you' and the natural equilibrium between them is restored. He puts his arm round her waist, lightly, to let her know he loves her.

But the organist is thumping out the notes too loudly and a headache that has been plaguing him since morning thuds insistently back into life, pricking the tightness behind his eyes, so that by the time the small congregation emerges, blinking, into the midday light, Andrew feels untethered from the ground, as though he is viewing proceedings through a pool of shallow water, his ears muffled so that everyone's speech sounds disjointed and slow.

He removes his sunglasses from his jacket pocket and slips them on. The crispness of the autumnal daylight is immediately softened by an overlay of sepia. He looks around and sees Caroline, standing underneath the spreading branches of a sycamore tree just in front of a cluster of faded and slanting gravestones. She is laughing, relieved to have her son back in her arms, able now to joke about the timing of his tears.

'Typical,' he hears her saying to the vicar. 'He's been good as gold all morning and then just at the moment . . .'

Good as gold, thinks Andrew. She never used to speak like that. It amuses him, this habit she has of picking up phrases like a magpie picks up glitter. She tries so hard to be someone else, something better and yet Andrew loves her exactly as she is. It doesn't matter how much he tells her this. She has no faith in herself, he thinks as he walks towards her. No faith at all. 'Happens all the time,' the vicar is chuckling amiably. 'I seem to have that effect on babies.' His mother is standing next to the vicar in a smartly tailored two-piece suit in royal blue. She laughs, causing the feathers on her fascinator to tremble. 'Our son was just the same,' Elsa says. 'You should have *heard* the fuss that Andrew made. Of course, he's been compensating ever since by being so terribly sensible.'

Caroline giggles, arching her eyebrows to show she knows exactly what her mother-in-law means, that she gets the joke.

Andrew edges into the circle of conversation, giving a non-committal smile. He holds out his arms to take Max, overtaken by the need to hold him, to feel him close.

'Are you all right?' Caroline asks and he sees that instead of giving him the child, she has moved to one side so that Max's face is obscured by the folds of her blouse, the silhouette of her hip.

'Fine, fine,' he says, putting his hands back into his pockets. 'Just a bit of a headache.'

Elsa looks at him. Her face, still beautiful through the wrinkles, is impeccably made up: blended brushstrokes of crimson lipstick, brown-black mascara, grey eyeshadow at the corners of her lids, lighter brown on the inside. She smells lightly of tuberose. 'Have you taken anything for it?'

He nods. Elsa pats him on the arm. 'Some champagne will do you good,' she says. 'When we get back, you'll sit down and I'll bring you an ice-cold glass of fizz.'

He sees Caroline frowning and then he remembers: they haven't bought any champagne. Caroline had thought sherry would be more 'appropriate'.

'But first, I insist on having a cuddle with my glorious grandson,' Elsa is saying, moving towards Caroline with elegant arms outstretched, a discreet gold bracelet hanging from her left wrist. 'Oh I could just eat him alive.'

The vicar gives a giant guffaw, arching his back so that his stomach protrudes over his waistband. 'Grandparents have the best of both worlds, don't they?' he says. 'They can always give the little blighters back at the end of the day!'

The vicar carries on talking, but Andrew is not listening. He is looking, instead, at the interaction between his mother and his wife. Elsa still has her arms outstretched, is still waiting for her grandson to be handed over. Perhaps it is the headache that makes it seem such an interminable wait, as though the ticking of time has slowed down until it is more pause than motion. But it seems to him as though Elsa waits for several long minutes, her arms gradually sagging and falling back down to her sides when she finally realises Caroline is not going to pass the baby over.

And in this new, slowed-down world his head is inhabiting, Andrew is able to see each minute sliver of reaction in perfect detail. He sees his wife give an almost inconspicuous shake of the head. He sees her smile become rubbery and false. And then he

39

sees her tighten her grip around Max's gown, lifting up the palm of one hand to his downy head, as though shielding him.

He sees Elsa, for the briefest of moments, look as if she has been slapped. And then, almost immediately, she masks her face with a blank politeness.

He is astonished by the clarity with which he notices all of this. When his thoughts click back into normal time, nothing appears to have happened. The vicar is still talking. Caroline is laughing easily again, saying apologetically, 'I'm sorry, Elsa, I think he needs changing. I'll just take him inside' and then Elsa is tucking a strand of hair behind her ear, giving a meticulously understanding smile.

'I'll do it,' Andrew says and he understands, as he is offering, that this is a test, that he is wondering how Caroline will react.

'Don't be silly, darling,' she says. She walks off towards the vestry with Max squirming in her arms. 'You know you can't change nappies for toffee.'

For toffee. Another phrase that doesn't fit.

He looks at her go, he hears the brisk clicking of her heels against the flagstones, the sway of her skirt as she moves.

He puts his sunglasses back in his jacket pocket and takes Elsa's arm. 'Come on, Mummy,' he says. 'Let's make a start on wetting the baby's head.'

She looks up at him, warmly.

'Good idea.'

They say goodbye to the vicar and walk towards the car, where they sit in a charged kind of silence until Caroline comes back. He notices as she approaches the passenger window that her face is unreadable: a freshly polished piece of silver.

'All done,' she says, as she straps Max into the baby seat, giving him a small kiss on his brow before getting into the car.

The hem of Caroline's dress catches in the door when she closes it. 'Hang on,' she says, opening the door and retrieving the dress, now stained with a smear of grease. 'What a nuisance,' Caroline says, tutting to herself. She clicks her seatbelt into place, then twists round to look at Andrew and gives his hand a squeeze.

'No one will see it,' he says automatically. 'Don't worry.'

'You're right. It's not as if anyone will be looking at me, will they?'

'No,' he replies, turning the key in the ignition. 'It's all about Max from now on.'

As if on cue, Max gives a grizzly little whimper from the back seat. They all laugh, lightly.

Andrew releases the handbrake and the car judders forward. Behind them, the church recedes, its steeple gradually disappearing behind the rising bend in the road.

PART II

PART II

Caroline

For Caroline, it had all started with a knock on the door. Ta-tat.

A quaver, then a crotchet, thumped out against the wood.

She thinks now how odd it was that they knocked when there was a perfectly good doorbell, a square box nailed to the wall with a circle-white buzzer so that every time she passed it she thought of an unfinished domino tile. Andrew had installed it several years previously, disproportionately proud of his prowess with the Black & Decker drill she had given him for Christmas. At first, he put it too high up on the doorframe so that no person of average height would be able to reach it. Then he moved it down several inches, but the wood remained dotted with holes where the doorbell had once been.

So the point was: they must have seen the doorbell and chosen to ignore it. Perhaps, she thinks, it was protocol, an anachronistic gesture of respect from a time before the installation of domestic electronics.

Whatever the reason, it was a knock that signalled Caroline's life was about to change. The knock seemed to echo more loudly than a buzzer, its staccato force reverberating clean and clear against the hallway tiles. It bounced off the buttermilk-painted walls, pinging its way like a pinball up to the top of the stairs where she was sitting cross-legged on the carpet in her jeans, folding freshly washed pillowcases to stack on a shelf in the airing cupboard.

She called to Andrew to answer. It was a Saturday and they had been out for the afternoon, shopping for things they believed they

45

needed but probably could have done perfectly well without: cushions for the conservatory chairs, a new fig and bergamot scented candle for the living room, a long-handled spoon for jars of marmalade to replace one that had mysteriously disappeared. On the way back to the house, they had stopped for tea at the vegetarian café and shared a slice of carrot cake, the vanilla cream icing melting sweetly in their mouths.

There was no answer from Andrew and Caroline remembers being irritated by that. She remembers flinging down the pillowcase she had been folding and making her way hurriedly downstairs, cursing her husband's absent-mindedness under her breath.

It seems so trivial now to have got upset over such a tiny inconvenience – magical, almost, to think that her life could have been so content back then that she had to invent reasons to be upset simply to give her day a bit of texture.

There was another knock before she got to the bottom of the stairs: three beats in quick succession.

Was it then that she began to sense that things were not as they should be? Was it then that she felt the first thump of blood to her head? She isn't sure. There is a temptation, in retrospect, to claim some psychic maternal intuition that all was not right. But she doesn't think she suspected anything. It had been a very normal Saturday up until that point. She does remember walking briskly across the hallway so that she wouldn't keep whoever it was waiting.

She was still, at that time, mindful of the necessary social politesse.

She walked down the hallway and looked through the glass-panelled front door to see a warped beige-blue darkness, an indistinct, lumpy shape that gradually shifted apart into two inky shadows. One of the shapes appeared to have yellow stripes on one shoulder but when it moved, the yellow dispersed, swirling into flakes of confetti with each dent of the glass. She squinted, unsure of what she was seeing and yet aware that it was somehow an echo of a thing she recognised.

Something about the way they were standing, erect, unbowed, certain, made the pieces fall into place. In her mind, the jumbled sparkle of a hundred kaleidoscope fragments slid into sudden formation.

Two men.

Uniforms.

A knock on the door.

This is what happens when soldiers die.

She felt a hole in the base of her stomach, as though something had unclenched within her and yet she kept moving towards the door. She turned the handle and opened it several inches but then she stopped, not trusting herself any further. Her eyes were shut, as if she were a child who could make something disappear by not seeing it.

'Is this 25 Lytton Terrace?' said the first man. 'Are you Mrs Weston?' He was dressed in charcoal grey and wore a gold signet ring on his little finger polished to an iridescent brightness. She didn't notice his colleague until much later.

Time slowed. The seconds dripped like treacle from a spoon.

'Would we be able to come inside?' the first man asked. And she knew, then. She knew.

She bent over before he could say any more, clutching at her waist, head dropping down so that she did not have to look at them. For a few seconds, she could make no noise. It felt as though the next breath would not come but remain, halted, just beyond her reach. She moaned. She said 'No,' and her voice when she heard it sounded far away: a whisper on the opposite side of an echoing cave.

She slammed the door shut. She leaned against it with her whole weight, pushing the glass with her hands, fingers splayed against the light. She pushed so hard that her flesh turned white and numb. And all the time she was saying no, no, no, feeling the lurch of desperate nausea in the pit of her stomach, the sweat breaking out underneath her arms and trickling down her spine. She was shaking her head, refuting the thought that this could possibly be real. It was not true. It couldn't be.

The two men knocked on the door again, saying her name, trying to be kind, but she couldn't let them in. She would not let them into the house. She would not listen to what they had to say.

She thought to herself that if she could stop them from speaking, if she could keep the door shut, if she could prevent them crossing the threshold, then everything would stay the same. She would prise open a gap in time, a velvety corner she could squeeze into where she would be safe, cocooned.

She heard footsteps running up behind her and for a moment she thought that the men had somehow got inside the house and were coming to get her, but then she remembered Andrew. Her husband.

She remembered with a rush that he existed, that he was with her, that she was not alone, that there was a rational shape to things, and then she felt his hands around her wrists, his warm, reassuring palms firmly gripping her throbbing veins. He was murmuring, saying something to her that made no sense, but his voice was familiar and soothing and the tendons in her hands relaxed as he prised them off the glass and held them tightly in his. She looked at his mouth and it was moving and he was making a sound but it took several seconds until Caroline could understand anything.

'We have to let them in,' he was saying. 'We have to let them in.' And his face was colourless and scared and she was shaking her head, but he simply kept repeating the same phrase over and over and she was lulled by the weird rhythm of his voice and then she felt exhaustion come over her and she slumped against him while he opened the door and let the two men in dark suits across the threshold.

And that is how she learned that her darling son was dead.

Later, the two men tried to tell her how Max had died but all Caroline could hear was a vague blur of voices. She had the overwhelming sensation of being too cold and then she went limp in Andrew's arms, as if she no longer possessed enough energy to expend on even the most basic of tasks. He half-carried her to an armchair in the sitting room, upholstered in a flowered pale-green fabric and she turned her head and pressed her face into the back of it so that she would not have to look at anyone.

She breathed in the armchair's comforting scent of hair and familiar sweat and felt the roughness of the material against her skin. She stared at a sun-faded lily stitched into the fabric, noticing the curl of the petals and the worn-away threads of the stalk. She did not cry but according to Andrew, she was whimpering – that was his word, 'whimpering' – like a broken-down dog limping to the side of a road.

Andrew managed to ask the relevant questions, to elicit the desired information, his voice flat and devoid of emotion, his hands placed carefully over the curve of each knee-bone. The two men said that Max had been on foot patrol in Upper Nile State, scanning the African countryside for pockets of resistance and ensuring the safety of the local villagers, when he stepped on a landmine. For some reason, they didn't call it a landmine. They referred to it as an Improvised Explosive Device, or IED. An acronym. It seemed wrong, somehow, to reduce his death to three slight letters.

The landmine had exploded directly underneath Max's feet. He was thrown backwards several metres, landing on his back and snapping his vertebrae. A two-inch piece of shrapnel sliced his chest in half. It lodged itself so close to his heart that the army doctor who got to him some time later could not risk extracting the metallic fragment in case it increased the bleeding. The doctor did what he could to staunch the flow of blood, pressing down with his own hands when they had run out of balled-up T-shirts and improvised bandages.

There would, she imagines, have been a few seconds when it could have gone either way: that fragmented moment that lies between the everyday and the nightmare. And then, in a faraway country, lying in a pool of his own blood, he stopped breathing. And that was it for Lance Corporal Max Weston, aged 21. That was it.

When the men had finished speaking, Andrew offered them a cup of tea. They said no, and she was relieved by that; relieved that they did not have to pretend or act normally.

Caroline had questions. So many questions.

What was Max's last thought?

Do you have last thoughts when you are dying?

Would his life have flashed through his mind as one is told it does, or would there not have been enough time?

What would his face have looked like?

Was his skull still intact, the smooth dip into the nape of his neck that she loved so much?

Was he always meant to die at 21? Was the shadow of his death hanging over them all during those times they had together? Had they simply been too arrogant or too innocent not to pay attention to it?

Did he think of his mother at all?

Did he know how much she would miss him?

Did he know that he was her life, her everything?

And: without him, how could she go on?

In the days that followed, Caroline would spend hours sitting in the kitchen, a mug of cooling coffee cradled in her hand, thinking back to the time when Max was a child, searching for any clues she might have missed about the path his life took.

But the irony of it was that Max had never played with soldiers when he was little. Andrew had once given him a much-cherished set of tin figurines, inherited from his own father, in the hope that Max would carry on the Weston family tradition of reconstructing interminable historic battles on the bedroom carpet. When Max opened the musty cardboard box and inspected the soldiers' minute Napoleonic uniforms greying with age, their bayonets blunted by the repeated pressure of other children's excitable fingers, he was distinctly unimpressed. He was nine years old – the perfect age, one would have thought, for playing with action men.

'You see, this chap here,' Andrew said, lifting up a portly-looking gentleman on horseback, 'is in charge of the cavalry.' And he passed the toy to Max, who looked pensively at his father before taking it wordlessly in his hand.

'Why is he on a horse?'

'That's how soldiers used to fight. In the old days. It meant they could move faster and cover more ground.'

Andrew looked up at Caroline and caught her eye and she could see he was delighted by Max's tentative curiosity. He up-ended the box and the soldiers tumbled out in a metallic heap. Max looked on warily, the cavalryman still clasped in his hand. He was an extremely thoughtful child, in the original sense of the word: he would examine everything with great care before deciding what to do about it. Unlike most boys of his age, he was not given to spontaneous outbursts of random energy or unexplained exuberance. Rather, he would step back and evaluate what was going on and then, if it was something that interested him, he would join in with total commitment.

He was selective about the people and hobbies he chose to pursue but Max's loyalty, once won, was never lost. From a very young age, he pursued his enthusiasms with utter dedication. After a school project on the history of flight, he spent hours making model aircrafts and would put each new design through a rigorous set of time trials in the hallway, recording the results neatly in a spiral-bound notebook. When he discovered a talent for tennis, he practised religiously, hitting a ball against the back wall of the garage until the daylight faded. He met his best friend Adam on the first day of primary school and although they did not immediately take to each other, they became close through a shared love of Top Trumps and were then inseparable, all the way to the end.

But in spite of Andrew's early optimism, he never could get Max to play with those tin soldiers. For weeks, they remained in a haphazard heap on the floor – the cavalryman standing disconsolately on his own by the skirting board looking on with despair at the unregimented jumble of his men – until Caroline cleared the toy army away, putting them all back in the box which stayed, untouched, underneath the bed in Max's room for years. In the days after his death, she took to going up to his room and sliding the box out. She liked to find the cavalryman and to hold him in her hand and to think that her son had also held him like this. It made her feel that she could touch Max again in some way, as if a particle of his skin might still have been lingering on the silvery-cool surface and they could make contact, even through the tangled awfulness of all that had happened. She sat for hours like that, feeling the time ebb gently away.

Perhaps Max was a gentle child partly because he did not have to compete for their attentions with other siblings. It had taken them years to conceive and then, just at the point where it had seemed to be hopeless, Max had made his presence known. The first time Caroline heard him cry after he was born, she instantly recognised it as the sound of her child. You could have put Max in an auditorium full of wailing babies and she would have known. Andrew made fun of her for that, but he couldn't have understood. He wasn't there at the birth – men in those days weren't – and she felt afterwards that he had missed out. Deep down, there was still a part of her that felt Andrew was never as close to their son as she was. And now, as she sat in the kitchen chair, the lingering acridity of coffee in her mouth, she genuinely didn't believe his grief could be as profound as her own.

The military was the last career either of them had imagined for Max. He grew into a popular, self-assured teenager, the kind of boy that seems to radiate light. He was good at everything: academically gifted, a brilliant sportsman and yet he retained an artistic temperament, a kindness around the edges that set him apart from his contemporaries. His friends all said so at the funeral.

He was made head boy even though he attended the local boarding school as a day-pupil and it was practically unheard of for a non-boarder to be asked. They were talking about Oxbridge, wondering whether to put him up for a scholarship, and then, without warning, Max announced over dinner one evening that he wasn't going to university.

'What do you mean you're not going to university?' said Andrew, his knife and fork hanging in mid-air.

Max laughed. He had this infuriating habit of defusing tension with laughter – it always worked because it made it quite impossible to be angry with him.

'I mean just that, Dad. I'm not going. I don't think it's right for me.'

Caroline looked at her son and saw that, despite the twitch of a smile, he was totally serious. She saw, all at once, that he would not be dissuaded. She had always imagined Max would be a barrister or an academic, someone who wore his success lightly and yet who was all the more impressive for it; someone who was impassioned by what he did and yet not defined by it. She could see herself talking about him to her friends in that murmuring, boastful way that proud mothers have, dropping nonchalant mentions of his latest achievement into conversation. She had wanted everything for her son, for him to achieve all the things she was never able to.

But his announcement shattered that illusion in a matter of seconds. Caroline forced herself to adopt a lightness of tone.

'Well, darling, what on earth do you intend to do? Sweep the streets?'

Max grinned and patted her hand. 'Fear not, mother dear. I don't intend to end up destitute or homeless.'

'And before you get any ideas, let me tell you I certainly won't be doing your stinky washing any more,' she said, punching him lightly on the arm. Max squinted with pretend pain. 'Ow!' He grinned. 'Mum, you don't know your own strength.'

She laughed. Then she saw Andrew out of the corner of her eye, his face set in rigid lines of worry and disapproval. She wanted to reach out to him, to rest her hand on his arm and tell him it was going to be all right. But she felt torn. She did not want Max to feel she was taking sides. So she waited.

'What are your plans, Max?' Andrew asked after a while.

'I thought I'd join the army.'

There was a stunned silence, broken only by the sound of Max chewing on a piece of steak.

Andrew put down his knife and fork.

'The army?'

Max nodded. He pushed his unfinished dinner to one side, the plate still heaped high with potatoes and limp green beans. The butter from the fried mushrooms was congealing at the edges, like wax.

'Where on earth did you get that idea from?' asked Andrew. Caroline looked at her son and noticed his eyes getting darker. She didn't want there to be a scene.

'We never realised you were interested in the military,' Caroline said, trying to be conciliatory. It seemed to work. Max's shoulders relaxed. He was still wearing his tatty brown denim jacket for

53

some reason. Perhaps he had been on his way out somewhere – he had an incredibly active social life – but the brown bagginess of the material combined with his uncontrollable mop of hair gave him the air of an enthusiastic teddy bear. She had to stop herself from reaching out and pushing the floppy strands of blond hair away from his forehead.

'It's something I've been thinking about for a while,' he said. 'I know it's not what you wanted or expected for me and I'm sorry for that, but you've always taught me that it's important to do what you love –'

'Within reason,' Andrew interjected.

'OK, well, I know I'm good at schoolwork and exams –'

'You're more than "good", Max. You're academically gifted. Your teachers are talking about Oxbridge.'

'Dad, please let me finish. I might be good at school but I don't love it.'

'What do you love?' Caroline asked.

'I love being part of a team. I love sports and being captain of rugby and people respond to me, Mum, they do. I'm a good leader. I like that about myself. But most of all I like the thought of doing something that counts. That really, truly counts for something.'

'Oh come on, Max,' said Andrew. 'Wanting to make a difference is not the same thing as offering yourself up to get killed.'

'Isn't it?' Max looked at them both steadily, still slouched on the table, his chin propped on his hand as if this were the most casual discussion in the world.

Neither Caroline nor Andrew knew what to say to that.

'How can you truly change anything unless you're willing to die for it?' Max asked and it sounded like something he had heard, a phrase to be played with like a picked-up pebble.

'Well, that's very philosophical of you, Max, but I don't think you know what you're talking about . . .'

'Have you thought of going to university first and then making a decision?' Caroline suggested. 'At least then you can leave your options open.'

But she could tell, even as she was mouthing the words, that there was nothing either of them could do to change his mind.

There was something about the way Max was talking, something about the utter certitude with which he met his father's eye, that made Caroline realise he thought he had found his vocation. She had never heard him so determined.

They found out later that a serving officer had been to speak at the school, invited by the politically correct careers department who were no doubt keen to introduce the pupils to a representative cross-section of society. In the same month, the school also hosted talks by a high court judge and the home affairs editor of a national newspaper. For whatever reason, Max was not enthused by what these two had to say. It was the army officer who inspired him and, as with the model airplanes and tennis practice and as with Adam, his best friend, Max had given himself over entirely to the idea of becoming a soldier and would remain loyal to it until he died.

To Caroline's surprise, Elsa gave her unequivocal backing to Max's decision. Part of her wondered whether her mother-in-law was doing it deliberately, to show her up for her failings, to show her that she had never deserved the privilege of being Max's mother or Andrew's wife.

Elsa's phone call came on a weekday morning, when she must have known Andrew would be at work. Caroline immediately assumed her brightest telephone manner, obscurely flattered by the fact Elsa had chosen to speak to her and her alone. Normally, she would only have gone through the motions with Caroline – how are you, how's Max, how's the garden, what are you having for supper, that kind of thing – until, after a reasonable interlude, she could ask to speak to Andrew, as if Caroline were simply some sort of conversational gatekeeper that had to be got through. But on this day, it was different.

'Caroline, it's Elsa,' she said, even though the kitchen telephone had already flashed up with her number.

'Hello, Elsa. How are –'

'You simply must allow Max to join the army,' she said, cutting in. 'He's told me all about it.'

'Max has told you about it?' Caroline asked, incredulous. When had he done that?

'Yes, he called me last night and he says you and Andrew are opposed to it.'

Caroline felt her shoulders tense. 'We're not opposed,' and a note of defensiveness crept in to her voice.

Elsa backtracked. 'No, I'm sorry, I didn't mean to say that. What he said was that you were trying to be supportive but he could tell your heart wasn't in it.'

'Well, Elsa, I don't think that's so surprising.'

Her mouth was dry. She disliked the idea of Elsa currying favour with Max, of exploiting a momentary lapse in her judgement. She disliked the thought of the two of them being close, forming an alliance that excluded her.

'No, of course not,' Elsa said. 'I'm sure it must be very difficult to think of your son in that kind of danger but Caroline, you must realise . . .' And the next words were so surprising, Caroline was not at first sure she had heard them correctly. 'You must realise that young men need to fight. They need to get it out of their system.'

Caroline was so taken aback that she did not think to question then why Elsa said it. It seemed such a curious statement of fact from an elderly lady whose only son was an accountant. What could she possibly know about a young man's need to fight?

Elsa carried on talking. 'I'm worried that if Max doesn't do this, he'll end up feeling he's never proved himself. He'll take it out on someone or something else. He'll make stupid decisions. He won't want to be thought of as a coward.'

'But . . .'

'There, I've said enough,' Elsa said, resuming her customary briskness. 'I'm sure you think this is none of my business, Caroline, but for reasons I can't go into, I feel very strongly about this.' And then she put the phone down.

Caroline did not tell Andrew about the conversation but she soon came to realise that unless she showed Max her whole-hearted support, she would risk pushing him away. He would seek out other friends, people who were more sympathetic to his ambitions – people like Elsa. The thought of this scared her. She did not want to lose him. So she gave Max her blessing. In time, Andrew had followed.

There was no stopping Max after that. He signed up to 1 Rifles, part of the 12 Mechanised Brigade based in Bulford and when his parents went to Wiltshire for his passing-out parade after thirty-eight weeks' basic training, he stood proud and bold in front of them, his hair shaved short, his shoulders broad and bulked-out underneath the uniform and Caroline wore a bright red hat and Andrew wore a dark grey suit and they clapped along with all the other parents and smiled and flashed their digital cameras and shook their heads in shared disbelief at how grown-up their children seemed. Max, surrounded by friends, his tired eyes gleaming, was in his element.

She has a photograph from that day of the two of them, taken by Andrew. In it, Max is laughing, his handsome head tilted backwards. He has his arm around her and Caroline remembers that the stiffness of his uniform made his movements unnaturally heavy. She has her hand on his chest, lightly resting just below his heart and her lipsticked mouth is stretched into a smile that manages to be both joyful and anxious. But Max . . . well, Max looks wonderful.

Sometimes, now, Caroline will see other bereaved families on the evening news who have been trotted out for the television cameras by the Ministry of Defence and they look like half-people, their ghostly outlines blurred from the ghastliness of their grief. They look slumped and shattered, shuffling forwards as if their spines are sagging, grey-faced and shaken and not quite comprehending the all-encompassing reality of what they have just been told. Often, these families will have a statement that they wish to read out. Most of the time, this statement will contain a line about how, in the midst of this terrible tragedy that has engulfed them, they take comfort from the knowledge that Paddy or Niall or Ian or Geoff or Ben died 'doing what they loved'.

Perhaps, Caroline thinks, it should give her succour now to think that Max died doing something he loved so much. But it doesn't. It makes her angry that he chose to put himself in danger. It makes her angry that no matter how much she loved him, it wasn't enough, that he needed something else. It makes her angry that he's dead. And, above anything else, it makes her angry that she was too gutless to stop him.

Because, after all, what is the point of a mother if she cannot protect her only child?

His body – what there was of it – was flown back on a military plane. They were driven up to RAF Lyneham in a plush black Mercedes provided by the army and although they held hands in the back of the car, Caroline felt completely separate from her husband. She rested her head against the window, watching the motorway service stations skidding by, the spindly trees caked in exhaust fumes, the dull, overcast sky that seemed to stretch for ever in a uniform pale brushstroke, and she could feel nothing. She was numb, empty, hollow.

'You OK?' asked Andrew, turning to look at her with dark-circled eyes.

She didn't answer. She tried to nod her head but it felt like a lie.

Once they got there, they lined up with the other bereaved parents in a surreal sort of welcoming committee. One of the mothers, a thin streak of a woman with badly cut hair, smiled at Caroline and then started crying so that for a moment it looked as though her face had been split into two halves in a game of consequences.

Three coffins covered in Union flags were carried out of the plane's hull in slow succession, each one held aloft on the shoulders of six uniformed men who walked with respectful sombreness across the tarmac. It was very windy and Caroline's hair kept slapping across her face.

The woman who had smiled at her was now crying uncontrollably, segments of a balled-up paper tissue in both hands. Her husband had his arm around the woman but kept looking straight ahead, his gaze masked, two thick wrinkle-lines etched from the corners of his mouth down either side of his chin.

Andrew's arms were crossed. His head was angled to one side so that she could only just make out the pinkish trace of a shaving cut on one side of his cheek. A tear, translucent and slippery as a slug's trail, was falling down his face. Caroline was surprised to see it there and she realised that, until now, she had never once seen Andrew crying.

The sight of him – vulnerable but trying not to be for her sake – moved her. She held out her gloved hand and he took it, gratefully. But then, with her hand in his, she started to feel trapped, as if she were betraying something, as if to be thinking of anyone else but Max in this moment was a form of disloyalty. For so long, she had relied on Andrew to be her rock. But now, she did not want him near her.

For her part, Caroline had no tears. She found that her grief was so vast it blanked everything else out. It was as though she were in the middle of a storm, perfectly calm at its epicentre but looking outwards at the whirling mayhem, the engulfing waves and thunder-split skies, the spiralling madness of normality ripped apart at the seams.

As she watched the soldiers carrying the coffins across the tarmac, she found herself remembering – of all things – the time she took Max to have his warts treated with liquid nitrogen at the hospital. He was 10 and his middle finger had bubbled up, the skin becoming hardened and nodular. None of the over-the-counter wart treatments worked, so they had driven one morning to the hospital, Max sitting in the front passenger seat, holding his finger up to the light to examine it better.

'Why can't I keep my wart?' he said in his plaintive, inquiring way.

'Because it's contagious.'

There was an effortful silence as Max considered this.

'What does contagious mean?'

'It means . . .' she pondered how best to describe it. 'It means other people can catch them.'

'Like a ball?'

'No, like the flu.'

That seemed to satisfy him and he was very brave with the doctor, pressing his hand down on to the table as he was told, trembling only the tiniest bit when the liquid nitrogen was applied with the tip of a cotton bud. But Caroline could tell it hurt because he blinked quickly three times which was exactly what he had done two summers previously after fracturing his elbow falling off his new bicycle.

As they walked to the hospital car park, she asked him whether it had hurt.

'Yes,' he said. 'But I don't know how it felt.'

She looked at him, surprised. 'What do you mean?'

'It felt really hot but it also felt really cold and I couldn't work out which it was. It hurt too much to know.'

Eleven years later, watching him come back to her in a box and a body-bag, that was how it was for Caroline: too painful to know what she was feeling.

The casualty visiting officer, a whey-faced woman called Sandy, told them that the army would pay for Max's funeral. She told them this as if it were a great favour.

'So you and Mr Weston won't have to worry about any of that,' she said, with a sympathetic expression that looked as if it had been ordered from a catalogue of necessary human emotions. Caroline was in the middle of making her a mug of tea. Instead of answering, she asked: 'Do you take sugar?'

'Yes, two please.'

Two sugars, thought Caroline, how common. She had stopped taking sugar years ago after Elsa had commented, devastatingly, on her 'terribly sweet tooth'.

Still, Caroline thought to herself as she stirred the loose leaves into the pot, there was no accounting for taste.

She brought Sandy's tea to the table. They were sitting in the kitchen, in the extension they'd had built after Max left for his training in Bulford. It had sliding windows that opened on to the garden and the light that day was streaming through, showing up the dusty streaks and cobwebs that Caroline hadn't got around to cleaning from the glass. You couldn't see the Malvern Hills from the kitchen but you could feel their presence, crouching like cats across the horizon.

Andrew, sitting across from Caroline with a file of papers in front of him, nodded at the officer absent-mindedly and made a note of something on the uppermost sheet of typed A4. Sandy was looking at her expectantly, clearly worried that Caroline wasn't taking anything in. 'The army will pay for the funeral, for everything,' she emphasised, enunciating each word with extra care.

Something about the way she spoke, in that patronising, slow voice used by teachers when a child is failing to grasp an elementary fact, made Caroline snap.

'Am I meant to be grateful for that?' she said. Andrew looked at her cautiously.

'The army will pay for his funeral? Well, that's terribly good of you,' Caroline continued, her voice squeezed tight. 'How kind. Still, I suppose it's the least you can do given that you were the ones who killed him.'

Sandy coughed uneasily. Andrew reached across the table and put his hand over Caroline's. She snatched it away.

'They are doing the best they can, Caroline,' he said in a level voice.

She stared at him. She could not understand why he insisted on being so reasonable.

'They killed our son.'

He shook his head. 'No, darling, no they didn't.'

'They sent him there.' Caroline could hear her words getting higher and more frantic. He had never listened to her, ever. He had never believed her opinions were worth having. She felt that she had to shout, to be louder than he was, just to make him hear what she was saying. 'They ordered him out on patrol so that he could step on a fucking landmine!'

The swear word sliced through the room. Sandy put her mug of tea down carefully on a coaster.

'Mrs Weston, I didn't mean to . . .'

'Don't . . .' she said. And then, more quietly, almost apologetic: 'I'm sorry, but you have no idea.'

She stood up with such a jolt that the chair toppled over and clattered against the floor.

'Caroline,' Andrew said. 'Calm down.'

It was those words that tipped her over the edge. Arms crossed, she dug her fingernails into the fleshy part of her bicep, to stop herself from letting go, to remind herself that she must act appropriately. But inside, she imagined lifting up her mug and hurling it at the wall. It would shatter on impact and spray the room with porcelain shards. She imagined a brown trickle of tea streaming down the paintwork and gathering in a pool at the skirting board.

But instead, she swallowed her anger and placed the mug carefully on the draining board by the sink. Then she walked out of the room, more briskly than she intended, and through the hallway and then to the front door and on to the street where she walked and walked and walked until she could no longer feel the soles of her feet. She was scared by her own fury, by the uncontrolled nature of it. When she came back, several hours later, she had no key. She had to ring the doorbell and when Andrew let her in, he took her in his arms and held her close. She should have felt relief. Instead what she felt was resentment.

'Do we have to go through with this?' she asked Andrew when they were sitting next to each other on the sofa, sifting through possible funeral readings. The vicar had given them a slim paperback volume of elegies, a gesture that had initially seemed macabre but that later proved to be extremely useful. They had already decided on one of the poems to read. Something about not grieving the life that was lost but celebrating how it had been lived.

'I'm sorry?' Andrew looked at her, vaguely. 'You mean choose the readings?'

'No, I mean the whole thing. The funeral . . .' she drifted off. 'All those people.'

Caroline did not like the thought of saying goodbye. Everyone spoke about how important it was to achieve 'closure' but she knew that she would never be able to let go; that any notion of closing the door on her son was unthinkable, almost heretical. She knew that they had to bury him and that proper procedures needed to be observed but at the same time she felt uncomfortable – sending out the endless emails to his friends and making those nasty little phone calls to distantly connected relatives – that she had to share Max with so many others who did not love him anywhere near as much as she did.

Andrew reached across and cupped her chin with his fingers. His hand felt cold.

He was still able to carry out the unthinking gestures of the everyday in a way that Caroline wasn't: the smile for the postman; the steady hand for his morning shave; the brush of a chair surface before he sat down. She wanted to shake him. And yet he could not see it.

'Of course we need to have a funeral, Caroline.'

He spoke tetchily, the sentence heavy with tiredness. Neither of them had been sleeping. They twisted under the duvet, their minds contracting in the darkness, willing the night to be over. Then, when it was – when the blank, white sunlight had once again slipped through the curtains like a taunt – they emerged with their eyes puffy and black, remembering all over again; the temporary grace that came with a snatched half-hour of unconsciousness, immediately stained by the inevitable spillage of knowledge.

And Andrew would simply roll over and kiss her chastely on the cheek, as if it had been just another normal night's sleep.

Perhaps, she thought, it was his way of coping. But that didn't make it any easier to live with.

Andrew held her hand for a few seconds longer and then withdrew it. He picked up the book of poems and started to leaf through it, pretending that his attention was absorbed. After a few seconds, he cleared his throat.

'I know this is hard for you . . .' he started and even that expression – 'hard for you' – made her cross. To Caroline, it seemed merely the sort of thing one said in a conversation about the difficulties of finding a reliable builder or locating a convenient parking space. It was not something you said about your son's death. It was not something you said when your world had collapsed. 'But it's hard for me too and we've got to get through this together, as best we can.'

She shook her head and moved away from him towards the edge of the sofa. 'You don't understand, Andrew.'

'I do understand, Caroline. I understand very well indeed.' He stopped. 'I lost a son too.' His voice quavered and he fell silent.

After a while, he exhaled, slow and long. He stood and went upstairs. She could hear the sound of a bath running.

But whatever he said, Caroline kept coming back to the same conclusion: she did not believe that Andrew could possibly have felt Max's death as deeply as she did. The two of them had been so close. Mother and son. Right up until the end.

She remembered the day Max got his A-Level results (straight As in History, English and Chemistry), when he went out in Worcester to celebrate with his friends. A group of them came back to the house in the evening – they were meant to have gone clubbing but couldn't get in because some of them were wearing trainers. Andrew and Caroline had just finished dinner and were watching the news when they heard the unmistakable sounds of cheerful drunkenness – the exaggerated shushing, the clomping, irregular footsteps, the clatter of cutlery and plates as they tried to make sandwiches from what was left in the fridge.

'Sounds like they're back,' Andrew said, hitting the mute button on the remote control.

'I thought they were going to be out until the early hours,' she said, picking up the packet of After Eights they had been working their way through. 'I suppose I'd better go and see what damage they're doing.' She smiled: part of her simply wanted an excuse.

Andrew reached up and took her free hand in his.

'I shouldn't bother,' he said, patting the sofa cushion. 'Why don't you relax? They can look after themselves.'

'I wouldn't be so sure about that.' She leaned down and kissed the top of Andrew's head, inhaling the musky fragrance of his shampoo undercut with something else, a scent that was indefinably his. 'I'll be back in a minute. Why don't you go on up?'

Andrew didn't respond.

As soon as Caroline walked into the kitchen there was a chorus of whooping and catcalls.

'Mrs Weston! Dudes, dudes, keep quiet. It's Max's Mum!' She laughed, finding it funny in spite of herself. There were five of them slumped around the kitchen table in various states of inebriation. Max was standing at the sink, filling up a pint glass with water, expression bright, his hair tousled.

'Where did you get that glass, Max?' she asked.

He turned to look at her and laughed. 'The pub, I think.' His friends disintegrated into hysterics as if this were the most comically insightful epigram anyone had ever uttered.

'OK, well listen, I just wanted to plead with you to keep the noise down –'

'Yeah, guys, guys, guys, shhhhhhh!'

'– because we do have neighbours –'

A couple of them started giving an out of tune rendition of the theme tune to the Australian soap at this point, '– so if you could *try* and be a little bit considerate, that would be great.'

Caroline looked over at Max, still standing by the sink, sipping his water. 'Now, would any of you like something to eat?'

'Mum, honestly, you don't need to bother.'

'It's no bother,' she said, wanting to stay in the room as long as possible. 'You shouldn't be drinking on empty stomachs.'

So she knocked up a round of fry-ups, the sound of sizzling eggs mingling with good-humoured banter, and when they had eaten their plates of food, leaving behind butter-yellow slicks of grease, they became quieter, more considered. The air hung thickly with the smell of fried bacon.

She felt a minor sense of triumph at having handled the situation so well. She had never enjoyed this kind of relationship with her parents. Her mother had been a lousy cook, forever sending Caroline down the road for fish and chips, with a saveloy on Fridays for her Dad. She could still smell the grease, clinging to her hair, still taste the tart tang of vinegar at the back of her throat. Once, when Caroline was seven, her parents had not come home from work as usual. She'd gone to bed scared, without washing. They'd rolled in at midnight, reeking of booze, and forgetting that she'd had to fend for herself.

'We thought Kathy was babysitting –' her mother had protested. 'Ah well, no harm done, was there? You're a big girl now.'

It was Andrew who'd taught her that wasn't normal.

'Mum, can we smoke?' Max's voice brought her up short. The vision of her mother disappeared. She shivered. He came up and put his arm around her and his face had that special pleading expression that he did so well.

'No, Max, you know your father doesn't like it.'

'We'll open the French windows.' Five pairs of eyes looked up at her from the kitchen table in expectation, like willing Labrador puppies.

She hesitated. 'Weeeell –' She knew Andrew hated the fact that Max smoked. He hit the roof when he discovered a packet of Marlboro Reds in Max's sock drawer and since then had expressly forbidden their son ever to light up in the house or anywhere near it. But Caroline also knew that Max still snuck in the occasional cigarette at the foot of the garden.

Sometimes she joined him there and shared the illicit pleasure of a few drags. It made her feel good, like she was young again and doing all the things that she should have done when she was 18. She could quite understand why Max would enjoy the instant, head-numbing hit of tobacco. And really, what harm would it do just this once?

'If you open all the doors and the windows . . .'

Max, scenting victory, gave her a rough kiss on the cheek. 'Thanks, Mum. You're a legend.'

His friends grinned at her. 'Yeah, thanks, Mrs Weston. That's really cool of you.'

'And part of the deal is that you have to give me one too.'

So they sat there, smoking in the kitchen until the sky was studded with streaks of daylight and then Caroline passed out sleeping bags and duvet covers and went upstairs to bed. She slipped in beside Andrew, trying to curve herself round him like a bracket at the end of a sentence, but he shifted on to his front and buried his head in the pillow. She could feel, without anything having to be said, that he was annoyed with her.

Andrew was distant for days after that. She would ask him what was wrong and he would do his usual thing of shrugging and saying, 'Nothing, why?' and so she left it. In the early days of being with Andrew, Caroline had felt so reliant on him, so eager to please and to be taught how to behave. But when they had Max, the need for this had ebbed. She had found confidence in being a mother, a confidence she had never previously imagined she possessed. In those long, hazy summer weeks after his A-Level results, while Max was preparing for army life and his mates were getting ready for university or gap years, their home became an impromptu hang-out for anyone who happened to be passing. Caroline got used to returning from the weekly shop to be greeted by a motley assortment of overgrown schoolboys, their limbs sprawled in every direction, munching crisps and leaving crumbs on the carpet, swigging bottles of beer and talking loudly above a hailstorm of thumping pop music. For all that they tried to be recalcitrant teenagers, Max's schoolfriends were always unfailingly polite. When her presence registered, the stereo system would be muted and everyone seemed to shift in their seats, backs straightening automatically until someone spoke.

'Hi, Mrs Weston, hope you don't mind, we were just . . . you know . . .'

And Caroline would smile because she was never as cross as she should have been. In fact, she was delighted to find them there. She loved hearing the house reverberate with noise. She loved making them snacks, collecting empty bottles, playfully swatting away feet from the furniture as if it mattered. She loved how happy it made Max. She loved feeling so needed.

'My Mum would never be as laid-back as this,' said Max's best friend Adam in the midst of one particularly raucous afternoon. He was helping her load the dishwasher and Caroline looked at him bent over the sink, rinsing each plate with such care it hardly needed to be cleaned.

'Your Mum is a much more sensible lady than I am, Adam,' she said but she didn't mean it.

He laughed and turned round. He was as tall as Max – well over six feet with a shocking mop of bright red hair and freckles that ran all the way down to his clavicle. When he smiled, it creased up the whole of his face.

'Well, we all really appreciate it, Mrs Weston.'

'Adam! I've been telling you to call me Caroline for bloody years.'

He blushed and she knew that she had embarrassed him so she told him to leave the rest of the washing-up to her and he strode out of the kitchen with the uneasy gait of a man who has not yet grown into his body.

In spite of herself, there was part of Caroline that rejoiced in the realisation that she had the power to make a boy blush.

And then Max went to Bulford and they didn't see much of him for weeks on end. It was difficult for Caroline to get used to his sudden absence after a whole summer of tripping over his shoes. The house became enveloped in the silence of it, a lack of sound so noticeable, it seemed as loud as thunder.

She was mildly depressed for a while after Max left. She went with increasing frequency to the bottom of the garden to steal a cigarette. She had taken to buying the odd pack of Marlboros, just to kid herself that he was still around. He phoned a couple of times, but his calls were sporadic and only ever lasted for a few minutes on a crackly line. He began to speak with the sort of professional jocosity that the military seemed to encourage in its recruits, never really saying anything much apart from the fact that he was enjoying himself.

'OK folks, I'd better go,' he would say at the end of a conversation.

'All right, Max,' Andrew replied from the kitchen phone.

'Love you,' she would say, sitting upstairs on the side of their bed, trying her best not to show her own emotion.

'Yep, bye, Mum. Bye, Dad.'

Then there would be the click of a receiver placed back on the hook and both Andrew and Caroline would stay on the phone for a few seconds longer, listening to each other's breathing.

'You still there, darling?'

'Yes, Andrew.'

'He loves you too, you know.'

'Yes. I know.'

Andrew was patient with her, sensing how hard she was taking it. He was quietly reassuring, never demanding her cheerfulness, always solicitous and affectionate. He did little things, like renting a video of a film Caroline had wanted to watch for months and surprising her with it. He took her out for dinner a couple of times and said she looked lovely. He held her hand across the table and talked about their future plans, about their shared past.

They went on holiday, just the two of them, to a self-catering place let out by a golfing acquaintance of Andrew's in the South of

France. They had a blissful week in clear sunshine just along the coast from Cannes. They spent the days reading books on the beach on rented sunloungers, ordering salade niçoise for lunch from the uniformed attendants. In the evenings, they would go out for supper. Caroline tried lobster for the first time. Her face grew burnt, then the redness turned to brown and a spray of freckles appeared across her nose. They talked more than they had done for years and Caroline felt the glimmer of that first excitement, of youthful love, re-ignite in the pit of her stomach.

For a while, everything had seemed to be getting back on track. But then, when they returned, Elsa got ill and much of Andrew's time was taken up with sorting out her affairs, arranging for Mrs Carswell to come in and care for his mother on a daily basis.

And then, Max died, and nothing was ever the same again.

The night before the funeral, they invited as many of Max's friends as they could to the house for a few drinks. They thought it would be a way of making everything a bit less formalised and they wanted the funeral to be as much for his friends as it was for the military brass.

They had asked them over from 5pm but no one turned up until 6pm, at which time there was a gentle trickle of his army friends – big, hulking men with young faces and careworn eyes, their skin creased with experiences they were too young to have endured. Some of them, like Pete, a signals officer who'd been on tour with Max when he died, Caroline had met before. Others, she didn't recognise but they all came up to her and introduced themselves, shaking her hand strongly, saying how sorry they were but she could tell they were deliberately not thinking about it too much, as though it would be unlucky to dwell too much on death.

With awful timing, the news that morning had been dominated with the story of a South Sudanese man who was being trained by the British Military Police and had turned against them, firing his weapon in the compound just as five of his teachers were settling down for a cup of tea. Four of them died; the fifth was in a critical condition in hospital. And there these boys were, stuck in the middle of a mess that was not of their own making.

The army men made straight for the drinks table. Caroline noticed a couple of them downing swift tumblers of neat whisky before helping themselves to the cans of lager Andrew had bought from the cash and carry that morning. They drank and drank and drank and yet they never got drunk. The alcohol seemed simply to warm them up, to get them to a point where they could cope with normal social interaction.

Then, after about half an hour, Max's schoolfriends arrived in a succession of large groups, taking comfort in numbers. They were much noisier, more boisterous than the others. It seemed, after a while, as if they had almost forgotten why they were there and the atmosphere of the house lifted with the sound of party chatter.

Caroline made a point of greeting all those that she knew by name and those that she didn't with a shake of the hand. They had a book open on the cabinet in the hallway for people to sign.

'Have you written in the book?' she would ask, smiling tightly as though she were making small talk, her voice brittle. 'You must. You really must.' And she would give them a pen and press the book to them and stand there while they wrote. Some of them looked uncomfortable in her presence, unsure of what to say.

There was a man called Tim, an army colleague who had turned up in a badly fitting suit, clearly bought some years ago for a special occasion and not worn much since. His hair was shaved clean against his scalp, the stubble growth glinting in the soft light of the standard lamp. He had a wonky nose that looked as if it had been broken more than once. His ears were misshapen and swollen. Caroline, recognising the injuries as the result of over-enthusiastic rugby tackles, asked him if he played and he grinned, showing a row of gold teeth along one side of his mouth. 'Afraid so, Mrs Weston,' he said. 'And Max was always a fast little bugger. Couldn't catch him.' And then he caught himself laughing and his smile vanished as quickly as chalk wiped off a blackboard. 'Sorry,' he said. 'I'm so sorry for your loss.' She nodded. She never knew how to respond to this, although she appreciated hearing it. It was important to Caroline to know that other people were sorry. The worst was for someone to make no reference to it, simply to carry on as though nothing had happened, as though she might forget if the person she was speaking to did not mention it. Like those strangers she met who, when they found out, would tell her that 'time is a great healer'. She didn't agree with that. Time meant simply that the actual event was further away so the shock of immediacy had subsided. The grief was still there, just as profound as it ever was.

Caroline didn't expect Tim's message to say much but when he passed the book back over and she read it, she saw that all he had written was: 'The best die young.' That was it. It was not an original thought, nor was it particularly poetically expressed and yet something about its very simplicity seemed to convey more emotion than any amount of flowery sentiment. The combination of Tim's straightforward masculinity with this quiet, considered epitaph touched her more than she could have expressed. So she moved on, without being able to thank him in case her voice broke.

There were a lot of girls there too – shrieking, giggling, slips of femininity who were uncertain of how to act. To Caroline, they seemed so slight, so insubstantial in comparison to the army men. Max had been out with a few girls at school – light-hearted flings that would start at a party on Saturday night and seem barely to last till the end of the week – but no one remotely serious. Only once did he bring one of them home to meet his parents, a waif-like girl called Angelique with thin arms and long, raggedy blonde hair. Caroline had cooked lasagne for supper and Angelique had barely eaten her portion, instead lifting dainty forkfuls of salad into her mouth and chewing interminably. When Caroline had cleared the plates away, she had looked at her with a limpid gaze and said 'Thank you, Mrs Weston, that was lovely,' even though she had left more than she had eaten.

'Ange has got a tiny appetite,' Max had said. He had turned and grinned at her, placing his hand on top of hers, covering her slender fingers as if they needed warming up. Angelique had met his gaze and smiled and, in that moment, she seemed to change entirely and the coolness of her stretched, white skin had been infused with warmth.

That evening, before the funeral, Angelique was sipping on a glass of white wine, her shoulders hunched, her face pallid and smudged with too much eyeliner. She was wearing skinny jeans tucked into flat-soled boots and a black, long-sleeved T-shirt with 'Kiss' emblazoned across the front in white sequins. Her hair hung down to her chest, unbrushed and held back from her face by a thin, silver-plaited hairband. No one seemed to be talking to her so Caroline went over, using the condolence book as an excuse.

'Hello, Angelique.'

She looked startled. 'Oh,' she said. 'Mrs Weston. You remember me?'

Caroline noticed she had that habit of going up at the end of a sentence even when it wasn't a question.

'Yes, of course I do. You came for supper that time.'

She smiled, and again the whole shape of her face appeared to change.

'I wondered if you wanted to sign this book . . .' Caroline said, passing it over to her. Angelique didn't take it. The two of them stood there, uneasily, for several seconds before Caroline closed the book and tucked it back under her arm.

'It's just . . .' Angelique said. 'I wouldn't know what to say.' She started to tremble, pulling the sleeve of her sweatshirt over her hand. 'I'm not good at that kind of stuff. Max was always loads cleverer than I was, but he was so sweet, you know?'

Caroline tried to smile. 'He would never look down on me. He, like, really cared. I miss him all the time. I thought he was stupid to join the army and we kind of stopped talking after he left. And I know I was never properly, like, his girlfriend and that he could do loads better than me.' She gave a short, sharp snort of laughter. 'I mean, I was sooo not in his league. But he was so, so . . .' She let the sentence trail between them. 'So *sweet*.'

Caroline did not want to hear any more. She walked away and left Angelique standing in the middle of the room with no one around her, cheeks wet and legs twisted around each other as if she were about to lose balance. She didn't feel like offering the girl comfort. At that moment, she felt that she simply didn't have enough of it to spare. Instead, she went to the kitchen, poured herself a neat tumbler of vodka and downed it in a single gulp.

Andrew came in just as she was screwing the cap back on the bottle. He raised his eyebrows.

'Dutch courage?'

'Something like that,' she replied.

He came across to Caroline and she could see that he was about to put his arms around her but something stopped him from doing so. He pulled back, cleared his throat and went to the sink to wash up some glasses. There were trays of untouched food still on the table – no one had seemed in the mood for eating – and she started to wrap some of it in cling-film. A joint of ham they had bought at Waitrose, its skin studded with cloves. A platter of smoked salmon blinis. A bowl of grated carrot salad that Caroline had stayed up late to make the night before. Looking at it all now, she was struck by how awful it was to have put on a spread. It seemed so wrong, as if they were celebrating something.

A strange, snuffling sound was coming from the sink and when Caroline turned towards it, she saw that Andrew's shoulders were shuddering uncontrollably. The tap was still running but his hands hung immobile at the lip of the sink. His head was bowed. She knew that she should go to him, but she couldn't. She couldn't face it.

They had asked Adam to say a few words and when Caroline returned to the drawing room, she could see he had positioned himself with his back to the fireplace, one hand in his pocket, one hand holding a glass of wine as if he were about to make a toast. When she looked at him, she could still see the traces of the boy who used to play with Max in the garden, small legs spinning, knees grazed, cheeks red. He looked ill at ease in his suit, the sleeves marginally too long for his arms, and Caroline wondered whether he had borrowed it for the occasion from his father. The thought of that made her well up so that her contact lenses misted over. She had to blink back the tears so that she could see clearly again.

'Excuse me,' Adam said, his voice hoarse. 'If I could have your attention for a few minutes.'

The chatter and the clink of glass subsided and Adam blushed deeply with the knowledge that everyone was looking at him, the

73

redness filtering out from the tips of his ears and spreading across his face. She wanted to reach out and touch him, to stroke his hair back so that the tufts of it that always stuck out just above his sideburns would be smoothed down.

She felt a breeze against her side and realised that Andrew had come in from the kitchen to stand next to her. She gave him a quick smile of support. He smiled back and put his arm around her, giving her right shoulder a squeeze. And then Adam started to speak.

'I'd like to start off with a question for all the ladies in the room,' he said, his mouth curling up at the corners. There were some vague tittering sounds as people looked at each other, bemused. 'Please raise your hands if you ever snogged Max Weston.' The titters transmuted into louder guffaws and a male voice from the back of the room started cheering as if he were at a sporting match. Caroline froze. She could feel Andrew tense up beside her.

'Come on, ladies, don't be shy,' said Adam, taking an enormous swig from his wine. That's it, she thought, he must be drunk, no one will take any notice of him.

But then, slowly, the hands started going up, each contoured arm rising to the ceiling like a string trailing a helium balloon. Caroline could see Angelique tentatively raising her hand, the fingernails glossed with black nail varnish. All around her, girls seemed to be putting their hands up. At first, they looked at each other with vague embarrassment but then they began to smile and it seemed that their shared discomfort was turning swiftly into a badge of pride. As more and more girls identified themselves, Caroline began to feel faint. But she was aware, simultaneously, that people were scanning her face to gauge her reaction. She told herself that she must be a good sport and so she tried to smile, fixing her lips in place so that no one could see how horrified she actually was.

There were dozens of them: brunettes and blondes, blue eyes and brown, the blow-dried Pony Clubbers like Amelia – the blousy girl that lived down the road – and the drop-out, creative types with too much make-up and translucent skin, like the girl by the door whom she didn't recognise with dyed red hair, her wrists weighed down with thick metallic bracelets. The girls seemed to have nothing in common, no defining feature that would enable Caroline to understand why Max had picked them. But the sheer number of them took her aback. She thought that she would have known if her son was out kissing a different woman every night, but apparently not. And not only that, but he seemed so, well, *indiscriminate* in his taste. How could she not have known? This Max – the man that Adam was describing – was not her Max at all.

'I thought as much,' Adam was saying. 'In case any of us were in any doubt, here is the physical evidence that Max Weston was a legend.' There were loud cheers and clapping. 'I have many favourite memories of my mate Max,' Adam continued. 'He was always game for a laugh, always braver than I was. I knew him from the first day of primary school and I don't think there was a single day that passed when Max didn't do something that surprised me.

'I remember once when we were teenagers and Max was staying over at my house, we climbed out on to the roof through the attic window. It was evening and the sun was just about to go down. We were having a cheeky beer –' he broke off and winked. 'And Max said to me – like, completely out of the blue – "I bet I can jump across to your next-door neighbour's roof." I was like, "Yeah, whatever, mate." But then he stood up and, before I could stop him, he only bloody went and did it. It was a good six-foot gap and he cleared it easily. Just like that. And then, afterwards, when I asked him why he'd done it, Max just said "Why not?" '

Adam's voice started to go. He stopped, pinching the bridge of his nose between his thumb and forefinger. 'He might not have lived beyond the age of 21,' Adam said, looking up, 'but he achieved more than most of us will have done when we're twice his age. So, here's to my mate Max.' He raised his glass and downed it in one. 'To Max' said the voices in the room, breaking into raucous applause as Adam stepped away from the fireplace.

Caroline remembered too late that she didn't have a glass in her hand so she had to stand there, with a forced smile on her face while all the time she could feel her chest constrict. The room started to spin around her and she thought how odd that was, how she had always previously imagined it was the type of thing that happened only in films or books and never in real life.

'Caroline?' She heard Andrew speaking but could not find the words to reply. She felt herself being guided out into the hallway. 'I think you need to sit down,' he said and then he found a chair and asked someone to get her a glass of water and something to eat and he told her to put her head down between her knees until she felt better.

'It's all been too much for you,' he said, stroking Caroline's hair with a gentle, rhythmic motion that was strangely soothing. 'They'll start to leave soon and then I think you should have a long, hot bath and get into bed.'

She looked up at him and circled his wrist with her fingers, drawing his hand to her mouth and kissing the back of it, which smelled, as it always did, of Imperial Leather soap.

'Thank you, Andrew.'

'There's no need to thank me.'

'There is. I know I've been . . . difficult to be around.'

Andrew coughed lightly. 'Well, we've both had a difficult time.'

Neither of them spoke for several minutes. They just sat next to each other, Caroline on the chair, Andrew crouched in front of her on the carpet, listening to the noises coming from the drawing room.

'You know,' Andrew said after a while, 'what Adam said in there, it's just young men letting off steam.' He broke off and then added, 'You mustn't take it to heart.'

'I haven't,' she said, trying to make herself believe that it was true. 'I know what Max was like. He spoke to me . . . Well, he spoke to me about everything.'

'Yes,' he said, nodding his head slowly. 'You were very close.' But something about his tone didn't ring true. There was a hint of condescension there.

'What he got up to in his spare time was his business,' Caroline said, her voice suddenly hard. 'I don't know why you're going on about it.'

Andrew, still sitting on the floor with his legs outstretched, let his head fall back so that it thunked against the wall.

'Andrew?'

He didn't answer.

'I'm going to start clearing away a few glasses,' she said, standing up and smoothing down her skirt. 'Perhaps that way they'll get the hint.'

Silence.

'Do you want to come and help?'

He turned towards her. Then, wordlessly, he stood up, unfolding himself a limb at a time.

'Feeling better?' he asked flatly.

'Yes, much,' she said. 'Thanks.'

They walked back into the drawing room.

It was a beautiful day for the funeral. Max was buried underneath a balmy sun and a blue, cloudless canopy of light, as though the world was deliberately showing them all what he would miss.

Caroline, still drained from the night before, found the service itself curiously empty of emotion. The ceremony of it was off-putting, as though everyone believed her grief would be assuaged by the neat precision of hymn and prayer. As the vicar spoke, inevitably, of life snatched away too soon and how we should be thankful not for the time we had lost with Max but for the time we had been given with him, she felt a furious resentment, as if her sadness were being belittled, as if it were no longer unique to her.

She cried only once, when Max's coffin was lifted out of the church on the shoulders of his pallbearers, draped in a Union flag. It was the flag that upset Caroline; the idea of something so big, so important – the emblem of an entire country – weighing down on the body of her little boy.

They did what was expected of them. They walked to the graveside and threw handfuls of earth on to their child's coffin, listening as it struck the wood with a scrabbling sound. They shook hands and nodded their heads and thanked people with small, sad smiles. They acknowledged the representatives sent by the army, straight-backed and proper and formal in their speech. They served tumblers of whisky at the wake and damp mushroom vol-au-vents that came, in bulk, from the supermarket. They did it all. And then, at the end of the day, when everyone had left and when Max had been buried under six feet of soil, they were left with the sudden emptiness of each other. Andrew and Caroline, with nothing in between. That was, until Elsa came to stay.

PART III

Andrew

IT IS A LONG drive to his mother's house but Andrew has always rather liked the journey. He enjoys the cocooned sense of being in a car on his own, going somewhere, moving steadily towards his destination with nowhere else to be and nothing else to do apart from shift gears and turn the steering wheel. He likes not having to speak to someone in the passenger seat, not having to feel responsible for their safety as well as his own and being able to take risks, go faster, brake more quickly than he would if there were other people in the car. He likes the comforting wide expanse of motorway, the tarmac smooth against the tyres and the soothing regularity of service stations, each one looking the same as the last with their coffee bars and amusement arcade machines and Cellophane-wrapped bunches of flowers limply propped up in buckets only to be ignored by the motorists passing through.

He stops off at one of these at the halfway point, about two hours into the journey from Malvern to Grantchester. It is only 10am and yet Andrew feels his stomach grumbling with hunger. He had been in a hurry to leave this morning and had not had time for a proper breakfast, choosing instead to butter a piece of bread and take it with him to the car, the crumbs falling messily on to his fleece top as he ate.

Caroline used to make his breakfast every morning before he left for work: a bowl of shop-bought muesli to which she added her own mixture of brazil nuts and raisins, two slices of wholemeal toast accompanied by butter on a dish and a jar of home-made marmalade with a long spoon so that the handle didn't get sticky.

She would get up when his alarm went off, kiss him good morning and then put on her dressing gown and go straight downstairs to get things ready while he took a shower. Andrew had loved the routine of it, the quiet but thoughtful ways in which their affection was expressed. He would dry himself off in the bathroom and the smell of toast would waft up from the kitchen. When he came downstairs, freshly shaven and in his shirt and tie, Caroline would put the kettle on and, after it boiled, she would warm the teapot before making the tea. Every weekday morning would be just the same, consoling in its familiarity. Andrew liked knowing what to expect.

She seemed to take pride in being his wife, in looking after him. He remembers the morning after their wedding day, when she had turned to him in the hotel room bed and said, blue eyes unblinking and wide: 'You saved me.'

He had been so startled by that, so unsure of what it meant. 'No I haven't,' he said, trying to brush the intensity of her words aside. 'I love you. I want to be with you.'

But she shook her head. 'No, you don't understand. I . . . I . . .'

She had been shy back then, nervous about expressing herself. 'I don't feel worthy of you,' she said finally, hiding her mouth with the tips of her fingers as though trying to put the words back in.

He had held her tightly to him and kissed her then, trying to dissipate her anxieties, to make her feel safe. He sensed that he held something terribly fragile in his arms, a damaged girl who wanted more than anything to be loved. Through the years, she had spoken to him only vaguely of her parents, but it was enough for him to get cross every time she mentioned them, to insist that she never had to see them again if she didn't want to. It sounded as if she had grown up in a household bereft of love, as though her parents saw her as an inconvenience, an obstacle to their own enjoyment. She told him that they had ignored her, treating her as little more than a domestic encumbrance as they carried on with their lives. Both of them had worked long hours – leaving the house early in the morning and returning late at night, by which stage Caroline was expected to have walked home from school and to have fed herself. It was too much for a young, sensitive girl.

Little wonder, he thought, that she had yearned to escape, that what she had craved all these years was a kind of acceptance.

He wanted, more than anything, to protect her. And he loved her, desperately, but he was aware that he had to be gentle, consistent, soft so as not to scare her off. She had grown to trust him and then, as the years passed, he noticed her beginning to change, to acquire the gloss of social ease. At first, it was almost imperceptible, those tiny accents of conversation that had once given her away – she started to use 'sofa' rather than 'settee', to ask where the 'lavatory' was, rather than the 'ladies', to say 'How do you do?' not 'Pleased to meet you.' The change accelerated in the early years of their marriage. She started ordering her clothes from the same shop as his mother – knee-length shift dresses and neatly buttoned cardigans, when he had always rather liked the mismatched, wayward way she used to dress. She cut her long hair so that it curled under, just beneath the ears, and dyed it so that it was flecked through with lighter, caramel streaks. She learned to cook. She sent Elsa carefully worded birthday cards, written in the round, simple writing that remained ineradicably hers. Her accent lost its rougher edges. Then, she had Max and, in many ways, her transformation was complete.

Perhaps he should have been happier for her, Andrew thinks, flicking up the indicator and hearing the familiar tick-tick-tick before turning carefully into the slip-road. He wonders why he wasn't more supportive of Caroline's obvious attempts to better herself but he thinks, deep down, it is because he never wanted her to change. He had loved her as she was: unvarnished; real. He had loved her because she wasn't his mother.

She had loved him too, of course. Of that he was certain. But now, he isn't sure how she feels about him. All her energies, all of her emotions seem to have been swamped by grief. It is as if, yet again, she doesn't have room in her life for anyone but Max.

He parks the car, carefully checking each of his mirrors as he reverses into a space. He is a precise, sensible driver and an excellent parker. Although Caroline had passed her test just before Max was born, she tended to leave most of the driving to him, which was a source of secret pride. Andrew liked the idea of protecting his woman, of delivering her safely to her chosen destination. But recently, he had started to wish that she took more of an initiative. He desperately wanted Caroline to get out of the house more, to visit some friends or go to that yoga class she had taken up when Max was sent abroad. Anything, really, to take her mind off things. Instead, she spent all day in her pyjamas, moping around in bed or on the sofa, watching daytime television and eating out of cans. And any time Andrew suggested doing something, she gave him that look, the one that left him feeling both ignorant and pathetic, as if he were incapable of knowing what she was going through. It would surprise Caroline to know how clearly Andrew sees what she thinks of him. But he can read her very easily. The merest movement of her eyebrow or the tiniest curl of her lip – these are the things one notices after almost thirty years of married life.

He switches off the ignition and un-clicks his seatbelt, stepping out of the car into the drizzly morning air. He breathes in deeply, stretching his legs and arms and groaning as he does so. It is a habit he has. Caroline used to poke fun at him for stretching every morning but he is convinced it kept his limbs supple. When they first met, Caroline had been charmed by what she called his 'old man ways'. But now, at 62, his physical age has caught up with him.

He walks into the service station, the automatic doors parting with a whirr as he approaches. Inside, there is a cacophonous noise of screaming children and the pinging of cashier tills, all somehow intensified by the unforgiving strip lighting that tinged everyone's face with green-grey shadows. He makes straight for the gents' toilets, which are being cleaned by a delicately boned Chinese man who is pushing around a trolley and a mop with a desultory expression on his face. Andrew never knows what to do in this sort of situation: should he acknowledge the cleaner with a smile and a nod of the head or would the man think it patronising? In the end, he can't decide and so settles for a curious half-grimace that makes the cleaner frown and leaves Andrew feeling uncomfortable. He has always been socially awkward. His mother, by contrast, had excelled at small-talk. Andrew is shy, gauche and finds it difficult to chatter away meaninglessly to put someone at ease. He is not sure why this is. Partly because of his height and his smoothly handsome appearance, people expect him to be charming and silken-tongued, to possess a certain sort of presence or arrogance, but Andrew has neither.

In many ways, Max had been unlike either of his parents. He seemed to have been born with an innate, quiet confidence that his way of doing things was the right way. At school, he had been popular without ever appearing to try. And yet he had still been able to see things from another person's point of view. Not many young men had that quality.

But he had his faults too, Andrew thinks as he puts his hands in one of those ergonomic hand dryers that never work as well as a towel. He is not as blinded to his son's weaknesses of character as Caroline is.

He thinks it is probably this that has been the source of much of the recent tension. There was that awful drinks party the night before the funeral, where Caroline had stood, stiff with disapproval, as Adam delivered his speech. Andrew shudders now to think of it: the sour way she had twisted her lips and crossed her arms in front of her chest; her utter refusal to accept any offer of comfort; her total ignorance of the fact that anyone looking at her could see quite clearly what was going on. She truly believed she had masked her real emotions, but afterwards Adam had come up to Andrew and apologised, saying he hoped he hadn't offended her. Andrew hadn't passed the sentiments on to Caroline because he knew she would pretend not to know what he was talking about. And, underneath, it would only make her feel worse. She prided herself on having such a good relationship with all of Max's friends, almost as though she were one of them.

She had been so convinced she knew every detail of Max's life but of course she hadn't. He was a young man and he did all the things that spirited young men do. Caroline tried to be too close to him, too much his equal, and Andrew knew that Max found it cloying.

That summer after his A-Levels, when Max had spent so much time at the house with his friends, he had spoken about it to his father. It was a hazy evening of dappled sunlight, the air tangy with the scent of freshly mown grass and the two of them had decided to walk to the pub after supper. There were two local pubs that they liked – one of them was up a steep hill in the centre of Malvern; the other was downhill towards Barnard's Green, a place that was effectively little more than an optimistically named roundabout, ringed with estate agents, off-licences and a fish and chip shop. Feeling lazy, they opted for the latter and strolled down to The George and Dragon. Andrew had bought the first round – a pint of ale for him; a pint of Guinness for Max – and when he laid them down carefully on the dark oak table in the corner that was their regular spot, Max had fiddled for several minutes with a soggy beer-mat and Andrew had known there was something on his mind.

'Anything bothering you?' he enquired, taking a long swig from his pint glass.

'Um, not really.' Max eased into his chair, rubbing the back of his neck with his right hand as he always did when he was trying to work out a problem.

Andrew left it for a few minutes, hoping that a companionable silence would tease out whatever it was he wanted to say. Andrew was good at silence. He had a placid, relaxing air of stillness about him and was quite capable of sitting for hours on the edge of a mountainside simply taking things in, contentedly alone with his thoughts. A friend had once told him he would make a good fisherman, but for some reason he had never taken up the hobby. Occasionally, at work, an employee would mistake his detached manner for aloofness or absent-mindedness but really it was neither of these things; it was simply that most of the time, he did not see the point in talking unless he had something important to say.

'It's Mum.'

Andrew waited.

'She's driving me mad,' said Max, looking his father straight in the eye. 'Can you have a word with her, Dad?'

'In what way is she driving you mad?'

'She's always . . . *around*. I just want to hang out with my mates before we all go off, you know, to uni or me to the army and Mum is just always there. She says I can bring people home, that she won't bother us and she'll "leave us to our own devices –" ' he made a quotation mark sign with his hands, 'but then she sits down with us and tries to be part of what we're saying or doing and . . .' He dropped his voice. 'It's embarrassing, Dad. She keeps asking us for cigarettes. She doesn't even smoke!'

'Well, she used to.'

'Yeah, exactly, she *used* to. She used to be young. She used to be my age. She isn't any more. My mates take the piss out of her as soon as she walks out the door.'

'That's not very fair of them,' said Andrew. 'Given how kind she is to them and how tolerant she is of having them around. Goodness knows, she's far more tolerant than me about that sort of thing.'

Max hung his head, a trace of shame colouring his features.

'It's a very hard time for her, Max. You're about to leave home and she's going to miss you terribly, as well as being worried about you going into the army.'

'It's only training.'

'Yes, but then you'll be sent away goodness knows where. You're her child, her little boy. Of course she's going to want to see as much of you as possible while she still can. You can understand that, surely?'

Max nodded.

'She would be awfully hurt if she knew we were having this conversation, let alone if I tried to talk to her about it.' Andrew paused. 'But I can see that you and your friends might want your own space, so I suggest you start spending time somewhere else, away from the house.'

He tapped gently on the edge of the table, his fingers making a soft thudding sound against the wood. 'Can't you go to Adam's house or, well, I don't know, go for a walk or something?'

Max snorted at the prospect of something so mundane and then, after a few minutes, said: 'You're right. Don't say anything to Mum. We can go somewhere else.'

'I know . . .' Andrew started and then pondered the wisdom of what he was about to say. He did not want to be disloyal to his wife but, at the same time, he wanted Max to feel that he understood. 'I know that Caroline can be quite . . .' he searched for the right word, 'intense, but it's only because she loves you so very deeply. You can see that, can't you?'

'It just feels like a bit of a pressure sometimes,' Max said, after a while. 'Being an only child.'

'Mmmm, I can see that,' replied Andrew, thinking sadly of how hard they had tried for more children when Max was young. 'Of course, I'm one myself. I know what it's like.'

He glanced at Max sitting across the table from him, fiddling intently with a beer-mat and not quite meeting his father's gaze. Andrew leaned forward so that he was in his eyeline. 'It's tough, feeling you're the receptacle for all your parents' hopes and fears, it is. I'm sorry about that, truly. But, look, Max, it won't be too long until you're leaving for Bulford and you won't have to worry about it any more. Now,' he said, draining his beer. 'Your round, I believe?'

Max laughed and sloped off to the bar and Andrew felt quietly pleased that his son had confided in him. And he had taken his advice too – from then on, Max and his friends spent far less time at the house. If Caroline had noticed, she had not said anything – deliberately, Andrew suspected, so that she would not lose face. She had always needed to be close to Max. Of course, all mothers cherish their children but he thinks it went deeper than that. It was almost as if she needed Max to love her to the exclusion of anyone else.

There had been all that business at Christmas – Max's last, as it turned out – when Elsa had come to stay. They had been gathered around the tree in the drawing room, Max sprawled out on a large floor cushion, Andrew and Elsa sitting in armchairs on opposite sides of the hearth and Caroline handing out the brightly wrapped parcels.

Caroline loved Christmas. There were many things about his wife that would always remain unexplained, unknowable, but he knew beyond doubt that she adored the festive period. She threw herself into the preparations, decking out the house in tinsel and holly boughs, making batches of mince pies and chocolate truffles, sending out the cards with meticulous precision (that year, she had even used an Excel spreadsheet to print the addresses). She liked the family being together and delighted in her role as hostess, accepting compliments with a beaming smile.

She put pressure on herself, each year, to come up with the per-fectly judged Christmas present for Max. Most of the time, she got it right. Sometimes, Andrew could see, Max would disguise his own disappointment so convincingly that Caroline never knew. But this particular year, he could tell that Caroline was especially pleased with the camera that they had bought him. She had spent hours researching the best model online, after Max had let slip one evening at supper that he would quite like to get into photography more seriously.

Andrew had left her to it. He had an inkling it might have made more sense to give Max the money and tell him to spend it on the camera he most wanted, but Caroline thought that giving cash was unimaginative and – this was her word – 'common'.

Traditionally, on Christmas Day, Caroline would give their present last, as if all of Max's other gifts were simply a build-up to the real event. So, when she handed over Elsa's neatly packaged box, at first nothing had seemed amiss. Caroline, her eyes bright, her cheeks flushed, had complimented Elsa on the wrapping paper.

'It's beautiful, Elsa,' she said, turning the gift over in her hands, admiring the curlicues of silver ribbon. 'Where do you find the time?'

Andrew braced himself, his ears finely attuned to detecting the subtle fragrance of implied criticism in any conversation between his wife and mother. He glanced across at Elsa, who looked unper-turbed, sitting upright on the sofa, her hand clasping a small glass of sherry. Caroline, a purple paper crown perched on her hair, was smiling broadly. Perhaps he had imagined it.

Max took the present from his mother and brought the box up to his ear, shaking it lightly. There was a rattling noise. 'A-ha. Granny. Is it a CD?' he asked, and everyone laughed. Elsa shook her head. 'A pair of socks?' he asked waggishly. 'Lavender-scented bath salts?'

'I'm afraid not, Maximilian,' she said, drily, 'I've let you down again.' She took a sip of her sherry, leaving a crimson imprint of lipstick on the rim of the glass. Caroline's smile grew tired. She hated Elsa calling him Maximilian. They had christened him plain old Max, she often reminded Andrew, with no longer version available to fall back on.

'It's like she's trying to prove she knows him better than us,' Caroline said.

'Oh don't be ridiculous, darling, I don't think that's it at all. It's because she's so fond of him, that's all.'

Caroline pinched her lips together. He'd left it at that.

That Christmas, Caroline had let the Maximilian comment pass, looking on as he unwrapped the parcel, kneeling on the carpet, her neck arched forwards to see better what was inside.

'Well,' said Max, keeping up a cheerful commentary as he began to open the package. 'This *is* intriguing.' The silver ribbon fell to one side; the paper crinkled and ripped and gradually, the contents emerged.

Andrew was the first to spot what had happened. He recognised the picture of the camera on the side of the box and then he focused on the name: Nikon 3580. It was exactly the same model that Caroline had bought. Andrew got up from his chair, sensing impending disaster but at the same time not being entirely sure what he could do to prevent it.

'Oh my God, Granny, how did you know?' Max was thrilled, his face positively beaming with joy. 'This is exactly what I wanted.' He leaped up from the floor and went to kiss Elsa effusively on the cheek.

Elsa put down her sherry glass to pat his arm. 'No need to fuss,' she said but Andrew could see she was pleased. 'I'm so glad I got the right one.' She cleared her throat and brought her hand delicately up to her mouth, the fourth finger circled by the dazzling emerald of the engagement ring she had worn every year since before Andrew was born. For a moment, Andrew was hypnotised by the stone's lucent sparkle, throwing out tiny refractions of light. Then he remembered Caroline. He went over to her and rested a hand lightly on her shoulder. She let it lie there, but did not respond to the touch. 'Well,' Andrew said, trying to preserve the jovial atmosphere that had existed until a few seconds before. 'Isn't that a coincidence?'

Max had already started opening the camera box, taking out leads and flashes and batteries and setting them all out on the carpet in front of him. He paused to look up at his father. 'What is?'

Elsa looked at him too and Andrew realised, not for the first time, how similar they were: their faces upturned at precisely the same angle, their profiles so pronounced against the warm light cast by the fire.

'Well,' said Andrew again, hopelessly. 'Your mother and I got you exactly the same thing.'

He forced himself to laugh and then Max, after a worried glance at his mother, started to chuckle too.

'Oh dear,' Max said. 'That's all my fault. I've obviously been banging on about it for so long . . .' He let the sentence hang in the air. Caroline, her face immobile, didn't laugh.

'I'm terribly sorry, Caroline,' said Elsa, instantly aware of the discomfort in the room. 'I should have spoken to you and Andrew about it. How silly of me.'

'Nonsense,' Andrew replied. 'No harm done. Max can take one of them back to the shop and spend the money on something else. What about a camera bag or one of those huge flashes that look so professional?'

Max nodded vigorously. 'Yeah, great idea, Dad. I'd actually really like a bag. You need it with a piece of kit like this.'

Everyone was looking at Caroline, waiting for her to say something, waiting for the inevitable denouement of this delicate dance of social politesse. Eventually, she stood up, brushed down her skirt and shook herself free from Andrew's grip. She smiled shakily and said, almost casually: 'I'm just going to see to something in the kitchen – if you'll all excuse me for a minute.' She slipped out of the door and Andrew knew, without even having to look at her face, that she would be crying. He felt a pang of frustration. Why did she take things so much to heart? Why couldn't she have made the effort to gloss over it like everyone else? He supposed he would have to go to her. But then, just as he was making his way to the door, Max touched his arm.

'Don't worry, Dad. I'll go.' The two of them exchanged a look. They both knew Caroline would rather see him.

Andrew walked back into the sitting room, headed straight for the drinks cabinet and poured himself a generous tumbler of whisky. His mother was still there, looking at him wryly.

'I think you need that,' she smiled, still seated elegantly on the sofa, her legs pressed together and angled at 45 degrees from the ground. 'Cheers,' she said, raising her sherry glass.

'Cheers,' Andrew replied, echoing the gesture.

After twenty minutes, Caroline and Max had re-emerged from the kitchen and peace had been restored, or so Andrew now recalls.

Odd, really, the things his mind is dwelling on now that Max has gone.

He walks out of the gents towards the coffee bar. As he joins the end of the queue, he hears someone calling his name. He does not immediately react because it is a girlish voice that he doesn't recognise and he cannot imagine why anyone would be trying to get his attention. But the voice is persistent and after a few seconds, he feels a tap on his shoulder.

'Andrew, I thought it was you.'

He turns around and finds himself face-to-face with a small, blonde woman enveloped in an oversized parka. Her hands are tucked into two pockets, set close to her chest like an old-fashioned muff. She is smiling broadly, her lips glossed with balm that smells of chemical strawberries. She is very pretty, in that artless, natural way seen in the fresh-faced girls in clothing catalogues, the girls who are picked because they are deliberately unintimidating, because the average female shopper will relate to them rather than feel threatened. He cannot place her straight away and is perplexed as to why she knows his name.

She laughs and a strand of hair escapes from her messy ponytail. 'It's Kate. From the office.'

'Of course it is,' Andrew says, flustered at his forgetfulness. Kate has been working at Weston & Barwell for the last few months, helping out with the increasing number of corporate accounts. She was a recent graduate and he remembers vaguely that there was some reason for her coming to Malvern, a sick relative or something, rather than heading off to the bright lights of a big city.

'I'm so sorry, Kate, my mind was somewhere else entirely.'

'Don't worry. It's probably the first time you've seen me in non-work clothes.'

'Yes,' he says and he has a clear image of her in a black two-piece suit with a pale pink striped shirt looking rather uptight and professional. 'And I suppose this isn't the most obvious place to run into one's work colleagues.'

She smiles and for a moment Andrew stares at her and then looks away. He feels embarrassed without knowing why. 'What are you doing in this part of the country?' he asks, to fill the awkwardness.

'Oh, me and a couple of mates are driving to Cambridge for the weekend. It's the first time we've gone back there since graduation, so we're going to try and recapture our youth.'

'I shouldn't think that will be too hard,' he replies. He hadn't known she'd gone to Cambridge. For some reason, this surprises him and he can feel himself beginning to take her more seriously. He'd always imagined she would be fairly unexceptional company. Why had he been so dismissive?

'Oh I don't know,' says Kate, looking directly at him. 'Sometimes I feel much older and wiser than my twenty-one years.' Her face is serious as she says this, her lips parted so that he can see the tip of her teeth as she breathes. After a few beats, she says, 'I'm really sorry, Andrew.' There is a pause. 'You know, about your son.' He does not respond because he doesn't know how. 'I never got a chance to say anything at the time but . . . well, now seemed a good opportunity.' She smiles, heartfelt, and then she does something strange: she reaches out with her right hand and touches him on his upper arm, her fingers grazing against the cotton of his fleece and the curve of his bicep. Kate lets her hand rest there and Andrew does not move away. 'If you ever want to talk,' she says, pressing down gently so that he can feel the weight of her touch on his skin.

He is mystified by what she is doing and yet he finds it pleasurable in spite of himself. He cannot imagine that this young, attractive woman is apparently trying to flirt with him but this is what seems to be happening. She has never before spoken more than three words to him. Had he simply never noticed her before today? Perhaps they had talked but he had been so distracted with Max and Caroline and everything that was happening at home that it had not made any impact. In his mind, it has been so long since he has been touched by a woman with any hint of affection or kindness or concern that Kate's small, simple gesture courses through him.

His thoughts are interrupted by a tinny rendition of Barber's *Adagio*. 'Sorry,' Kate says, removing her hand and taking a sleek-looking mobile phone out of her pocket. She swipes the screen with her index finger to answer. 'Yeah?' he hears her saying. 'I know, I'm just here . . . No, by the Costa Coffee . . . do you see me? OK, come over.' She giggles at something the person on the other end of the line is saying and Andrew feels oddly exposed, discomfited. He makes a sign to indicate he is going and it has been nice to see her but she holds out her other hand to motion for him to stay. 'See you in a sec.' She touches the screen again to hang up. 'Sorry about that,' she says, chewing on her bottom lip in a way that Andrew finds distracting.

'Well, Kate, it was nice to see you,' he says, deliberately brisk and authoritative. 'I'm sure we'll bump into each other on Monday.'

'Yes,' she answers, looking straight at him in that disarming way. 'I'd like that.'

Andrew walks quickly out of the service station and back to the car, turning the key in the ignition before he has even put on his seatbelt. He drives for several miles before he remembers that he forgot to get his coffee.

When he sees his mother, he is taken aback by her appearance. Elsa is sitting in the hallway waiting for him when Mrs Carswell opens the front door and beckons him inside.

'Come on in, Mr Weston,' she says, cheerily. 'No need to stand on ceremony for us, now is there?' Mrs Carswell addresses the question to Elsa, who doesn't respond. Andrew, brushing the rain from his coat, walks in, remembering at the last minute to bend down so that he doesn't hit his head on the doorframe.

There are no lights on even though the day is gloomy and at first he doesn't see his mother, who is sitting to one side, by the table with the telephone, her features overcast by shadow. But then, when he sees her properly, he has to stop himself from exclaiming at the change in her over the last month. She seems to have shrunk, as though her bones are collapsing in on themselves. Her shoulders are hunched forwards, leaving a deep valley of skin on each side of her collarbone. Her face is pinched and sallow, her eyes hooded by the protrusion of her forehead.

She is wearing a checked blouse, like a lumberjack shirt, done up in haste so that the buttons are not in the right holes and give her a lopsided look. There is an indistinct red-brown stain on the collar, the edges of which are fraying. Her hair has clearly not been set for several weeks and has grown into a straggly grey, the brittle texture of candyfloss. Her mouth, pale and thin and puckered, is set in a downward curve that makes her look mournful and lost. He thinks to himself: I should not be surprised; this is what happens when you are 98 years old. And yet he is shocked because Elsa had always taken such punctilious care of her appearance. Age did not seem to have worn her down in the same way that it had his father. She remained a good-looking woman well into her eighties and the force of her personality, her strength of character, had always shone through. The stroke earlier this year had taken away much of her ability to express herself, but even then, she had still looked recognisably the same.

He feels guilty that he has not seen her enough, that he has not been here to look after her better. He starts to say this to Mrs Carswell, but before he can get the words out, she pats him on the arm and shushes him. 'Don't you be so hard on yourself, Mr Weston,' Mrs Carswell says. 'You've had enough on your plate lately.' There is an uneasy pause and then she adds, quietly. 'I was ever so sorry to hear about Max, Mr Weston. Ever so sorry.'

He thanks her and then asks for a glass of water so that she leaves him alone. He feels crowded but does not wish to be rude.

When she has gone, he leans across and kisses Elsa on the cheek. 'Hello, Mummy.' She doesn't recognise him, so he says 'It's Andrew,' before adding pointlessly, 'your son.'

Her eyes swivel towards him and she murmurs something, the sound of it slurring and imprecise. He wants to believe she is saying 'Of course I know who it is, you bloody fool' and he smiles, thinking that although her appearance might have altered, perhaps a glimmer of the old Elsa remains; perhaps, inside her head, everything is as it was.

Elsa

ELSA IS BEING TAKEN to her new home. She is in the passenger seat of Andrew's car and the seatbelt is rubbing uncomfortably against her neck but she has no strength to move it. She watches the motorway signs scudding by: bright blue squares with white lettering that she feels too dizzy to make out.

Mrs Carswell has quite deliberately made it seem as though Elsa is simply going on an extended visit to Andrew's house, but she is shrewd enough to know this is a lie. She has noticed her own sharp disintegration over the last few weeks: buttons she was unable to undo; light-switches she could no longer press; words she had forgotten the meaning of. She could not even get out of bed on her own.

She is baffled and upset by the way her body and her mind are letting her down and by the fact that she is now entirely reliant on other people for any kind of existence. It is as though her decrepitude has diminished her personality to a tiny pinprick, so that it is no longer big enough to take up the requisite space. She cannot fill a house any more; is not deemed worthy of it. And Elsa had always so cherished her independence.

After her husband Oliver had died, Andrew tried to persuade her to move out of their Grantchester home to somewhere more manageable but she had refused. She had loved that house, despite its ludicrous pink-painted exterior. It was the only place she had ever felt truly comfortable, safe in the knowledge that she could do exactly what she liked within its walls and that visitors had to abide by her rules.

Elsa remembers her first morning there, just after they moved up from London. She had woken in the upstairs bedroom and got dressed with Oliver still sleeping, the rhythm of his breath rising and falling softly beside her. She noticed the birds first of all: the tinkle and chirrup of their song and the muted yellow of warm sunshine pushing through the unlined curtains. Intrigued by the unfamiliar clarity of light, Elsa walked across to the window and lifted the corner of one curtain. She saw the dense, dark green grass of a meadow stretching into the distance, lush with the previous day's rainfall. She could just make out the river, dotted with the freshly laundered white of swan feathers. She gasped with happiness at the sight. It was so much more beautiful than she had anticipated. At last, she had found a home for a family of her own.

And now, she was leaving it behind and there was nothing she could do about it. She could not even put her sadness into words. When she tried, her tongue would loll uselessly to one side and she would fail to convey whatever it was she wanted to say and this would make everything so much worse that, in the end, she simply gave up trying. She became, to all intents and purposes, mute: a sentence rubbed out; a pause at the end of a line; a space where once there had been a person.

'Caroline is looking forward to seeing you.' She hears Andrew speaking but cannot make sense of what he is saying. She lets his voice wash over her and then, once the wave has been sucked back by the tide, she picks up the left-behind words like shells on a beach, playing with their textures one by one until she understands them.

Caroline. She turns the name over in her mind. A face does not immediately come to her. She thinks longer, harder, and then the image begins to emerge from a swirling circular fuzziness, like melted chocolate being poured into a bowl of cream. Of course, she thinks, Caroline. And then she remembers her as she first saw her. She was a mousy-looking girl wearing a skirt that accentuated her plumpness, so that when her blouse rode up, Elsa could see a creamy roll of flesh spilling over the waistband. She had always believed that being overweight, even mildly so like Caroline, was indicative of a lack of discipline. Her first impressions of her were not favourable.

No, she hadn't taken to Caroline, even though she could tell the girl was desperately eager to please. There was something about her Elsa couldn't quite place, other than knowing she came from a different kind of background. She certainly hadn't thought she was marriage material. Not for Andrew, in any case.

But then, Elsa thinks bitterly, she'd got her claws into him after all.

Andrew is looking at his mother sideways, still concentrating on the road, his hands on the steering wheel in an exact ten to two position. 'You remember Caroline,' he is saying now, indicating to overtake a lorry in the lane in front of them. 'My wife.'

Does he honestly believe she's that far gone? Of course she remembers. Elsa nods her head, opens her mouth to say 'Yes' but it comes out as a sibilant sludge of Ss. She is angry now, frustrated both by Andrew's condescension and her own incompetence. She can recall, years ago, that she had lent Caroline a book. It comes back to her now, with absolute precision. Caroline and Andrew had driven up for the weekend, bringing with them a moody, teen-age Max who spent most of his time unsuccessfully trying to catch fish in the Cam with Oliver's old rod.

Over tea and slices of Dundee cake on the Saturday afternoon, Elsa had discovered through the course of their conversation that Caroline had never read Thackeray's *Vanity Fair*.

'Oh but you must,' Elsa said. 'You simply must, mustn't she, darling?' She looked at Andrew for confirmation. He nodded his head but his mouth was full of cake, the crumbs falling on to his napkin.

'It's one of my absolute favourite books,' Elsa continued. 'I'd take it with me on my Desert Island.' She laughed, lightly. 'I'll lend it to you. I'm sure I've got a copy knocking around here some-where.'

Caroline, who was stirring two heaped teaspoonfuls of sugar into her tea, looked up.

'Oh . . . that's very kind of you, Elsa, but . . .' The sentence trailed off. 'Well, the thing is, I'm not a big reader.'

Elsa glanced at her, astonished. 'Nonsense,' she said briskly. 'Everyone reads.'

Caroline blushed, shifting uneasily in her seat. Elsa noticed that she was wearing new shoes. They were high-heeled, with a small gold disc on each toe and looked expensive. They were not like her normal scuffed shoes at all. In fact, thought Elsa, they reminded her of a similar pair she had owned years ago.

'Yes, you're right of course, Elsa,' Caroline said, nodding her head too quickly. 'I'm sure I'll love it. I'm bound to, if *you* think it's good.'

Elsa raised her eyebrows. She wished her daughter-in-law didn't try quite so hard.

'Why don't you go and track it down, Mummy?' Andrew said. 'I wouldn't mind rereading it myself.'

She had found it eventually in the bookcase in the spare bedroom – a dog-eared paperback with a Hogarth reproduction on the cover. But before handing it over to Caroline, she had done something unusual: she had written her name on the top right-hand corner of the inside page in blue ink. Elsa realised, as she moved her fountain pen quickly across the paper, that she did not trust Caroline to return it. And the curious thing was, she never had. Elsa had never seen the book again.

Remembering this now, she feels a surge of irritation, even though so many years have passed, even though the book itself never really mattered. And she is scared, too, that Caroline, a woman she has mistrusted for so long, will feature largely in this new, unasked-for life.

She is familiar with this feeling of being beholden, of being trapped. Because, of course, it has happened to her before.

Elsa, 1919

S HE IS 6 WHEN her father comes home from the war. On the
day of his arrival, Elsa cannot sleep. She wakes early, when the
morning is still unworn, before the milk bottles have been left on
the doorstep. She tiptoes out of bed in her nightdress and sits at the
window-seat in her bedroom, overlooking the faded blue of a
hydrangea growing in a clay pot in the back garden.

Until a few months ago, her window had been covered with a
dense black material that was meant to protect them from something called a Zeppelin. Once, in the early evening, the blind had
lifted all the way up until it was at right angles to the wall, where
it stayed, levitating, for several seconds. There had been no wind
and Elsa had been frightened when she saw it, that the Zeppelin
would come, but it never had. No one had ever explained to her
what a Zeppelin was, they just assumed she knew. To her ears, it
had sounded fun and jolly, the sort of name one might give a magi-
cian from overseas who pulls rabbits out of hats and has a twirly
moustache and a dashing red coat.

Now the black material has gone and Elsa has her old curtains
back again. She is fascinated by the curtains. They were sewn by
her mother out of thick, beige material that was scratchy and dense
to the touch. The fabric was delicately etched with country scenes,
the pale pink lines of shepherdesses and oak trees spreading outwards like bloodshot veins leaking into the white of a tired eye.
Elsa had asked her mother once where the material had come from
and had been told that it was French and called Toile de Jouy. Her
mother had written it down for her on a piece of paper in her

elegant copperplate, the T and the J leaning to the right; trees swayed by the wind.

Elsa had folded the paper and hidden it underneath the loose floorboard in the corner of her room where she kept all her most precious possessions. There was a marble shot through with a liquid purple flame that she had won in a game with Bobby Farrow from next door; a miniature Bible, the paper thin and translucent, edged with gold and crackly to the touch; and a dog-eared post-card, the image of a village church dulled with the years. On the back of the postcard, her mother had written in brown ink: 'Dear Mama and Papa, We have arrived safely in Broadhembury and are pleasantly ensconced in clean rooms in The Drewe Arms (which faces the church you see pictured overleaf). The weather is warm and a little overcast. Tomorrow, we hope to summon up our energies sufficiently to go exploring. Your loving daughter, Alice.' When she first discovered this postcard, nestling among the pages of a musty-smelling scrapbook, Elsa had been confused as to who the 'we' referred to. She had never known Alice to exist as any-thing other than her mother. If Elsa had not been with her on this trip to Broadhembury, then who had?

'Why, your father of course,' her mother had said, a gentle smile on her face. She stroked Elsa's light brown hair and patted it down flat with the palm of her hand. 'We took a trip to Devon shortly after we got married.'

Elsa crinkled her nose. 'Why was I not there?' she asked, confused.

Her mother laughed. 'Because you weren't born yet, my darling.'

The thought of this seemed so extraordinary, so against the nat-ural order of things, that Elsa had not known what to do with it. The idea of her mother travelling somewhere without her, in the company of her father, a man whom she thought of as a rather austere, remote figure, was too much to take in. She knew him only through a photograph on the mantelpiece above the fireplace in the drawing room. It is in a silver frame and it shows a man standing upright and stern, his face unsmiling through the dusty sepia. Although he has a moustache, it is not twirly like a magi-cian's but instead neatly trimmed and workmanlike, the edge of it cut flush against his top lip. His eyes are large, a bit bulging and he is gazing beyond the frame at something unexplained, as if he has just left the house and forgotten something he needed. His name is Horace.

For all her life up to this point, her father has existed only as a distant, unfocused idea in her mind. Her mother says Elsa has met him once but she was too young to remember and he has been away ever since, fighting the Germans in France. Sitting on the window-seat now, she finds it difficult to connect the photograph with the solidity of an actual person. She knows that her father is real, that he is coming home today, but still, in her mind, he remains intangibly trapped in two dimensions. He is like an illustration in a book. He is like the Zeppelin: a concept that she accepts without ever really knowing what it is.

They wait for him all day, sitting in the drawing room, stilted and silent, both too nervous to move. Elsa casts sideways glances at her mother and notices that her hair looks different, more plumped-up than normal. She is wearing a blouse that Elsa has not seen before, made of creamy silk, with a high lace collar, elegant puffed sleeves and tightly buttoned cuffs that emphasise the slenderness of her wrists.

At teatime, Bobby Farrow appears at the door to tell them that he has seen Mr Brompton at the railway station. 'He's back,' Bobby says, breathing hard because he ran all the way up the hill and now has to bend over with his hands on his knees to recover. 'Mr Brompton. He's coming up the street now.'

And so they rush to the door and peer out and there he is, just as Bobby said, walking towards them with a limp and a sagging kit bag slung over one shoulder, a grey-green cap on his head that looks like a flattened mushroom and shades the upper half of his face against the sunlight so that Elsa cannot make out his expression.

'Are you glad he's back?' Bobby asks.

'Yes,' she replies without thinking. But, in reality, she is not glad at all. She is nervous at the thought of this stranger coming to live with them. She thinks of the postcard, hidden away underneath the floorboards upstairs, and feels a quivering in her throat.

And then, all of a sudden, he is through the door and standing in front of her. He is a tall man with a surprisingly slender frame. His arms hang down to his mid-thigh, long and shapely and almost feminine. He has pale brown hair and his moustache turns ginger at the edges. His expression is fierce. There is something about his appearance that makes him look old even though Elsa knows he is 27, not that much older than her mother. But his face has the unhealthy look of uncooked pastry, the flesh pouched, swollen and shiny with light perspiration.

He does not particularly resemble his photo, the stillness of which had made him seem calm and controlled. In real life, his movements are quick and sharp and constantly wary, like a small, tense animal. He does not smile when he walks into the house.

Her mother steps forward to greet him, putting her hands on his shoulders hesitantly and politely kissing his cheek. This new, unknown man does not respond, other than to pat Alice stiffly on the back. 'No need to fuss,' he says, breaking off from the uneasy embrace to remove his cap, which he places carefully on the glass-panelled cabinet at the bottom of the stairs.

'Who's this then?' he says, turning towards Elsa, his voice gruff and blank. His face is impassive as he looks at her and it feels to Elsa as though he is examining something he is about to buy, measuring it up in his head to see whether it would fit in the hall-way. She does not reply, but stands shyly clinging on to the thick wooden banister pole so as to occupy her hands. She twists her right foot around her ankle, unsure of what is going to happen next.

'Elsa, it's your Papa,' her mother says in the brittle, shiny voice that she normally uses for strangers. Elsa sees that her mother's mouth is trembling at the corners, as if she has been smiling too hard. She lets go of the banister with great reluctance and steps forward into the shadow cast by her father.

'Hello, Papa,' she says, quietly.

She wants to like him but instinctively she shrinks away. He seems to carry within him a sort of darkness, an impenetrable shadow that surrounds him in a circle of stillness. But it is not an aura of calm; rather it gives the sense of a violence being contained; a blackness that is pushing and scrabbling to get out of him.

Without a word, he holds out his hand. For a moment, Elsa is not sure what he expects her to do. Is he leading her somewhere? Is it a game of some sort? She stretches out her own hand timidly and he takes it firmly in his grasp, shaking it up and down with great vigour. Elsa can feel bristly hairs on the back of his thumb. His clothes smell damp. She notices that the edges of his boots are caked in a grey-coloured clay but that it does not flake off on to the carpet like ordinary mud. There is a livid red scar at the point where his neck meets his jawbone, knotted and twisted like a coil of rope.

'Good,' he says, letting go of her hand with another dry little cough. He stands up straight and places both arms behind his back, his face tilting upwards as though he is sniffing the air to check it smelled the same as when he had left it. Elsa slinks back to her place by the banister, already aware that she must not make too much noise. She does not want to upset him. She has some instinct, some child's intimation, that it would unleash something bad.

'Would you like some tea, dear?' asks her mother brightly. 'I think Mrs Timmins has prepared some cold ham for you.'

He nods. 'Yes, that would be –' A muscle twitches just below his right eye. '*Nice*,' he says with precision. He strides up the stairs without another word, the heavy male footfall unfamiliar to Elsa's ears.

A few days later, her father lights a fire in the back garden. The flames are straggly and weak and buffeted by the wind so that the smoke snakes in through the window frames and lingers, acrid, in the house. Elsa is sitting with her mother in the drawing room, carefully trying to read a book that has too many words for her yet to make sense of. But she likes the pictures, especially the burnished green-gold front cover that is decorated with looping, elegant pink roses. There is a picture of a girl in a bright red coat with long, curly blonde hair like an angel's and the girl is bending over to push a key into a hidden door in the middle of a thick, dense hedge. The book is called *The Secret Garden*. Elsa likes secrets. She likes the idea of having a key to a place that is hers and hers alone, that no one else will ever be able to discover.

When she asks her mother what the fire is for, Alice replies that Papa was burning his uniform.

'Why?'

'Because it holds bad memories for him,' she says. 'Besides, he doesn't need to wear it any more. The war is over.'

'Is it?'

Alice puts down her embroidery and looks at Elsa, frowning.

'Why yes, you knew that,' she says, insistent. 'You remember when Mrs Farrow came over and we heard the church bells ring out even though it wasn't a Sunday? And we went into town and there were lots of people smiling and cheering?'

Elsa nods. She remembers clearly that her mother had been wearing her black voile dress and the hat with the feather that was normally only reserved for special occasions. Mrs Crawford, the butcher's wife, had hung a string of triangular flags across the front of the shop window. Elsa had liked watching the flags blow gently in the breeze, seeing the colours and lines warp and blur in the white sunlight. Shortly afterwards, a man had come and removed the blue paint from all the street-lamps. She had known they were celebrating the end of the war because her mother had told her, but she hadn't fully realised the implications. She had thought it was like a school holiday: a temporary interruption before things got back to normal. She sees now that she hadn't understood.

'Well,' her mother continues, 'that was the end of having to fight all those nasty Germans.'

Elsa considers this statement for a moment, and then asks: 'Does that mean Papa is staying?'

She stares down at the line made by the white lace hem of her dress against the thick black wool of her stockings. The leather of her buttoned-up boots is pressing against her big toe. She has grown a lot over the past year and all her clothes now seem either too small or too big. Her mother takes up her sewing so that when she answers, her head is bowed and her profile is silhouetted against the gas-lamp and she does not look at Elsa as she speaks. 'Yes,' she replies. 'Yes, it does.'

Elsa feels anxious. She is uncomfortable with this new, masculine presence in her home. Her mother now seems distant, more detached than before. She wishes, more than anything, that she and her mother could run away and live in a house of their own. She imagines this dream house down to every last detail. Her mother would have her own floor filled with all the pretty objects that she knew Alice loved: the green-and-white china vase in the living room; the Toile de Jouy curtains; the oil painting of a bend in a river near where Alice had grown up. In this house, they would exist in perfect peace with no one to disturb them. Mealtimes would be whenever they felt hungry. Elsa would paint her bedroom a cornflower blue just because she could. There would be no strange man, laying claim to things that were not his own.

Her reverie is interrupted by her father coming in from the garden, stooping even though he is several inches clear of the door-frame. 'All finished,' he says.

'Well done,' says Elsa's mother and then, because there is a crackle to the silence that follows, she adds: 'You managed to work up quite a good blaze in the end.'

'Yes.' He sits down on an armchair, lifting a pinch of trouser leg with each hand as he does so. Her mother puts aside her embroidery in readiness for conversation but Horace does not speak. Instead he stares vaguely into the distance, his hands resting lightly on his knees. Elsa, who has been sitting by the fireplace with her book, feels that she should also suspend any activity out of politeness. She puts the book down on her lap but the shiny cover slips against the fabric of her dress and falls on to the tiled hearth with a sudden, loud slam.

At the noise, her father jumps in his seat. He makes a wet, whimpering sound and for a moment, Elsa wonders where the noise – so oddly vulnerable – is coming from. When Elsa looks up, she sees that he is pushing his shoulders forwards, curling himself tightly into a ball in the armchair. His mouth is twisted; his lips are pale blue against the red flush of his skin and an arm is raised up to shield his head. He is shivering. And then, as quickly as it started, it stops and he unclenches his muscles, as if nothing has happened.

The whole episode is over in less than a few seconds, but Elsa cannot stop staring.

He catches her eye and straightens up with a snap. His face, which just a second ago had been ashen and scared, now becomes contorted with anger.

'Can't you sit still for one second?' he says and although his voice is level, spittle appears at each corner of his mouth. The room echoes with the question. He stands up and strides over to Elsa and his height makes her feel very small. She hangs her head, not wanting to make eye contact. She realises she is trembling and this makes her nervous that she might do something else wrong and that this might enrage her father even more.

'Well? Speak up, child. What do you have to say for yourself?' His words are harsh. He is trying to control his voice but the question comes out almost as a scream. Elsa puts her hands over her ears. She fears that he might lose control completely if she does not say the right thing. He is so close, she can smell the tang of his sweat.

'Sorry, Papa,' she says in a whisper. He bends down, grabbing her chin and forcing her head up.

'Kindly extend me the courtesy of looking at me when you apologise,' he says. Elsa meets his gaze. Tears obscure her sight.

'Sorry, Papa,' she says hoarsely.

'Good.' He lets go of her face and she can feel the pressure of his fingers against her skin. 'Now get out.'

She picks up the book, one corner blunted with the impact, and places it on the card table in front of her, sliding it on to the surface of the wood as softly as she can. Without warning, her father lifts the book and throws it with all his force into the fireplace, the spine of it breaking and bending back on itself so that several pages rip loose and scatter like leaves across the coal. Elsa cries out and moves towards the fireplace, unable to stop herself. Her father swings back and slaps her across the face, so swiftly that she curves inwards with the strength of it, her body becoming concave before she crumples on to the floor, overcome by the sheer, hot pain of the blow.

'Get out,' her father says, pointing towards the door.

She can hear her mother interjecting. 'Horace,' she was saying. 'Do you think . . .'

'She has to learn,' he says. 'You've been too lenient with her, Alice.'

For a moment, Elsa is too winded to move. Then she tries to push herself upright. Her mother stays seated, her expression inscrutable. Eventually, Elsa manages to stand but the effort of it makes her gasp. She wants to disappear.

She walks to the door, trying to make as little noise as possible. She fumbles for the handle. It releases. She feels relief, then stumbles out of the room, pulling the door shut behind her. She makes it up to her bedroom where she lies on the bed, allowing the sharpness of the pain on her cheek to subside gradually into a dull, persistent thud. She is not sure what she has done wrong but she knows it must have been something awful to have been so badly punished and she is upset with herself for misbehaving. If only she could learn how he wanted her to be. She tries to tell herself not to be weak, but it doesn't work. She wants, more than anything, to hear her mother in the hallway and for her to hold Elsa tight and to make it better.

After a bit, she moves carefully to the window-seat so that she can search out the comfort of a familiar view, but she can focus only on the charred black patch of deadened grass where the fire had been. She notices a piece of something reflective on the ground, shining in the day's dissolving light. It is smaller, smoother than a stone and yet it looks misshapen, dented. She realises it must be one of the brass buttons from her father's serge tunic and her tears fall more insistently than before until her breath can no longer keep up and she starts hiccuping. A numb tiredness sweeps over her and, eventually, she dozes off on the counterpane, her legs and arms curled together in front of her chest.

When she opens her eyes some time later, the walls are stained with darkness. Her first thought on waking is that her mother still had not come.

She realises then that she is on her own.

*　　*　　*

The next morning, she wakes to find a new copy of *The Secret Garden* beside the lamp on her bedside table. The cover is exactly the same: the same gold lettering, the same pink roses, the same girl pushing a key into the lock of the concealed door. Elsa frowns. She wonders, for a brief moment, whether she had dreamed the events of the previous day. Perhaps her book had not been thrown into the fire after all.

She touches her cheek with the tips of her fingers and then goes to the glass hanging on one wall to look at her face. A tiny bruise is leaking out of the corner of one eye. So she had not imagined it after all. The pain seems to have moved down, towards the edges of her ribcage. If she breathes in deeply, there is a sharp discomfort in her chest.

At breakfast, no one mentions what had happened. Her father sits at the top of the table, his back erect, his two forearms flat on the polished wood, waiting to be served. Her mother, sitting next to him, seems not to be able to look at Elsa directly. Her eyes skitter to and fro, from the mantelpiece to the rug to the teapot, never settling on one firm location. She is fidgeting with her cup and saucer, chattering away with a forced brightness punctuated with the occasional, uneasy laugh. Elsa does not speak. She does not feel hungry, but she manages to eat a few forkfuls of kedgeree, the rice sticking lumpenly to her throat as she swallows. She tries to imagine herself somewhere else. She thinks of herself deep in a secret garden, surrounded by the heady scent of crimson flowers and the squawking of exotic, big-beaked birds. She imagines climbing a tree, clambering deep into its branches so that she is hidden by the leaves. From up here, she can look down on the plants and the grass and the animals. From up here, she can see the four thick stone walls, the heavy door that only she possesses the key to, and she feels safe.

'Elsa.' Her mother's voice is sharp. The flowers pop and burst in her mind. 'Elsa, answer your Papa.'

Elsa looks up, blindly.

'I wondered if you found your present this morning,' he says. He seems expectant, almost nervous. The twitch under his eye is more pronounced than usual.

Unsure what is required of her, she waits before answering, scanning his face for clues.

He looks at her levelly and then wipes a speck of egg off his moustache with the bunched-up edge of a napkin. 'The book, I mean,' he continues. 'Did you find the book I bought you?' He places the napkin on the table and then repositions it, ever so slightly, as though it had not been straight enough.

Elsa nods her head, slowly. Her mother looks at her with an expression of panic. 'Yes, Papa,' she says. When she speaks her voice is scratchy and she realises these are the first words she has uttered for hours.

'Good,' Horace says. He looks as though he is about to carry on speaking, as though he has something more he wants to say. Instead, he clears his throat. 'Good,' he says again. And then he smiles.

It is the first time Elsa has seen his smile and for a second, his face seems young, unlined. She cannot help but smile back at him. And she realises she still wants him to like her.

'Thank you,' she says and then she pushes her knife and fork together neatly on the plate, trying not to make too much noise as she does so.

Caroline

THEY ARRIVE WHILE CAROLINE is watching the television news. She is sitting on the sofa, with the light from the screen sending her into a semi-hypnotic trance, when she hears the car draw up in the driveway. She reaches for the remote control and mutes the volume, but her gaze is still fixed to the screen. They are showing footage of a procession of hearses driving through a provincial English town, each one containing the coffin of a dead serviceman. It isn't raining but the first car has its windscreen wipers on because so many flowers are being thrown by the gathered crowd that the driver is finding it impossible to see where he is going through the density of petals and stalks. To one side, a white-faced woman in black clothes is pressing a tissue to her mouth. She seems aware that the television cameras are on her; that she is being watched; that her emotions are being probed for wider consumption.

Outside, Caroline can hear the opening and shutting of doors, the metallic crunch of Andrew attempting to unfold Elsa's wheelchair and then the muted sounds of struggle as he tries to transfer her from the car seat. Caroline makes no movement to get up. Until recently, the thought of Elsa coming to stay would have sent her into a spiral of self-doubt and manic preparation. She would have wanted everything to be just so: the carpets hoovered, the bookshelves dusted, the dining table polished. And yet, no matter how hard she tried, there would always be something for her mother-in-law to find fault with. It was never explicitly expressed, Elsa was too clever for that. It was always a dangerously subtle comment, slipped in around the edges of conversation so that no one but Caroline would notice.

'You *are* lucky,' Elsa would say, looking around her with that imperious gaze. 'Such an easy house to clean.'

Or if Max were playing on the computer, it would be: 'Is he all right up there?' accompanied by a slight smile, a gently raised eyebrow. 'All on his own in front of a screen. It can't be good for him.' And if Caroline ever felt hurt or defensive, Andrew would tell her not to be so sensitive, that his mother was only trying to help. She wasn't, he said, implying that Caroline's parenting was somehow defective, of course not. But Caroline knew better. It was a war of increments, but it was a war nonetheless.

She had so wanted for Elsa to admire her . . . No, she thinks, it was more than that. She had wanted Elsa to love her. But now Caroline feels that the fault was hers all along: whatever she did, she could never be lovable enough. Something about her was wrong; some characteristic fatally lacking.

The front door slams shut. 'We're here,' Andrew calls out. Caroline pushes herself up off the sofa. It takes three goes before she manages it and then her mind takes a while to click into place. Her thoughts are misted up, like condensation on a bathroom mirror. She cannot think how to speak, what words are required of her.

'Caroline?' She shuffles out into the hallway and realises, almost as an afterthought, that she has forgotten to get dressed and is still in her pyjamas and slippers.

'I'm here,' she says and then she sees Elsa and she breathes in sharply at the sight of her. Her mother-in-law has changed beyond all recognition. In the wheelchair, she looks scrunched up and small, a squashed fruit with skin that has lost its moisture. The last time Caroline had seen her, Elsa had been in bed recovering from her first stroke. But despite the circumstances, she had been draped smartly in a cashmere scarf held in place by a cameo brooch and was able to issue orders to the hospital staff and speak to guests with her customary gusto. Her face had still been her own. Now, Caroline is taken aback to see that Elsa's skin has been overrun by liver spots, blending into each other in splodges of yellow and brown. Her head is bent to one side and her left hand is curled in on itself.

'Hello, Elsa,' she says, trying to mask her surprise.

Elsa swivels to look at her. She groans and Caroline can see she is trying to say something but the words come out in an incomprehensible slurry.

'She's been like this all the way down,' Andrew says, his hands still on the wheelchair handles. He is speaking quietly, as if Elsa won't be able to hear.

'It's lovely to have you here, Elsa,' she says, feeling the weight of the lie as it drops out of her mouth. 'We've prepared a room for you downstairs. We thought that would be . . .' she searches for the right word. 'Easier. More convenient.'

In truth, it is Andrew who has done all the preparations, moving the old furniture out of the downstairs study, assembling flat-pack furniture and ringing round various care agencies to get the necessary equipment. In the last few days, they have taken delivery of a bed with a sliding metal bar at one side, a mechanical hoist to lift Elsa off the mattress when necessary, several industrial-sized packets of baby wipes and a red panic button alarm device that is worn round the neck. So much paraphernalia. The process reminds Caroline of the provisions they had made for Max's birth – stocking up on nappies and Babygros, building the cot, hanging the mobile – a natural symmetry between the beginning and end of life.

Caroline has let it happen. She has found no energy, no strength to help. She cannot even think how many days have passed since Andrew first mooted the idea of Elsa coming to live with them. The weeks have melted into each other since Max died.

She has taken refuge, instead, in the twenty-four-hour news pumped out by television and radio stations. Her days are defined by the glossy faces of newsreaders, the movement of their painted lips conveying the details of yet another atrocity: a suicide bomber killing seventeen in a crowded marketplace; a soldier maimed by sniper fire; a grieving mother calling for a government inquiry into why her son died.

It is the mothers Caroline has become obsessed with. They become her companions, these women she has never met.

'I'm going to settle Mummy in,' Andrew says and he wheels Elsa through the hallway, leaving faint black marks on the tiled floor. Caroline does not reply. She returns to her spot on the sofa, yawning. She hits the mute button so that the sound of the news headlines once again floods the room.

The first story is one about a regiment that has returned safely from South Sudan. The cameras are following the men as they walk into a large anonymous space that looks like a school gymnasium, decorated with brightly coloured 'Welcome Home' banners and trestle-tables dotted with polystyrene cups and urns of tea. The soldiers are dressed in light khaki and their faces are tanned from months under the African sun. As they walk into the hall, their families rise to greet them.

Caroline watches one woman with dyed blonde hair and a tiny, sparkling stud on one side of her nose. She has a baby in her arms, swaddled tightly in a pink blanket, and although the woman is smiling, there is also something else – nervousness, maybe, that her husband will have changed. The woman is wearing a light grey velour tracksuit. When she turns away from the camera, Caroline sees that the seat of her trousers is covered with loopy gothic script that spells out the word 'Juicy' in an arc just above her bottom cheeks. Her figure is slim, almost child-like. Now she is passing over the baby to a man in a beret and the accompanying voiceover is saying that this is the first time Sergeant so-and-so has met his two-month-old daughter. Then the commentator says something else about 'our boys' and what a relief it is to their families that they have returned and Caroline shrinks back. She has always hated those words. 'Our boys.' The casual possessiveness of it. They aren't *their* boys, she thinks to herself. Max is hers alone. While Max was alive, she could persuade herself that this was a purely superficial ownership, little more than a display of jingoistic patriotism on the part of strangers. But now that he is dead, she feels powerless. It is as if he has been swallowed up by the country, as if the man has become subsumed by the greater narrative. When the one hundredth British serviceman was killed in South Sudan two days ago, the *Daily Telegraph* had devoted its whole front page to 100 passport-sized photographs of the dead, reprinted against a black background. Max was there in the eighth row down, two in from the right, like a square on a crossword puzzle.

It makes Caroline sad that his smile is no longer just for her. Other people can see it now, gleaming out at them from a smudge of newsprint. People who have never met him. People who will not even notice his face amongst all the others.

The newsreader moves on to a different story about a state visit by the Queen to Canada so Caroline switches over, searching through the channels until she finds one that is talking about the Sudanese conflict. She alights on a daytime chat show. Across the bottom of the screen, written in white bold type against a blue background, is the question: 'Is the government letting our servicemen down?'

A man in a suit and tie, not much older than Caroline, is speaking into the microphone, jabbing a finger as he makes each point. 'I want to know three things,' he is saying in a strong Yorkshire accent. 'One: was my son given the right body armour when he was sent out there? Two: If he wasn't, why wasn't he? Was it some penny-pinching exercise by those crooks in Westminster? And three: if the government's at fault, then I'd damn well like to know what they're going to do about it.' The man's face is reddening. His collar looks too tight for his neck. As he sits back in his chair, the chat show host gives him a peremptory pat on the shoulder. 'Thanks for that, John,' says the host, nodding his head in an understanding manner, gleaming with faux sincerity. 'I'm sure your story will touch many people watching at home.'

Caroline stares at John through the screen. He has loosened his tie and is breathing more easily. But his cheeks are still mottled and his muscles seem tightly coiled, as if the effort of sitting still is almost more than he can bear.

Body armour, Caroline thinks to herself. Would Max have been wearing body armour? She wonders who she can ask about this. Sandy, the visiting officer, perhaps. She is hopeless on military details. Until now, she has never wanted to take an interest, has never wanted to know too much in case it made her even more worried for Max's safety. But now, she thinks . . . well, now there is nothing to lose.

'Caroline,' Andrew says, his voice slicing sharply through her thoughts. 'Where are . . .' He breaks off and glances at the television. 'You must stop watching this stuff, it can't be good for you,' he says, walking up to the set and pressing the power switch so that the television goes black. Caroline keeps staring at it, watching her own reflection in the glass.

'What do you mean,' she says, ' "good for you"?'

He turns to her from where he is standing on the other side of the room and she notices how stressed he looks, how angular his shoulders have become.

'I mean just that. It can't be helping.'

'Helping? There's nothing that can *help*, Andrew. We've lost our . . .'

But before she can finish the sentence, he snaps back. 'Look, Caroline, I don't have time for this. I'm only trying to think of you, to do what's best. You must know that.'

She wishes he would stop talking.

'Now, I've got to go and settle Mummy in. I came to ask where you keep the sheets.' He pauses. 'You don't seem to have got round to making the bed.'

Caroline frowns, stung by the criticism.

'You didn't ask me to.'

'I did . . .' he starts, but then he shakes his head and doesn't complete the sentence. 'Look, it's fine, you obviously don't remember.'

'I wouldn't forget something like that.'

'It's not your fault, it's those blasted pills. I keep telling you . . .'

'Don't start,' she says. 'Please don't start that again.'

He notices she is upset and he kneels down in front of her and takes her hands in his.

'I'm sorry, darling,' he says but the words sound rushed. 'I'm just worried about you, that's all.' She sits there, listless, unresponsive. 'Now, could you tell me where I can find some sheets? I don't want to leave Mummy sitting there for much longer.'

Caroline presses her lips together and slides herself forward off the sofa, letting the blanket drop from her shoulders.

'You don't have to show me,' Andrew says. 'I didn't mean for you to get up.'

'It's easier if I do it.' She pushes past him to go upstairs to the airing cupboard.

When she opens the cupboard door, she is assailed by the warm, fresh smell of washed linen. The shelves are scrupulously labelled with stickers on which she has written in clear, rounded lettering: sheets (double; single; fitted), pillowcases, towels. She laughs when she sees the stickers, she actually laughs. They seem so pointless, so ridiculously unnecessary. Yes, the rest of my life is in chaos, Caroline thinks, but thank God my sheets and pillowcases are all in the right place. Thank God for that. She takes out the bedlinen for Elsa and goes back downstairs. She can hear Andrew trying to make conversation in the downstairs room. Elsa makes no reply.

As Caroline walks down the stairs, two words stick in her mind, the letters whirling and bursting into flecks of light like fireworks studded against a night sky. Body armour. She sees the four syllables written out, hears the sound of them. The idea has lodged inside of her, has taken root.

Perhaps, she thinks, that's the answer. Perhaps, after all, there is someone to blame for his death.

For the first time in weeks, she feels a tiny spark of hope.

Elsa

S HE SENSES IMMEDIATELY THAT she is lying in an unfamiliar bed. It takes a moment for Elsa to place herself, to arrange her thoughts so that she can understand what has happened. In this short, confusing period between sleeping and waking, she has to remind herself not to panic or cry out and to remember that the answers will come to her soon enough. She tries to take a deep breath, but her mouth feels dry and her inhalation is wheezy and slight. Where is she? What is she doing here?

The questions press against her, trampling over her chest. They come at her one after the other, taunting her, jeering, because she does not know the answers. She has no idea where she is. She casts around the room, frantically trying to alight on some familiar object but there is nothing she recognises. There is instead a dressing table with a mirror cracked in one corner, a pine chest of drawers with round handles, a painting of the seaside. The sun shines thickly through the window, making her sight blur and blacken. Elsa squints, blinking away the brightness of it.

Because there is nothing she can attach herself to, no furniture to jog her memory, no solid shapes to channel the wateriness of her thoughts, Elsa feels her grip on herself begin to slip. The tight knot of terror in her stomach is unravelling and she knows that if she gives into it, if she lets the shadow darken, there will be no return. She must be on guard, alert, cautious. Patience, she tells herself. She has to be patient. This is what happens when you get old. Your faculties need more time to click into place than they used to. Calm, she says. Calm.

And slowly, slowly, her mind comes back to her, each glimpse of an explanation shooting forward like an iron filing to a magnet until there are enough of them collected together to make sense.

The first thing she remembers is that she has been taken away from home.

Then: this is because I can no longer look after myself.

Her son drove her to his house, she thinks, and it was a long, long journey.

She is thirsty and too hot.

She has been here for what feels like years but might only be minutes.

Mrs Carswell packed her a . . . a what do you call it? Leather. Square. A thing. A watch? No, that wasn't it, not quite. A newspaper? No, no, it's something you use to put clothes in, to transport them. A *suitcase*. That was it.

The word slots into place and she feels triumphant. But now she wonders: what is her son's name? She can visualise him as a tall man with greying hair but she cannot put her finger on what he is called. She is frustrated with her stupidity. Why can she remember Mrs Carswell's name and not that of her own child? Stupid old woman, she thinks to herself. Pathetic, ancient old biddy making a nuisance of herself, not even able to go to the lavatory on her own.

She shifts against the sheets, attempting to prop herself up against the pillow so that she can further examine her surroundings. She notices that her bed is surrounded by a metal bar and the mattress feels crackly underneath. She wonders why this should be and then realises someone has put on a waterproof undersheet in case Elsa has an accident. The humiliation of this is unbearable.

She can see her suitcase, still buckled up, on top of a trunk at the end of her bed. She wishes she could open it herself. Elsa never liked to delay unpacking. It had always been the first thing she did on holiday, almost as soon as she walked into the hotel. The sterility of an unlived-in room had unsettled her. She had wanted, as soon as possible, to make it recognisably hers, to hang her dresses and prop up her toothbrush in the bathroom water glass. Until she had done this, it had always felt as though someone were about to ask her to leave.

To her left in this new room, there is a bay window that is letting in a stream of sunlight so strong it is making her head hurt. She lifts up her hand to shade her face but it is too tiring to keep it there and, after a while, she drops it back down on to her lap, defeated. She stares at her hand on the blanket, its flesh pitted and wrinkled like a packet of limp, wilting carrots past their sell-by date. Her fingers are furling into her palm. There is a smattering of liver spots just below her knuckles, fenced in by a stringy protrusion of veins.

No one expects this when they are young, she thinks to herself. No one understands how magical it is to have two, fully functioning hands until it is too late. No one appreciates the beauty and cleverness of the design, those four fingers and a thumb, working so easily in tandem to do the most complicated things: unscrewing jam jar lids, dialling a telephone number, wiping the sweat from a brow. She would do anything to have her slim, elegant hands back as they were – her fingers rapid and precise, her white-pink palm soft and smooth, her newly cut nails shiny with two coats of clear varnish.

Until recently, Elsa had worn a small gold watch on her left wrist, given to her by her husband Oliver for their thirtieth wedding anniversary. The watch had become looser over the years as the flesh on her arms had shrivelled and sagged. Now, she noticed, the watch was not there any more. Mrs Carswell had stopped putting it on a few weeks ago, telling Elsa in a loud, forceful voice that she didn't want to risk losing it and wouldn't it be safer on the bedside cabinet?

Perhaps, now that she was so old, they thought she didn't care about time any longer. But Elsa can't help hoping that Mrs Carswell had remembered to pack the watch in her belongings. She did not like to think of it abandoned in her bedroom back home, dust settling on its strap, the ticking by of the days gradually dimming its sheen.

Outside, a bird is making a shrill sound like a ringing telephone. She wishes someone would open the window so she could feel the breeze on her face. Upstairs, a door slams. Elsa jumps. Andrew. That's it. That's what her son is called. Her thoughts align themselves with perfect clarity as though the suddenness of the noise has unblocked a mental dam. Andrew lives in a house in Malvern. This is where he has taken her. She feels cheered by the fact she has remembered something so concrete. And then it goes on: Andrew is married. Andrew has a wife and her name is . . . is . . . Carla, no, that's not it, Catherine? No. No it's . . . it's . . . that's right, her name is Caroline. Elsa smiles, relieved. Still life in the old bat yet, she thinks to herself. Yes, she remembers now that she had seen Caroline when Andrew brought her into the house. It must have been only yesterday even though it felt like a decade ago. They had met in the hallway. Caroline had mouthed her usual pleasantries but something about her had changed. She looked as though she had fallen in on herself, Elsa thought, standing there wearing a lumpy dressing gown, the white of it dulled by too many washes. She had never been of the opinion that her daughter-in-law was a great beauty – attractive, perhaps, if viewed in a certain light. Still, she could see what Andrew found titillating about her – Caroline had always possessed creamy skin and a womanly figure, curvy and soft. It was the kind of thing certain men liked and Andrew had always been a rather needy child, constantly in search of comfort and hugs and the kind of tactile reassurance Elsa found it difficult to give. It was not that she had not loved him. It was more that she had found it almost impossible to express that love, as if to put it into words or gestures would be to diminish its power. Looking back, she wonders if she should have tried harder.

The sun is getting hotter and Elsa turns her head to face away from the window, so that a welcome coolness bathes her cheek. There is a rectangular frame hanging on the wall and within it are three photographs, set side by side and mounted against a pale green background. The central image is a group of three figures. She cannot at first make out who they are, but the more she stares at the frame, the clearer the faces become. There is Andrew, smiling gently, wearing a brown corduroy jacket. And there, on the other side, is Caroline, laughing with her mouth wide open, wearing too much make-up, her hair parted to one side and flicked out at the ends. In between the two of them is a man in a uniform. For a second, Elsa notices the brass buttons and the stiff khaki collar and she thinks it is her father. The man has the same blue eyes as Horace, the same slanted cheeks, but he stands taller, more assured. He does not have Horace's stooped-over shoulders or his tense, downturned mouth or the livid red scar. This man, the one in the photograph, is happy. This man, she thinks, would not hurt her. And then, she remembers.

This man is Max, her grandson. He was a soldier too. But unlike her father, Max had never come home from the war. He had been killed. It comes to her now in a flurry of memories: the phone call from Andrew, almost too distressed to speak, and then the black-edged card that had arrived on her doormat and she remembers that she had gone to find all the photographs of Max she had ever taken, all the letters he had ever sent her, all the messy crayon pictures he had ever drawn her as a child, and she had asked Mrs Carswell to burn them in a fire in the garden because she didn't want to think about him any more. She couldn't. The sadness was too much to bear.

Max had been her only grandchild and she had adored him. The vociferousness of her love had taken her by surprise when he was born because she had always been such a cautious mother, but it was different with a grandchild, she discovered. You didn't have to worry about discipline or putting them to bed or feeding them the right food or any of the agonising stuff that made you feel, as a parent, you were always doing something slightly wrong. With Max, she could simply shower him with attention and presents and home-baked cakes and then send him home, comfortable in the knowledge that her fondness for him was requited, that no one was judging her or accusing her, silently, of not being good enough.

She remembers one of the last times he came up to Grantchester. His school had wanted Max to apply for Oxbridge and encouraged him to go to various open days at Cambridge colleges. Elsa had put him up in the box room that used to be Oliver's study, overlooking the willow tree in the front driveway.

He arrived late on a Friday, having found his way from Malvern on public transport despite her insisting that he should have taken a taxi from the station and that she would reimburse him.

'But where's the fun in that, Granny?' he had said. 'You don't meet as many interesting people that way.'

And over a supper of fish pie and green beans, he had regaled her with his encounters with strangers on various trains and buses.

'One guy on the train from King's Cross was coming to meet his birth mother,' Max said, draining his glass of Rioja. Elsa had always thought it ridiculous not to allow young people to drink alcohol in moderation.

'His what?' asked Elsa.

'His birth mother. He'd been adopted as a baby and his parents only just told him.'

'Gracious,' she said, picking at an overcooked bit of potato crust from the pie. 'What an awful thing.'

'Sometimes I wonder if I'm adopted.'

'Don't be ridiculous.'

'No, I'm only joking, obviously, but it's just . . .'

She stayed quiet, waiting for him to continue.

'Mum and Dad sometimes seem so different from me, you know?'

She cocked her head to one side. 'How so?' she asked gently, starting to clear away the plates. She was always very careful with Max not to let her real feelings about Caroline show. It was the right thing to do, she thought, and she was quite scrupulous about it.

Max sighed and scratched his head. His hair was too long, Elsa noted. Caroline really should tell him to get it cut. She filled the sink with warm water, squirting in Fairy Liquid and then put on a pair of bright yellow rubber gloves. She liked to take care of her hands. You could always tell a woman's age by her hands.

'I don't even know if I want to go to university,' he said after a long pause.

Elsa turned to look at him. He was twisting his empty wine glass round and round by the stem, sending shifting prisms of candle-light across the linen tablecloth. She examined his face: the long straight nose, the angularity of his cheek, like slate. He was so handsome, she thought. He got that from his father.

'Oh Max, what's brought this on?'

They had a long talk then, about what he wanted to do with his life, how he wanted to make a difference, to do something that counted. Elsa was inclined to dismiss most of it as youthful naivety. She teased him about it and he took it in good humour. By the next morning, she felt that he seemed lighter, less preoccupied.

When she drove him back to the station after breakfast two days later, he gave her a hug on the concourse. 'Thanks, Granny,' he said. 'For putting me up. And for the chat.'

'It's been a pleasure, Max,' she said, not meeting his eye, embarrassed all of a sudden at how emotional she felt. Silly really, how he had the power to affect her.

'No, I mean it. It really helped talking things through.'

And she said, almost without thinking: 'There's nothing worse than wasting years of your life being forced to do something you don't want to do.' She scanned the departure board to find his platform while she spoke, avoiding looking at him. 'It can ruin you. It can make you into someone you don't want to be.'

Max squeezed her shoulder. She had not realised until later that she was talking from experience but, of course, she had been. She had been talking about Horace. And also, in a way, she had been talking about herself.

She waited to wave Max off, watching him stride towards the train with his battered leather satchel slung across his chest. He seemed so unaware of the effect he had on other people: the admiring glances from girls as he passed, the physical space he commanded just by being in it. She felt so proud of him, in a way she never had with Andrew.

Was that a terrible admission?

He grinned at her, waved and then disappeared into the carriage. She waited for the train to pull out and stood on the platform, staring silently for a moment at the empty tracks. She did not want to miss him but still she felt his absence.

After a while, Elsa made her way to the car park. She concentrated more than she needed to on the drive back home. When she got back, she put the *Goldberg Variations* on the record player and turned the music up as loud as she dared. She poured herself a whisky, sat back on the sofa, and for a few, solitary minutes, closed her eyes and allowed herself to feel depressed.

'Right, that's that,' she said, after the harpsichord had stopped. 'Onwards and upwards.'

Elsa smoothed down her skirt and, with her hands clenched in downward fists on either side of her, managed to propel herself upwards, feeling a muscular twinge in her back as she did so.

For the first time then, she began to feel old. Not physically, but mentally, as though her mind were becoming blunt, her thoughts empty of meaning. She missed Max, she knew, and at the same time, she would not allow herself to. She felt, already, that she was losing him. She felt, perhaps, they all were.

Caroline

SHE BEGINS TO MAKE more of an effort. She gets out of bed, dresses herself, tries to regain some semblance of normality. Each task seems endless, as if she is trying to gather up spilt sugar from the linoleum only to find the next day that there are still sticky granules of it crunching underfoot. Still, she keeps on trying.

Part of it is guilt: she knows she has been neglecting Andrew and that he is upset by this, although he would never say so. But part of it is that, with Elsa in the house, Caroline cannot help but feel it is self-indulgent to carry on as she has been.

Her mother-in-law has been with them now for almost a month and Caroline can see the pleading desperation in her face every time she walks into her room. Although she can barely speak, Elsa's discontented anger is there in her every gesture: the clenched fist on the counterpane, the narrowed eyes when the curtains are opened, the way she twists and turns when they try to change the bedclothes. And when Caroline witnesses this, it feels cruel, some-how, to choose to be in bed all day when Elsa so furiously wishes to be elsewhere. Until now, her mother-in-law had never displayed any hint of fragility in front of Caroline. She had been impenetra-ble. To watch this sudden disintegration is not upsetting exactly – Caroline had never been fond enough of Elsa for that – but it is disjointing, as if the natural order of things has once again been thrown out of kilter. First Max; now Elsa. She feels that she must do her bit to maintain some kind of continuity.

She tries, without success, to remember how she used to be, to reassemble the scaffold of her previous self bit by bit. One morning, she is able to brush her hair. The next, to put on a load of laundry. Within a week, she has cut her fingernails and filed them neatly. Of course, there are still things she struggles to do. She does not like to leave the house. She has not yet risked driving the car. Sometimes, she cannot get dressed and she disappears into a thick mist, unable to hear what is going on around her, unable to communicate or answer questions that are asked of her. And no matter how well she seems to be doing, there is a point, every day, every single day, where she will collapse on to the carpet and curl up and cry. The smallest thing can set her off. Yesterday, it was the appearance of Max's name on her mobile phone screen. It had pinged up without warning when she was looking through her text messages and there it was, the last text he had ever sent her: 'Hi Mum. At Brize Norton about to get on plane. Missing you and sending you lots of love. Save me some apple crumble for when I get back. Xxxx.'

She had no words for how she felt about seeing that.

Tonight, Andrew is preparing dinner. He has asked that they eat, not with trays on their laps in front of the television as has become their custom, but around the kitchen table and he has laid it beautifully with candles and a jam jar filled with pale pink blossoms from the garden. Caroline is trying to be pleasant, to nod her head and listen to what he is saying but the fine grain of conversation keep slipping through her fingers before she can catch hold of it. Her head is blocked up from too much crying.

'I can't understand her,' Andrew is saying, tipping the edge of the frying pan over a platter of poached salmon, covering it with a greasy trickle of lemon-butter. The silence goes on for a fraction too long and Caroline realises she is meant to respond.

'Who?' she asks, vaguely.

He turns to look at her. 'My mother. Elsa. We've just been talking about her.'

'Sorry. What about her?'

He is about to sigh but then he stops himself, unaware that it is too late. She has already heard the whisper of irritation.

'I was just saying I can't understand the things she's trying to say to me.' He waits, expectantly.

'Maybe you're trying too hard?'

He brings the food to the table, placing a too-full plate in front of her. Looking at the food makes her tired.

'What was that?' Andrew asks.

'Maybe you're trying too hard to understand each syllable when actually you should just let it all wash over you and get an impression of what she's trying to say.'

He lets this sink in. 'Yes, maybe. That's a good thought,' but his voice suggests precisely the opposite. She has noticed, in the last few weeks, that Andrew has begun to dismiss what she says, almost as if he expects her to fail him.

'Sorry. Forgot the salt.' He stands up from the kitchen table, holding the back of the chair with one hand so that it will not tip over. She wonders if he honestly thinks it would matter if the chair fell, if the worst thing it would mean is that one of them would have to bend down and pick it up?

She concentrates on slicing a boiled potato into quarters, lifting a piece to her mouth, forcing herself to swallow. It is not good for Andrew to see her upset. Recently, he has been making comments about Caroline 'not being able to cope', questioning whether the pills are 'doing her any good', asking whether she wouldn't prefer 'to talk to someone'. Caroline finds the thought of this, of not having the trap-door of chemical numbness through which to escape, too awful to contemplate. She reminds herself: I must pretend to be on top of it all; he expects me to be getting better. I must get better. I must put on a show of it.

She takes a deep breath and Andrew sits back down next to her, stroking her arm lightly with the tips of his fingers.

'You're right,' he says, soothing, conciliatory. 'I'm too worried about getting each word and so often she gets things the wrong way round.' He opens the packet of Maldon sea salt and pinches a clump of white crystals between his thumb and forefinger.

'The other day she called me her daughter,' he says, sprinkling the salt liberally over his plate.

'Yes. She did that with Max.'

He looks momentarily taken aback. 'You talked to her about Max?'

'She brought it up,' Caroline says.

'Oh.' He is obviously taken aback.

'She pointed at Max's photo on the wall.' Caroline pushes the salmon around her plate. The smell of the fish makes her sick. 'You know,' she gestures vaguely. 'The one in that room. Of his passing out parade.'

'Ah,' says Andrew, his forehead crinkling. 'How interesting. Well, I'm glad she remembers that much at least.'

'Why wouldn't she? Remember Max's death, I mean.' Caroline senses that her words are coming out in the wrong order, that she isn't being clear enough. 'She adored him.' A pause, and then she cannot help herself from adding: 'She seemed to think she was closer to him than I was half the time, don't you remember?'

He looks at her, quizzically. 'Oh darling, you were always too sensitive about that.' After a while, he adds: 'It's just that normally she hates talking about anything to do with war ... the military ... Or she did at any rate.'

Andrew polishes off the last of his salmon, pushing it against his fork with a sliver of potato and a piece of broccoli, then wiping round the plate to soak up any leftover sauce. He is so precise, she thinks, even when he eats.

'Had enough?' he asks.

Caroline nods. 'I'm sorry. Not terribly hungry.'

He clears away the plates, loading the dishwasher without rinsing them first, which used to drive her mad. He turns on the cold tap, letting it run before filling up a glass of water. He drinks two litres a day, is religious about it.

'Why doesn't she like talking about the war?' Caroline asks, deliberately not watching as he drinks. She can't bear it. The routine of it. The way he just carries on as if nothing has happened. She wonders, not for the first time, if her love for Andrew has dried at the edges: a shallow stream on a hot, hot day.

'Oh you know, all that stuff with her father,' says Andrew, coming back to sit next to her. 'I mean, yes, he survived the war, but was never quite the same. I think he was a difficult man to live with when he came back.' Andrew tips back the glass in his hand and downs the water swiftly in a series of gulps. He exhales, satisfied, and wipes his top lip. 'Mummy's never really spoken to me about it though. Not in depth, at least.' He leans across, touching the back of her hand with his palm. 'As you know, she's not particularly good at opening up about that sort of thing.'

He smiles, trying to re-establish some of their old intimacy but when she looks at him she feels tears welling inside and she cannot help it. He registers that she is about to cry and withdraws his hand quickly. The tears start to trickle down her cheeks even though she doesn't feel especially sad. She wipes her nose on the cuff of her sweatshirt sleeve.

'I'm sorry –' she starts and then she realises there is no point. 'It was a lovely dinner.' A lie. Another one. She imagines the lies in a small pile, accumulating like dry twigs for a bonfire. She gets up, pushing back with two hands on the table to steady herself. She finds she is shaky on her feet nowadays and when she moves too quickly, her head is flooded with a tight, constricting blackness dotted with pixels of blurred light. The other day, she had knelt down to scrub out the bath and felt she was about to faint. She had to lie down, cold-clammy with sweat until the nausea subsided.

'Where are you off to?' asks Andrew.

'Just going to see what's on the box,' she replies, walking down the hallway.

'Do you think that's wise?'

She considers answering and then decides against it. She pushes open the sitting-room door and sinks gratefully into the sofa, feeling the familiar cushioned contours shift to accommodate her shape. She reaches for the remote control, which is lying at exactly the same angle where she had left it on the coffee table. The screen jumps into life and she feels intense relief as the voices start. It is the male newsreader she likes, the one with the Welsh accent and the side-parting. The first item is about the rise in tuition fees. Caroline jiggles her leg, impatient. If they carry on talking about this, she will turn over to the satellite news channel. But then, as if the newsreader has heard her thoughts, the next story is about the parents of a dead RAF man taking the Ministry of Defence to court.

Andrew thinks it is bad for her, this constant need for information about the war. He says that she was never interested before, when Max was serving, so why should she be now? He says she will never be able to move forwards if she insists on raking over the past. He says he is telling her this not because he wants to cause her pain but because he loves her, because he wants to look after her. She can understand his sentiment but she does not feel it in any real way. And if she tried to explain why she watched, she knows she would be unable to put it into words.

The parents of the dead RAF man are on screen now, sitting in a café, talking to the reporter. The mother's face is puffy, but her features are delicate. Her hair has been dyed blonde but it is growing out so that there are dark roots across the crown of her scalp.

'What do you want to achieve from this case, ultimately?' the reporter is asking.

'I want someone to be held accountable,' the mother replies. 'I want to find out why. I wasn't there when my boy most needed me in life. But I'm going to make sure I'm here for him now, in death.'

That's exactly it, Caroline thinks. That's exactly how she feels. And looking at this woman, there is a filament of recognition. She is seized by an idea. She remembers the words that had been floating in the recesses of her mind for days: body armour.

Later, she goes upstairs to the study. She sits at the desk, waiting for the computer screen to jump into life, listening to the internal machinery of it whirr as she presses the 'on' button. She types 'body armour' and 'foot patrol' into the search engine and hits the return key.

At the bottom of the second page of search results is a small news story published in the *Observer* a few weeks ago. Caroline is surprised that she had not seen it at the time, but she and Andrew subscribe to the *Telegraph* and it has taken her a long while to be able to look at any newspaper after Max's death. Until recently, she had not wanted to read any reports of her son's death, had not wanted to submit to the journalistic stringing together of a series of clinical sentences. She had not wanted his death to become part of the historical record, appropriated by others.

She clicks on the link to the *Observer* article. It is headlined: 'Questions Raised Over Soldiers' Deaths' and, when she skims through it to get the general gist, she learns that a support group of 'grieving families' had written an open letter to the paper which decried the lack of equipment given to their sons and daughters on the front line. She clicks on to the link so that she can read the letter in its entirety.

'Dear Sir –

We, the undersigned, call upon our government to do more to equip our armed forces in the light of a number of worrying incidents concerning the failure to supply the latest body armour to our troops on the front line.

All of us have experienced the loss of a loved one, killed in action while serving our country in various conflicts abroad. We believe it is time for our troops to be afforded the respect that they deserve. If they put their lives on the line in our name, we believe that the very least we can do is provide them with the best protective equipment.

Yours faithfully –'

There followed a list of names, most of them female, with the italicised details of the relative they had lost in brackets. Caroline reaches for a piece of paper from the printer and, spreading it on the desk, starts to write down the names. The ballpoint of the biro makes a scrabbling sound against the wood as she moves across the page, her writing slanting and slipping in her haste to get all the information down.

She clicks back to the longer news story. The journalist had written that the families concerned were using the Freedom of Information Act to determine whether eight soldiers killed in Upper Nile State earlier this year had been given something called 'Osprey body armour'. Apparently, there were concerns that the soldiers in question had been using old, out-of-date kit that did not offer comprehensive protection.

When she reads this, Caroline emits a small cry of surprise. She is startled by the noise, as though it had come from someone else.

But then, she feels relief and that sensation turns into something more tangible, something approaching certainty. Did Max have the right body armour? Because if these men and women didn't and if they were fighting in the same region as Max had been, facing the same kind of dangers, the chances were that he too would not have been provided with the right equipment.

The official cause of death given to Caroline by the army was that a piece of shrapnel had sliced into Max's chest, severing the aortic artery. She had requested that they send her the full post-mortem, despite Sandy, the casualty visiting officer, cautioning her against it.

'It will contain some uncomfortable details,' she had said, with an expression of concern that looked tired, as though it had been worn several times before, on other occasions like this one.

'More uncomfortable than the fact that Max is dead?' Caroline had replied. There had been no response. She had found herself getting pricklier, more defensive, in the aftermath of Max's death. In the dark stew of grief, she found that these small victories – points scored against an invisible enemy – made her somehow feel stronger, more like herself, more like the person she once was.

She remembers herself as she had been that very first time she met Elsa: young, insecure, scared and completely out of her depth. She feels no fondness for her younger self, only embarrassment mingled with an anxious desire never again to slip into the patterns of that person's behaviour. As soon as she and Andrew had married and bought the sprawling, red-brick house in Malvern, Caroline had set about re-inventing herself. She cut off all ties with her parents. There had been no dramatic showdown, simply a gradual cessation of communication, a distancing, and, as Caroline had suspected, they made no effort to bridge the gap. They had died within a year of each other shortly after Max was born: her mother of cancer and her father of a heart attack. She had sold the flight-path bungalow, complete with the dingy three-piece suite and the flock wallpaper stained yellow with cigarette smoke. When she had shifted her parents' double bed to hoover the carpet upstairs, two empty gin bottles had slipped to the floor. 'You only live once,' her mother had been fond of saying. 'Might as well enjoy it while you can.'

Caroline had felt no grief at her parents' death and, at the time, she was pleased by this, pleased by the thought that she had so successfully managed to eradicate any feeling for her flesh and blood. She dismantled her memories of them, of the sour disappointment they trailed, the small-mindedness of their ideas, the constant nagging at their only child. She pushed the thought of them out to sea.

And then Caroline concentrated on her own family, on raising Max and looking after Andrew and winning Elsa over by scratching away any trace of her less than acceptable past. She found it was surprisingly easy to assume the outward appearance of a respectable middle-class housewife, the kind of woman who wore espadrilles on holiday in the South of France and could rustle up a good lasagne at a moment's notice. She listened to Radio 4 and picked up the tricks of received pronunciation. Her voice became deeper, her vowels more lengthened. There were little things she learned just by watching carefully: the fact that people who are comfortably off do not like their possessions to look brand new, for instance. Their BMW estates will always be slightly battered; their designer cashmere casually bobbled at the edges. The first time Caroline bought a pair of tasteful cream-coloured Converse trainers (so practical for the school run and rushing around the supermarket, don't you find?), she was careful to scuff them gently before she wore them.

She had done it all for love, all of it. How odd that was.

And Max, in a way, had unwittingly been part of it. She had always been so afraid of letting him down, of her own son looking at her and realising she wasn't what she should have been, that she had spent a whole life trying, as though the exercise of effort would be enough to make her lovable.

Because what a waste it all seemed. Now that he had gone, what did any of it matter?

Turning back to the computer, Caroline starts to type the relevant search terms into Google. She runs her finger down the piece of paper she has written on, making sure she doesn't miss anything out or misspell any of the technical words. The keyboard becomes slick with the sweat from her fingertips. A lock of hair falls forward from her clipped-up ponytail and sticks to her cheek. She does not brush it away. She does not notice that it is past midnight and Andrew has already gone to bed without saying goodnight. She does not feel tired but instead is gripped with a kind of manic energy. She hasn't felt this alive for months.

Within a couple of hours, Caroline has amassed a sheaf of documents, printed out in 12-point Times New Roman. She discovers, leafing through them, that the Osprey kit offered good front and back protection whereas the older version – the enhanced body combat armour – did not fully cover the sides of the torso, meaning that fragments of shrapnel could slip through, sometimes fatally. But the Osprey was, inevitably, more expensive and there seemed to be a concerted effort by the Ministry of Defence to avoid paying for it – the more she searched, the more comments she found made by politicians claiming that the Osprey body armour was too bulky and heavy; that the older kit enabled soldiers to move more freely and carry more equipment.

'They would say that, wouldn't they?' she hears herself muttering. The more she reads, the more convinced she becomes: slowly, all the pieces seem to fall into place. She feels her rib-cage constrict with the conviction that this is what had killed Max. He didn't have the right body armour. How else would the shrapnel have sliced through his chest? As yet, she has no proof. But whatever it is – mother's intuition, a woman's instinct, call it what you like – she knows. She just *knows*.

There is an indistinct image on one of the sheets of paper, taken from an internet discussion forum on the war in South Sudan. It is a photograph of the Armed Forces Minister, a podgy-faced man named Derek Lester who has the appearance of a self-important rural bank manager. In the picture, his tie is skewed, with a small, tight knot. His cheeks are florid and plump, suggesting that Derek Lester does not refrain from indulging in the finer things in life. She looks at this picture and then, quickly, she finds herself scribbling across his face in pen until his features are hidden under a tangled mass of black ink.

Caroline switches off the computer. It fizzles and snaps and the screen goes black. She gathers up the sheets of paper and puts them neatly in the top drawer of the desk. Then she goes to bed, sliding in beside a sleeping Andrew and trying not to wake him. Automatically, she flexes her feet away from his legs so that he will not feel the coolness of her toes. She closes her eyes but she does not sleep. It will be morning soon, she thinks, and then it will begin, all over again.

Andrew

H E GOES FOR A long afternoon walk through the Malvern
Hills, striding forward with swift purpose, shaking the dust
from his thoughts. It is cold, a late autumn Saturday when the
winter seems to be gathering in around the edges, slipping through
the cracks. As he walks, following the public footpath up to St
Anne's Well, his wellington boots pick up strands of frost-dried
mud and fragments of leaf.

He has no particular destination in mind, but he had been overcome, all of a sudden, by the need to get out of the house. So he
had left Caroline sitting at her computer upstairs, staring at the
screen, the desk covered in bits of paper.

Andrew has noticed that countless forms and official documents
seem to appear from the ether when someone dies unexpectedly.
Everywhere, there are ripped-open envelopes and sheets of foolscap
and, for some reason, a sudden surge in the number of electrical
cords. The house was full of thick, tangled wires leading nowhere.

This morning, he had woken and felt overwhelmed by lassitude,
by the sense that he couldn't muster up the energy to keep going.
He had got Elsa her breakfast and spoon-fed her mashed-up
banana as usual, but today she had been sulky and uncooperative,
turning her head away when he tried to feed her, wrinkling her
nose and mouth. He knew she did not do it maliciously, but a frustration had seeped into him. He had snapped at her and then,
immediately, felt guilty about it.

'I'm sorry, Mummy,' he said but he couldn't be sure that she
understood or that she even heard him. Or perhaps she was taking

it all in and that, in a way, would be worse. In the end, Elsa closed her eyes and he felt relief that he no longer had to look at their blueness, alive, still, beneath the murkiness of cataracts.

Once he had cleared up the breakfast tray, he thought a walk might clear his thoughts. He called upstairs to Caroline to let her know he was going.

'I'm off out,' he shouted from the hallway, his Barbour already halfway on.

She hadn't acknowledged him.

'I'll see you in a bit,' he said, more loudly.

Still nothing.

He has begun to feel resentment for his wife where previously there had been only sympathy and love. It is a change that worries him and he is anxious to discover the cause of it, so that he can tackle it, so that he can turn it into a logical problem to be fixed.

But now that he is out on the Hills on his own he finds that instead of the walk clearing his mind, it has left him feeling unsettled, preoccupied. He is worried about Caroline, about her strange obsession with this body armour stuff. She has, over the past week, acquired a wild energy, printing off reams and reams of what she calls 'research' and presenting them to him at all times of day and night. He wishes she would spend her time more usefully. Would it really be so much to ask for her to cook the occasional meal? Or to look after Elsa from time to time?

Yesterday, he had been soaking in the bath when she came in without knocking, bearing a fresh sheath of paper slipped into a clear plastic wallet.

'There,' she said, passing him the folder, and there was a peculiar triumph in her voice. 'See what you think about that.'

Her hair was askew and her shirt buttons were in mismatched holes so that she looked unkempt, half-crazed. She used to be so lovely, he found himself thinking, and now she is old and too skinny. He took the folder with damp fingers and scanned the top document, noticing that she had marked several passages in highlighter pen.

'I'm afraid I don't quite see . . .'

'Oh Andrew, come *on*,' she said, impatiently snatching back the paper. 'It says here that the European Court of Human Rights is expected to rule our servicemen have a right to life; that by ignoring the military covenant our government . . .'

He stood up in the bath, letting the water drip from him, trying to block out what she was saying. He finds it is best to allow Caroline to wear herself out with these theories, not to take any of it too seriously. At the start, he had tried to be supportive but, increasingly, he has come to fear that she is losing her grip on reality, that her mind has become inflated with the idea of a conspiracy that doesn't exist.

'Caroline, darling, stop,' he said, wrapping a towel around his waist. 'Stop this.'

She looked at him, wounded.

'Don't you care?' she asked and he knew he had hurt her. 'Don't you see, Andrew, that this is what we need to prove that Derek Lester . . .'

Andrew groaned. He couldn't help himself. If she mentioned that bloody man's name one more time . . .

'You know I care,' he said. 'But you've got to let it go.'

Her gaze was vacant.

'I don't understand . . .' she started, her voice quiet. 'If Derek Lester . . .'

'Sod Derek Lester,' he said, surprised by his own outburst. 'Sod the lot of them. You're working yourself up for no reason . . .'

Caroline turned and dashed out of the bathroom. His first reaction was not of sympathy but of intense irritation. He noted this and it caused him a moment's pain. There seemed to be such a breach between them. He could not imagine ever being close to her again.

He dried himself quickly, put on his dressing gown and went in search of her. He found her by the computer, hunched up in a chair, her shoulders heaving. She was making no sound. He went to her and tried to take her in his arms but she shrank away from him.

'Go,' she said. 'Just leave me alone.'

And although he should have stayed, although he should have said sorry, he did as she asked.

As he walks towards the crest of the hill, he admonishes himself for being too harsh with her. He can understand why Caroline needs someone to be responsible for Max's death, but he simply doesn't believe that any one individual can answer that particular charge. Max died because he was in a war zone. Not only that, Andrew thinks, letting his breath unfurl against the sky, but he died because he chose to be in that war zone. He chose to join the army. He knew what he was getting into.

And yet, he can't deny that Caroline has been getting better. Whatever he thinks of her obsessions, at least they have given her a reason to get up in the morning, a reason not to slouch around half-dressed and silent and unreachable. For that, he is grateful. He picks up pace again, hands clasped behind his back, head pushed forward in the direction of movement.

He walks up a steep stretch of hillside at a steady speed so that he does not feel the need to stop for a rest and start again. An experienced mountaineer had once told him this was the key to reaching the top: endurance rather than haste. The method worked, but he has to keep reminding himself not to sprint ahead; to have patience in the slow, almost geriatric steps he is taking.

Still, it gives him the chance to take in the view as he goes. He notices that almost all the leaves have been buffeted off the trees by the shrill wind and, when he looks up to gauge how many hours of daylight he has left, he is surprised to see the sky is veiled by a canopy of interwoven branches, like clasping fingers. Andrew has hardly paid any attention to the outside world over the last few months. It has all been internal: the careful mapping and charting of the tiniest change in grief's gradient or contour.

As the ground begins to level out, there is a turn-off signposted to St Anne's Well. A family of four, wearing brightly coloured waterproofs and matching climbing shoes, are consulting a map just where the pathway forks. Andrew keeps his head down, not wanting to be diverted, not wanting to have to acknowledge their presence, to nod his head and give an amiable 'Hello'. Instead, he cuts through the trees to avoid the weekend crowds. He has done this walk hundreds of time before and he knows every dip and curve of the territory: he can loop past the Well, wend his way through this clump of trees and then rejoin the path further on when the tourists have thinned out.

For a few seconds, he experiences that simple gleam of satisfaction one gets when a minor, practical problem had been solved, but then his mind returns, as it always does, to Max. He remembers the last time he saw Max, when he had come down to Malvern for a couple of days' leave before being sent to South Sudan. He had turned up late on the Friday night, blaming a delay on the motorway that meant his bus had been caught in traffic, and yet although the dinner was cold, although Caroline had been anxiously biting her nails for hours, although Andrew had tried repeatedly to call Max's mobile without success, the sight of him on the front step, the familiar lopsided smile, shoulders hunched to get through the doorway, had made all of the nervous strain dissipate almost immediately.

'Parents,' he said, opening his arm wide in a deliberately grandiose gesture, letting his rucksack slip to the floor. 'Great to see you.' Caroline went straight to him, giving into his crushing hug.

'Well, well well,' said Andrew, not quite allowing himself to smile. 'The prodigal son returns.'

Max laughed, then beckoned for his father to move closer. 'Come on, Dad, there's plenty of room in here.'

What was it about Max that meant all tension was defused with such ease? Why was it impossible ever to be cross with him?

They had stood there for several minutes, embracing, the three of them locked in place. It was Andrew who had broken it off first, patting Max on the back, embarrassed by how emotional he felt to see him.

'Your supper is feeling rather sorry for itself,' he said, lifting up Max's bag and leading the way to the kitchen. 'Still, it'll be better than what you get on the base, I imagine.'

Max, his arm still around his mother, followed him down the hallway. 'Anything that isn't a pasta bake, a chicken fricassee or a beef stew will be fine with me,' Max said. 'I've become a man of simple tastes.'

He ate an enormous portion of shepherd's pie and then went straight to bed, where he slept for thirteen hours straight until it was almost lunchtime the next day. Caroline and Andrew had spent the morning inventing pointless little tasks that would keep them in the house in case he emerged from his bedroom, both of them valiantly pretending not to be disappointed that they weren't getting to spend more time with him. Andrew was better at the pretence than Caroline. He was acutely aware of the need not to put too much pressure on their only child, not to make him the unwilling recipient of all their neediness and expectation. But, by the time he woke up, there was not much they could do with the rest of the day apart from walk into town for tea.

They went to a hotel that Caroline particularly liked but which Andrew had always found a touch twee and stuffy. The best thing that could be said about it was the view, which stretched out beneath a long panoramic window at one end of the dining room: the twisting pathways of the town, lined with terraced houses along the green-brown slopes. The hotel had been built at the very edge of the valley, so that if you pressed your forehead against the window glass and looked down, you could imagine you were floating in space. This was something Max used to do as a child. He had never been scared.

On this particular day, they had taken the long route up to the hotel, tramping up a series of back roads that looped around the Malvern Priory before cutting through the graveyard. The ground was dotted with damp bits of confetti, pale pink and cream blotches stuck to the tarmac like multi-coloured pinheads pierced through a velvet cushion. One of the confetti pieces fixed itself to the edge of Andrew's shoe and he was trying to shake it off without halting, so his attention was momentarily elsewhere when he noticed Max running away from the church towards the high street.

'Max!' Caroline called after him. 'Wait!'

Andrew looked over. There were two men standing on the other side of the railings and one of them was gripping the other by his shirt collar. A blue car had been abandoned in the middle of the road, the door by the driver's seat left open. One of the men – the one under attack – was wearing a grey suit and a loosened tie. He was trying to say something, but the other man kept shouting, his face red and sweaty and screwed up. At this distance, Andrew couldn't make out what they were saying, beyond the occasional jarring snap of a swear word.

Max, running at full pelt, had almost reached the men. Caroline, lagging behind him, had stopped to recover her breath, bending over and resting her hands on her waist. As Andrew drew up alongside her, she pointed helplessly towards the unfolding scene. 'Andrew,' she panted. 'Do something.'

He glanced towards the street. The suited man was shouting now, his voice loud enough that Andrew could hear him.

'Get your hands off me,' he was saying, but Andrew could tell, even from this distance, the pretence of his bravado. 'I told you I didn't see you.'

'Yeah? That right, mate? You didn't fucking see me when you pulled out like that in the middle of the fucking traffic?'

The red-faced man tightened his grip. He drew his right arm back behind his head and, swiftly, landed a punch square on the other man's jaw. The man slumped and groaned. At just the moment that the attacker was going in for another, clenching his fist in readiness, Andrew saw Max climbing over the railings to get to the fight.

Andrew started to sprint. He could see, as he ran, that Max had placed himself between the two men, holding out his arms at full span to separate them. The red-faced man was trying to push forwards, his arms flailing. Andrew noticed Max's lips moving but could not make out the words. By the time he got there, Max was saying 'Cool it. The two of you. No need to fight.'

He had done something to his voice, Andrew noticed, so that it no longer sounded quite so well spoken. His accent had become rougher around the edges, the glottal stop more pronounced and yet what he was saying, the way he was saying it, seemed all at once infused with authority.

The red-faced man allowed his shoulders to slump. 'This is none of your fucking business, mate,' he said, but the power seemed to have gone out of him.

Max put his hand on the man's arm. 'Whatever you're fighting about, it's not worth a police record, is it?'

The man smirked, then disengaged himself. He shifted away from Max and walked back to his car. 'Fucking pillock,' he said, as he slid into the driving seat. He turned the key in the ignition and a thumping beat started up from the radio, drowning out the shriek of the engine. The blue car swung out into the road amidst a chorus of beeping horns, then sped up the high street.

'All right?' Max was saying to the man in the suit, who was touching his bruised jaw, his body slackened by shock. Max inspected the man's face. 'It doesn't look like too much damage has been done, mate. But I'm sure it hurts like hell. Listen, is there anything we can do for you? Do you need us to call anyone or take you anywhere?'

The man shook his head. Then, after a pause, he said: 'Thank you for . . . you know . . .' His voice was slurred. Max grinned. 'Don't mention it. Guy was a nutter.' The man nodded, then returned to his own car and drove off, the exhaust stuttering as he negotiated the steep hill start.

Andrew, unaware until this moment that he had been holding his breath, exhaled. He was still a few yards away from his son and he realised he had been standing there for several seconds, simply watching the drama unfold in front of him, unable to move or intervene. He walked towards Max now and called out his name.

'Sorry, Dad,' Max said, his shoulders relaxed as if nothing had happened. 'We can go to tea now. No more hold-ups, I promise.'

'Max,' Andrew protested. 'You could have been hurt.' But he knew, as he said the words, that he was ashamed of himself, of his own weakness. It was Andrew's natural inclination never to get involved in fights he did not understand. If he had passed two men in the street in the grip of a violent argument, Andrew would have stepped back and allowed someone else to sort it out. It was only now, watching his son, that he realised his own cowardice.

Caroline was running up behind them, arms folded across her chest to stop her cardigan from flapping open as she moved. 'Max, sweetheart,' she was saying, her breathing irregular.

'It's fine, Caroline,' Andrew said. 'He's fine.' But she went to Max and hugged him tightly to her. Max, reddening, did not put his arms around her. 'Mum, honestly . . .' He let his voice trail away. 'Let's go and eat some scones, shall we?'

'What were you thinking?' Caroline said, playfully slapping his chest. 'God knows what could have happened. They're not worth it, darling.' She tried to regulate her voice so that it appeared light, breezy.

'Come on,' Andrew said, walking up and putting an arm around her, 'Let's get going.' She kept looking at Max, her eyes shining. She did not move away from Andrew's touch but she did not respond to it either. As they resumed their course towards the hotel, he saw that she had reached out to take her son's hand but either Max didn't see or he chose to ignore it.

After Max died, Andrew found that this incident kept rising in his mind, floating on the surface of his thoughts like pond-weed. Partly, it was because it had been the last time he had seen his son alive. But it was also that, looking back, Andrew realised it was then, seeing Max resolve the fight between those two men, that he finally understood what kind of a soldier he was. He had never previously realised that Max's sense of injustice, of unfairness, was so sharply cultivated. But he saw, that day in the churchyard, that Max's desire for right to prevail would override his own instinct towards self-preservation.

Was that recklessness or was it bravery? Andrew supposed it depended on the context. And, yes, there was also a touch of arrogance about it, of over-confidence: the idea that Max could step into a precarious situation and sort it out simply because he believed so strongly in himself, in his own honourable motivations. Was that a symptom of his youth? Would he have grown out of it if he'd had the chance?

All at once, Andrew is assailed by a desire to stop walking, to lie down on this patch of ground and go to sleep. He refuses to give into it and keeps moving forward, concentrating hard on the precise pattern of indentation left by his wellington boot sole on the mud. There is no point dwelling on those questions. What good would it possibly do to know the answers now?

The inside pocket of his Barbour vibrates and he fishes out his Blackberry, irritated that he had not remembered to switch it off. He thinks it will probably be a quote from the stonemasons for a memorial stone they have commissioned to be placed in the gardens of Max's old school. It was Caroline's idea but, like everything else these days, she had left it to Andrew to organise.

Yet when he looks at the screen, he sees it is not an email but a text he has received. The name flashes up immediately: Kate. Automatically, he feels a stirring in his chest without admitting to himself he knows the cause of it.

'Hi Andrew,' the message reads. 'Thanks so much for a lovely drink last night. Next time, it's on me.' The message ends and he notices that there is a single, provocative kiss attached to the last sentence. He wonders briefly about replying and then, before he has time to change his mind, he erases the message and slips the Blackberry back into his pocket.

It had been a pleasant evening, he thinks, as he presses forward, feeling the heat rise from his muscles as he walks, ignoring the growing thirst at the back of his throat. They had both been working late on a new account and, when Andrew got up to leave for the evening shortly before 8pm, Kate had suggested 'a quick pint'. He had been surprised by the offer, assuming that she would have better things to do on a Friday night than spend time with her fusty old boss and he told her so.

She laughed, switching off her desk lamp. 'You're not *that* fusty,' Kate said, reaching for her coat from the hat-stand. She looked at him and for a moment he caught her eye. She blinked slowly, almost drowsily. He smiled and she turned away, but he noticed a pale flush rising up her neck.

They had spent an enjoyable hour in the pub. It had felt good to be in a pub again, inhaling the malty smell of sweat and beer-mats. He had sunk his first pint fairly easily and he was surprised to see that Kate matched him, drink for drink. Caroline never liked to drink too much. She had told him once it was because the thought of losing control terrified her. But Kate seemed not to care. She was relaxed in his company, chatty and smiling and never running out of conversation and it was nice, after months of never being able to say the right thing, to feel he could be charming, that a woman wanted to listen to him. No – more than that – that a woman wanted to flirt with him.

He stops himself short. He mustn't think like this. He has never been unfaithful to Caroline, never so much as looked at another woman. But she had always been so attentive to his needs, so sexually available, that he had never wanted to stray. Now, his wife seems to have folded into herself, seems no longer to need his intimacy.

Once, after they had been seeing each other for a few months, they went to St Ives for a long weekend. They booked a room in a bed and breakfast in the centre of town, with a small balcony over-looking the seafront. Every evening, they sat on the balcony with a glass of wine and watched as a small crowd of onlookers gathered along the edge of the pier to see the lifeboat being taken out of its shed for a practice run.

In the mornings, they woke to the cawing of seagulls and, after breakfast, took long walks along the cliffs towards Zennor, over-taking other stragglers and tourists in their haste to get to an isolated outcrop of rock, where they sat, their shoes dangling over the edge, looking out at the vastness of sea and sky. They talked about nothing in particular, or they fell silent, knowing that they did not need to speak.

On the way back from one of these walks, Caroline had shrieked and stumbled when she saw an adder, curled on a rock like a loosening knot. He had laughed at her, Andrew remembers now, and had been astonished to see hot tears of frustration in her eyes.

'What's wrong?' he asked.

She shook her head, not trusting herself to speak.

'I didn't mean –' he reached out to touch her and she let him draw her close. 'There's nothing to be scared of.'

He stroked her hair, pressing his lips to her temple. He realised, then, that she thought he was laughing at her, that he was some-how mocking her perceived stupidity.

'Caroline.' She did not look at him, so he tilted her face towards his. 'I love you.'

It was the first time he had spoken the words. He hadn't been sure, until then, that he was going to say them or, even, that he felt so profoundly. But something about Caroline's vulnerability in that moment, her obvious childishness, had clutched at his heart. She was less sophisticated than any woman he had ever known – in the sense that her emotional reflexes were instant and easily decoded – and he found that he valued this about her, that he cherished her unspoiltness. She did not seem to want to play games with him. There was no manufactured coolness to her. Her affection for him was worn without concealment, as though it were a thing to be proud of rather than disdained.

She looked at him, astonished, and then squealed with delight. 'Andrew,' she laughed. 'I can't believe you said that!'

He chuckled. 'Well,' he started. And then, again: 'Well, I hope you . . . like me too.'

'Of course I do.' She spun away from him, grabbing his hand so that he fell towards her and then, into her arms. 'I've loved you for ever.'

'You haven't known me for ever.'

'But it feels like it.'

They kissed. The salt-scented breeze rushed up from the water so that Caroline's hair whipped against his cheek. He could feel his nose beginning to run with the cold, but he ignored it, placing both gloved hands around her face, pressing her closer to him, until he was not sure where her lips began and his came to an end.

He had no idea how long they stood like that or how much longer they would have stayed there, had not a group of ramblers suddenly appeared over the crest of a hill, interrupting their romantic reverie with a blur of cagoules, bobble hats and walking sticks.

'Terribly sorry,' the lead rambler said. 'Didn't mean to interrupt.' He was a man with a ruddy face and a plastic-wrapped map hanging around his neck who appeared so flustered at finding Andrew and Caroline mid-embrace that they couldn't help but giggle.

'No harm done,' said Andrew, stifling his laughter. 'Please, carry on.'

'You too,' the man said, gruffly.

They were unable to stop themselves after that. A mild hysteria trailed them all the way back to St Ives.

A year later, they were married.

The light is dusk-bruised and he realises that it is almost 4 o'clock. He feels guilty that he has left Caroline on her own for too long. He picks up his pace and soon reaches the edge of the valley, with its sweeping view of the town below. He has worked up a sweat from his walk and he takes off his Barbour, spreading it over a tussock of grass and sitting comfortably on the lining so that he can spend a few minutes looking out across the low horizon. The ground and sky are beginning to melt together: the syrupy brown of the soil merging with a strip of cloud that gives way to a clear wash of blue. Andrew breathes in, feeling the coolness of the late afternoon trickle into his lungs. Briefly, his mind empties and there is a glimpse of contentment.

And then he thinks of Kate, of Elsa, of Caroline, of the varied responsibilities he has to all these women and his mind is crowded with a perceptible sense of failure. He wishes Max were here. He wishes he could talk to him, listen to his problems and feel like a father again. He shakes his head and then, pressing on, makes his way back down the hillside.

Elsa, 1923

S HE KNOWS NEVER TO talk about it. She has learned, finally, to be silent and acquiescent, to nod her head when it is required, to speak only when spoken to. Her father has drummed it into her and although, deep down, Elsa knows that she is pretending to be good, she does it so well that he seems to have no complaint. She does not mention her father's behaviour, does not even think of it much any more. She comes to believe it is normal, because it is easier that way, easier to assume it is happening in other houses on the same street, in the same city, to the same kind of children.

She is determined that he will have no excuse to hit her so that, when he does, when he unbuckles his belt and twists it round his hand and flicks it halfway up behind his shoulder, then brings it back down on her, whipping her flesh with a stinging force that takes her breath away, when he does this, she knows. She knows he has no reason for it. He is simply doing it because he is a bully; a bully and a broken man.

'You must not test his patience so,' her mother said one morning, before she went to school. Elsa looked up at her from the dining table. She saw that her mother's hair was turning grey, strands of it flecked with white. Before, she would have said something, would have stood up for herself and replied 'But I don't, Mama. I don't do anything to upset him.' Now, though, Elsa knew better. She knew that the appearance of things was more important to adults than the truth of what lay beneath. She knew that they wanted her to be meek, not difficult. She knew that her spirit must be split in two, her ardour for life dampened until she was no longer a challenge to them.

She had been doing things wrong all this time, Elsa thought to herself as she folded her napkin, and no one had told her. She felt foolish, as though her mother had deliberately led her into a trap, encouraging her to behave one way, only to have her father come back from the war and undo it all. She looked at the empty place at the head of the table where, later, her father would take his seat. She knew she was a disappointment to him and although she tried not to care, although she tried to hate him for what he was, Elsa found that she couldn't. Not entirely.

'He is under a great deal of strain,' her mother continued. 'There are things perhaps you do not understand . . .'

'About what, Mama?'

Her mother walked over to the mantelpiece, busying herself with the winding up of a carriage clock, so that from where she was sitting, Elsa could see only her smooth, long back and her shoulder blades pressing against the silk of her blouse like jagged wings.

'About how he left the army.' She kept winding the clock. 'They said he was a coward. They said his nerves couldn't cope. It was agony for him, to hear them say that, the men he had fought with.' She was trailing off, speaking to herself more than Elsa. 'All through that last year of fighting, Horace was being cared for in a hospital and all the time, I thought . . . I thought . . .' Her voice was breaking. 'I never knew. He never told me. He seems . . . he seems ashamed.'

Ashamed.

Coward.

She was not sure what those words meant, but there was a part of Elsa that understood she was being told something of crucial importance and that there was shame attached to it, to the notion of her father not fighting. She took this in, silently looking at her mother's silhouette against the fireplace, careful not to say anything that would upset the tender balance of what had just happened. Elsa clutched the secret tightly to her, unwilling to let it go, hiding it away as if it were another treasure to add to her hidden stash underneath the floorboards.

She thought then of her father's strangeness, of the way he tried to disguise his occasional stammer by using words that did not begin with a 'p' or a 't', of the way he jumped at the sound of a door slammed too quickly. The way he did not like to walk past the butcher's shop because he could not abide the smell of uncooked flesh or the sight of blood-red meat set out on big cool slabs for customers to buy. The way that when it rained, he refused to walk outside in case he got mud on his shoes.

Was that because he was a coward? Was that how a coward acted?

She thought, too, of a day long ago when she had seen a woman in a blue-black dress following a man over Putney Bridge. The woman had touched the tip of his elbow and the man had turned around and then, with a curious kind of smile, the woman had handed him a white feather. It was her smile Elsa remembered. It had seemed so out of place.

Coward.

She plays with the two syllables, heavy like marbles in her mouth, and, as she says them out loud, she cannot help but think of a bovine face, limpid eyes and milky udders.

Coward.

Is that what her father is?

It is night. She tiptoes along the corridor from her bedroom. Her purpose is clear, but she is not sure what drives it. The door to her parents' room is pushed to, but not closed. She presses a single fingertip against the wood and the door swings back, incrementally, so that she can peer into the darkness.

Her father is lying on the side of the bed closest to her, the covers wrapped up tightly around him, the pillows covering his head so that only his nose pokes out of the blankets. How can he breathe? she thinks. And then, before she can stop the idea, she imagines what would happen if he suffocated, if his next breath never came. How different her life would be. She whispers the word then, hearing the two languid syllables unfold themselves as she stands by the door, one hand on the cool brass knob.

'Coward,' she says. She holds her breath. She stands there for a moment longer to see if he has heard. There is no movement from underneath the bedclothes and she goes quietly back to bed. She feels stronger for having said it.

It is daytime. They walk past a man in Richmond Park and there is something odd about his face. Elsa knows she shouldn't stare but she cannot help it. As they approach, she sees that although half of the man's face is moving normally as he speaks and smiles and lights up his pipe, the other half is completely immobile. As they walk closer to him, she sees that he is wearing a mask, forged out of the lightest tin and painted expertly with the mirrored imprint of his face. From a distance, you would not have thought there was anything wrong with him. Up close, the mask seems sinister, something one might see in the circus. Elsa shivers when she sees it and turns away, quickly. But her father stops dead in his tracks.

'Horace?' her mother says, lightly touching his elbow with her gloved hand.

Without explanation, her father starts walking rapidly in the other direction. It is a hot day and by the time they reach the welcome shade of the nearest copse of trees, his cheeks are drained of colour. He is pale and sweating, his moustache damp with heat. Her mother trails some steps behind, leaning heavily on the handle of her parasol, her breaths shortened by the tightness of her old-fashioned corset. She looks to Elsa like a long-stemmed lily – the petals curling brown at the edges, the pollen-heavy stamens lolling downwards in the warmth of a summer's day. Something about her visible frailty seems to anger him. 'Keep up, woman, can't you?' he shouts. Her mother pauses, looking up at him, squinting in the sunlight. Elsa, straight-backed, stands silently next to Horace waiting for her to reach them. He glances at her, his face shaded by the brim of his hat.

'You're a good walker,' he says to Elsa, then turns his face away.

She wonders if she has heard him correctly. She does not want to look at him in case that is the wrong thing to do, but out of the corner of her eye, she sees a flush on his cheeks. She knows then that she is not mistaken. He has paid her a compliment and now he does not know how to act.

Elsa keeps her features expressionless but inside, she feels a small tingle of pride. He does not say anything more.

It is one of the only times she will feel close to him.

But then, later, when they get home, he beats her with a belt for dropping a china plate. Her fingers had been wet and the crockery had slipped from her grasp but she knows better than to try and explain. She can see his face, looming over hers, the mouth skewed as he grunts with the physical effort. She feels the leather of the belt burn against her thigh and she knows there will be a bruise there later, dark as ash. She blanks his face out. She submits. She allows the blows to fall because she knows he cannot touch her, not inside where it counts.

It is evening, the light is dusky. Elsa walks into the drawing room and sees her father sitting in an armchair in the half-gloom. He is crying. Elsa has never seen a man cry before and she is shocked. The tears roll thickly down her father's face, gathering in streams underneath his nose. His quiet sobs are catching in his throat as he tries to regulate his breathing. His shoulders are shuddering and his limbs are bent out of shape, angular and spiky like the spokes of a broken umbrella. He lifts up a hand to shield his face, not wanting to be looked at but Elsa keeps staring. He has not seen her. But still she keeps looking. She wants to remember this, to remember what it was to see him look so weak.

Coward, she thinks. And she allows herself a small smile before she turns back into the hallway and walks softly up the stairs.

Caroline

T HE PILE OF PAPERS is growing on her desk. Typewritten
sheets of military jargon, photocopies of newspaper dia-
grams, jottings of place names and telephone numbers and email
addresses, a relevant fact heard on the radio and written down
quickly on the back of a bank statement before she forgets it. All
of this information spills over itself, an endless chain of words that
seems to point to something, even though it is not always clear to
her what that might be. The physicality of the paper reassures her.
If it exists in black and white, she thinks, it will not disappear. The
proof of it cannot be disputed. She will not be made a fool of
because she will be able to say 'Look – here, here it is' and they will
have to listen to her, they will have to admit there is evidence that
she is right.

All her adult life, she has felt embarrassed by her lack of educa-
tion, by the unstructured mess of her mind. But now she has a
purpose. Now she can prove that she is as good as the rest of them
at ordering her thoughts, at presenting a case.

Caroline is sitting cross-legged on the floor in her study, sipping
on a cup of strong black coffee that is still too hot to drink. Each
sip burns the roof of her mouth, but she does not notice. She is too
busy, sorting out the papers into different sections of an ancient
filing cabinet she had asked Andrew to bring back from the office.
Her system for organising is haphazard – sometimes alphabetical,
sometimes numerical. Occasionally, the fuzziness of her mind
means it is difficult to remember which word she has used. Anything relating to Derek Lester, for instance, is either under 'L' for

his surname, or 'D' for his first name or sometimes even 'A' for 'Armed Forces Minister'. She giggles at her own absurdity – a sharp sound she had not expected to make.

She glances at her watch and notices she has put it on the wrong wrist so that the gold of the strap clashes with the platinum of the ring Andrew gave to her when Max was born. It is half past seven in the morning and she has been up for three hours. Caroline opens the bottom drawer of the filing cabinet and reaches her arm far into the back corner. She retrieves a slim brown envelope, the tongue slipped into itself. Opening the envelope, she takes out a small silken package, a wrapped-up square of bright blue fabric. She places it on the floor and unwinds the silk. There are twenty-three white pills still left. She has further stocks hidden in different places around the house so as to avoid Andrew's disapproval. He thinks she has reduced her dose.

She counts out the pills, lining them up along the carpet: a trail of breadcrumbs. She looks at them for a few seconds, pressing one of them down with the pad of her thumb, feeling its smoothness against her skin. Then, quickly, she takes one and swallows it with a gulp of coffee. She sniffs. Her nose is running but she has no time to wipe it. She has work to do. She must get on.

But then her gaze fixes on the blue silk square and she remembers that Elsa had given it to her, years ago when Max was still at school. Elsa had just returned from an Italian holiday – one of those culturally improving package tours she went on yearly with Dorothy, her bridge-playing friend – and instead of heading straight home from the airport, she had come to stay with them for a few days.

Over dinner, Elsa had talked them through the whole itinerary in painstaking detail – the Duomo in Florence, the Frari church in Venice, the 'simply breathtaking' Tintoretto museum – until Caroline could feel her eyelids drooping with the weight of tiredness. Max had already gone up to bed when they took coffee in the drawing room.

'Are you not having any, Caroline?' Elsa asked, resting the cup and saucer flat on the palm of her hand.

'No, I'm afraid not,' she said, as though she had done something wrong. 'It keeps me up all night.'

Andrew winked at her. His mother didn't notice. After a while, Elsa had rummaged in her handbag and produced two neat packages, wrapped in paisley-patterned paper.

'These are for you –'

'Oh Mummy, you shouldn't have,' Andrew said because he always said that sort of thing.

He unwrapped his first and lifted out a pair of bright gold cufflinks, each one engraved with the image of a Madonna and Child. He got out of his chair and strode across to his mother, dipping down to kiss the top of her head. 'They're exquisite,' he said. 'I shall never take them off.'

Caroline tried to summon up the necessary gusto she knew would be required when she opened her present. Her enthusiasm for these little gifts of Elsa's always sounded so false to her ears. She had never found any use for the trinkets that Elsa brought back from her travels abroad. She was beginning to feel that the gifts were not an exercise in generosity but in showing off.

She ripped the wrapping paper apart, too late noticing her mother-in-law's silent disapproval (Elsa liked to keep wrapping paper to re-use) and when she saw the blue square of silk, threaded through with glimmers of swirling silver, she was not sure what to make of it. It was pretty but, when she unfolded the fabric, she saw it was not quite big enough to be a scarf.

'How lovely,' Caroline said. 'Is it a handkerchief?'

Elsa looked at her levelly. 'I daresay you can use it however you see fit,' she said, icily. 'But I certainly wouldn't blow my nose on it.'

'No, I didn't mean –'

'Anyway, I suppose I should be getting on up to bed,' Elsa continued, ignoring her. 'I've taken up enough of your time.' And then, not looking at either of them: 'Thank you for a delightful evening.' She walked out of the room without another word.

'Oh dear,' Andrew said, getting up to follow her. He patted Caroline's arm as he walked past her. She felt ashamed, her face hot. She had not meant to cause any offence. But there was a part of her, a diamond-hard sparkle inside, that felt glad she had. She switched the lights off, leaving the coffee cups to wash up the next morning.

On the upstairs landing, she could make out the low, conciliatory murmur of Andrew's voice: 'Didn't mean any harm . . . would be mortified to think . . . no, no, that's not it . . .' And then, after these snatches of half-caught conversation, she heard Elsa's response with perfect clarity. 'Perhaps you should teach her not to be so ungrateful.'

Caroline's mouth went dry. Her throat thickened with the shock of those words. How dare she, Caroline thought. She was so bloody superior. So righteously convinced of her own course of action. She would never be able to please Elsa, never.

But although her indignation was real, it lasted only for a second, and then she was overcome with guilt and anxiety. How could she have been so stupid, so thoughtless? Why did she never understand how to do the right thing? All that work trying to get Elsa to like her and now this!

She had gone to the bathroom, put down the loo seat and sat there, for several minutes, to compose herself. She did not want Andrew to see that she had been upset. And, when he eventually emerged from the guest room some ten minutes later, he didn't say a word.

The next morning, Caroline had set the alarm earlier than usual so that she could go downstairs and make breakfast. She wanted to show how sorry she was, rather than attempt to explain it, because she knew her words would get muddled and over-emotional and that Elsa hated any show of hysteria. She laid the table with extra care, folding linen napkins on each side-plate, rubbing down the toast rack with the edge of a dishcloth to make it gleam and placing a small vase of peonies in the centre. She defrosted a packet of croissants and, although normally she would have made herself a quick cup of instant, she took out the cafetière to make a proper pot of coffee. She decanted the milk into a jug, hand-painted with blue and white flowers.

By the time Elsa came down, Caroline had her apron on, a spatula in one hand, ready to scramble the eggs.

'Good morning, Elsa,' she said, brightly. 'I hope you slept well?'

Elsa, resplendent in a knee-length red cardigan, drew the belt more tightly around her waist. 'I did, thank you.' She sat down, unfolded the napkin on her lap and laid her hands lightly on the table, her fingers tapping ever so slightly up and down on the wooden surface. 'This all looks delightful,' Elsa said.

'I'm glad –' started Caroline but at exactly the same moment, Elsa said something. 'I'm sorry, I didn't hear what –'

'I said I think I owe you an apology,' Elsa said, the words stumbling out in a pile. Caroline looked across at her mother-in-law and saw that she was embarrassed and that what underlay this embarrassment was the slightest tinge of something else; of nervousness. She was so startled by Elsa's show of remorse she forgot to answer and stood there, the spatula still raised, unable to speak.

'I overreacted,' Elsa continued. 'I'm not sure why.'

She glanced up at Caroline briefly and then down at the table again, fiddling with a curl of hair, moving her knife a millimetre to the side with her free hand.

'Elsa, you don't need to apologise, honestly. It was a beautiful gift. I – I – oh I don't know. I was too stupid to realise what it was. It was my fault. I'm so bad at . . . you know, at finding the right words.'

Elsa smiled. 'Words can be treacherous,' she said. 'At the best of times.'

'Let's forget it ever happened. Let me make you something to eat.'

After that, they had enjoyed a relatively pleasant breakfast of scrambled eggs and if Elsa had noticed that the croissants were slightly limp around the edges, she didn't say so. In fact, she was unfailingly polite for the remainder of the morning. When Andrew left for work, it was Elsa who suggested they go out furniture shopping at a nearby antiques shop in Upton-upon-Severn.

'We could make a day of it,' she said. 'I need to find a bookshelf for the downstairs sitting room and you're so good at that kind of thing.'

Caroline, taken aback, reddened. 'No, I'm not!'

'Nonsense. Just look at this house. You've done wonders with it,' Elsa said, avoiding eye contact. 'We could have lunch. My treat. As a way of . . .' There was a pause. 'Well, what do you say?'

So they had driven into Upton, Caroline more nervous than she should have been at the wheel, conscious, as she always was, of the probability that Elsa was judging her, examining her from the corner of her eye. It took her three goes to get into a parking space on the high street.

'Sorry about this, Elsa,' Caroline said, pulling the stiff steering wheel towards her. 'I'm terrible at parking.' She laughed, too loudly, and hated herself for it. 'It's a lack of spatial awareness. I don't have that kind of brain, not like Andrew or Max. They know exactly what fits into where and at what angle. You should see the two of them playing snooker together down the pub, it's amazing . . .' She carried on in this vein, the sentences babbling out of her and although she wanted to stop talking, she found that she couldn't. She needed to fill the silences.

When they got to the antiques shop, they found a 'Back in Five Minutes' sign on the door.

'Honestly,' said Elsa. 'It's the middle of the day! You'd think they'd be thrilled to have our business.'

'Yes, quite.' The shop had never been closed before. This day of all days, Caroline thought to herself. Typical. 'We could go for a cappuccino just across the road if you like?' She signalled towards a nearby café, the windows misted up with condensation. 'We'll be able to see when he gets back.'

'Good idea.'

They sat at a window table with their mugs of coffee. Caroline ordered a square of millionaire's shortbread.

'Are you sure you wouldn't like one?' she asked.

'Good Lord no,' Elsa said, the note of criticism implicit. 'We've only just had breakfast.'

To begin with, neither of them talked and Caroline found herself anxiously scanning the room, as if the surroundings could offer up a suitable topic for conversation.

Then, out of the blue, Elsa spoke. 'The thing is,' she said. 'I miss him dreadfully.'

For a moment, Caroline was not sure she had heard her properly.

'Oliver?' she asked, tentative.

Elsa nodded. 'I know it's been a year, but I just can't seem to shake this feeling of . . .' She broke off. 'Churchill called it the black dog, didn't he? A good description, I've always thought. A black dog, trailing me around.'

Caroline stared at her. Her mother-in-law had never once confided how she felt and now that she had, Caroline was not sure what to do.

'I think it's only natural, when someone you've spent your life with passes away . . .'

'He died, Caroline. Let's not prettify it,' Elsa said. Her face was pale, the lines on her forehead pronounced. 'I can't bear it when people mince their words. Pass away. Gone to a better place. Fallen asleep.' She waved her hand indistinctly in the air. 'All of that guff.'

'I'm sorry.'

'Don't apologise. I don't want you to say everything will be all right. God knows, I've got enough people doing that. I just . . .' Elsa lapsed into silence. Then she looked across the street. 'Ah. The antiques man is back.'

'Oh yes,' Caroline said, confused. 'But what you were saying about . . .'

'Please, forget it,' Elsa interjected. She opened her handbag, took out her lipstick and applied it briskly without a mirror. She smiled, but her eyes remained dull. 'I shouldn't have bothered you with it. There's no reason why you would understand.'

Caroline felt the blow of the last sentence like a physical slap.

'No,' she said. 'Of course.'

They crossed the road and opened the door to the antiques shop. A bell rang out. The proprietor, a man with white hair and half-moon spectacles, came across to greet them. 'Anything I can help you with?'

'Yes,' Elsa said. 'I'm looking for a bookcase. About two feet high, good quality wood.'

'I've got just the thing,' he said and he led them down the stairs towards a French-style dresser, painted in a pale green.

'Oh that's beautiful,' Caroline said.

'No,' Elsa said sharply. 'I'm not fond of all this painted furniture one sees nowadays.'

The man met Caroline's gaze and shrugged. 'Of course, well, we do have something rather special that you might prefer. If you'll just come this way . . .'

The two of them wound their way through a narrow corridor, lined on either side by rows of curve-backed chairs and a series of large, gilt-framed mirrors, the glass speckled with age. Caroline hung back, unwilling to follow. She felt tears prick against her eyes and was frustrated at her own weakness. She must stop taking things so much to heart.

Caroline took a step forwards and, stretching out one arm, she traced the edge of the French dresser with her hand. The wood felt smooth to the touch. When she looked down, she saw a smudge of dust on her fingertip.

The phone rings. Caroline gathers up the blue handkerchief and bundles it back into the filing cabinet before picking up the extension in the spare room.

'Malvern 668723.'

'Mrs Weston?' says a posh, female voice.

'Yes.'

'Oh hi there, it's Camilla here from Derek Lester's office.'

She holds her breath.

'Oh. Right. Hello.'

'I understand you've been wanting to make an appointment to see the minister,' Camilla is saying and Caroline can hear the tac-tac-tac of someone typing with their fingernails in the background.

'Yes.'

'He's terribly busy at the moment with the by-election,' Camilla says, 'and he's asked if you can get back in touch with him a few weeks from now . . .'

'A few weeks?'

'Yes,' Camilla says, and Caroline gets a clear image of how she might look: an averagely pretty blonde girl with pearl earrings and thick mascara, just out of university. 'He asks me to send his apologies but I'm afraid there's nothing he can do for now.'

'Right,' Caroline says. 'Thank you.'

Camilla does not even say goodbye. She simply hangs up. Caroline lets the phone rest by her ear, listening to the dialling tone until she feels calmer. She supposes she shouldn't be surprised that Lester is stalling for time. In fact, it simply solidifies her suspicions that there is something amiss, that he is trying to hide the truth. She feels a throbbing in her wrists. Her entire body seems electrified, tense.

Then, just as she is about to return to her filing, there is a cry from downstairs, followed by the clatter of something falling. She wonders briefly whether a fox has broken into the house through an open window. And then, too late, she remembers Elsa.

She takes the stairs carefully because her steps seem wobbly and the carpet appears to be shifting beneath her. When she reaches Elsa's door, she can hear a soft whimpering from the other side. For a moment, she hesitates, then she pushes the door open and a bright yellow light glares out of the room so that Caroline has to refocus her gaze.

Elsa is sitting slumped in the armchair, where Andrew must have put her, and her head strangely angled so that her chin is sliding into her shoulder. Her eyes are stuttering, the lids beating out a frantic metronome. There is a narrow line of brown where the iris is still visible through the translucent, twitching skin. Her mouth is slack, the lower jaw hanging loose as if she is on the brink of saying something but can find no words, only the disjointed, mournful wail she is now making.

Caroline notices how skinny Elsa is, how prominent her skull has become, how, in places, her skin is stretched tightly across her slender body like the surface of a drum. She is moaning gently and a thin line of saliva is trickling out of the corner of her mouth, her lips slack as loose elastic.

'Elsa?' Caroline says, hurrying across to her, kneeling down by the armchair and automatically reaching for her pulse. She can feel the brisk thump of it against the tips of her fingers. There is a faintly metallic smell in the air. Caroline draws back the checked blanket from her lap to find a spreading dampness across the seat of the chair, the edges of the stain creeping outwards. She slides her hand round Elsa's back and finds that her skirt and the bottom edges of her blouse are soaking, the urine warm and clammy to the touch. She sees that Elsa is looking straight at her and that her jaw is moving uselessly up and down but no words are coming out.

'It's all right, Elsa,' she says, patting the back of her hand, but something about her mother-in-law's eyes – impenetrable, unmoving – starts to scare her. She tries to manoeuvre Elsa out of the chair. 'It's all right,' Caroline says, wrapping Elsa's arms round her neck. 'Don't worry. Now, let's get you out of these wet clothes.'

The old woman has no strength in her muscles and her arms slip back down almost immediately, like wet bags of sand. Her head is lolling to one side, creasing the thin layer of flesh at the top of her neck. Caroline bends down so that her face is level with hers and she tries to lift up her arms once more. Elsa's breath smells mossy. It reminds her of damp autumn leaves trodden into mulch at the side of a pavement. Caroline winces.

'Now, Elsa, I'm going to need you to try and hold on while I lift you up and get you on to the bed,' she says, deliberately modulating her voice so that it is clear and firm like it used to be when she had to tell Max off for some minor infraction. Elsa seems to squint her assent. Her hearing aid is emitting a high-pitched squeal.

Caroline puts Elsa's arms around her neck once more, holding on to them with one hand, while she loops the other one round Elsa's back and attempts to lever her out of the chair. It proves impossible to shift her. Although Elsa looks frail and shrunken, she is a dead weight. Caroline, sweaty and frustrated, straightens herself up.

She is out of breath with the exertion and decides to try and take off Elsa's skirt with her still sitting in the armchair. At least that way, she would be able to clean her up a little bit. She looks for a clasp or a zip but then realises that the skirt has an elasticated waistband, so she starts to tug at the hem but it is stuck fast to Elsa's thighs. She rolls Elsa to one side, more roughly than she intended, and struggles to pull the skirt away. Eventually, it comes off, leaving Elsa's puckered limbs exposed. Her legs are shrivelled and bony. The dirty-white cotton of her pants is almost see-through. She sees Caroline looking at them and tries to move her hands down to protect her modesty, folding them clumsily over the faded patch of her pubic hair, just visible through the fabric. Elsa is embarrassed and Caroline finds that, in spite of herself, she is moved by this realisation; by the knowledge that however incapacitated she is physically, inside she is still the same old Elsa, a woman who takes pride in her appearance; who likes everything to be just so.

Caroline balls up the skirt and leaves it crumpled on the floor in the corner of the room to be washed later. Then she goes to the kitchen to fill up a bowl of warm soapy water. She takes a new sponge out of the cupboard underneath the sink and treads carefully back down the corridor, the water splashing against her wrists.

When Caroline re-enters the room, she sees that Elsa is trying to undo the buttons on her blouse, her fingers plucking at the small pearl circles.

'Elsa, just leave it,' she says, putting the water down by her feet. Caroline kneels down next to the bucket and looks her in the face. 'I'll do it.'

Elsa looks at Caroline but there is no spark of recognition. Her eyes are blank and then, without warning, the pupils contract.

She shouts out, flapping her hands with great agitation, her neck muscles rigid.

'What is it?' Caroline says, holding on to her wrists, trying to calm her down. Elsa manages to get her hands free and looks at Caroline with such loathing that she has to stop herself stepping back. 'Calm down, Elsa, it's all right, it's all right.' She takes the sponge and dips it into the water, thinking that if she can make Elsa dry and clean, then she might relax, but when Caroline tries to wipe it across her thighs, Elsa starts to writhe in her seat, clawing at the air with her hands. She seems to have rediscovered her strength and the more she squirms, the more difficult it is to sponge her down and the more irritated Caroline becomes. 'Oh come on, Elsa, I'm only trying to help,' she snaps. 'Stop moving around.'

And then, without warning, Elsa slaps her. It is a light slap, a weak imitation of what it should have been, but there is no doubting the forceful intent behind it. Caroline looks at her, stunned.

'What the . . .'

Elsa is twisting her lips as though chewing something and Caroline realises, all at once, that she intends to spit at her. She moves away, quickly, on her haunches.

'Away,' says Elsa, her voice clear and vicious. 'Get away.'

Then, as quickly as she had transformed, Elsa slumps back into the armchair, her head bent down, the chin sinking back into her chest.

Caroline is sitting in the corner of the room and the edge of the skirting board is pressing into her lower back. Her hands are trembling and when she lifts them, there is a fuzzy indentation on each palm from the pressure of pushing on to the carpet. She is there for a long time, waiting to see what will happen next, unsure of what Elsa will do if she tries to go over to her. After a while, there is a gentle grunting sound, like the clicking of a bicycle gear that has not quite shifted into place. Caroline looks up and sees that Elsa is asleep and snoring lightly. Caroline is intensely – almost absurdly – relieved. She acknowledges, as if for the first time, that her nervousness around Elsa had always bordered on fear. Her mother-in-law had possessed such a forceful personality, underlined by the sense – unspoken, concealed – that she could turn, that her temper was never far from the surface.

Caroline gets up from the floor, hearing her bones crack in protest at the sudden movement. Something clicks painfully in Caroline's upper arm and her muscles ache from the attempts to wrestle Elsa out of her chair. For a brief second, she thinks of sponging Elsa down while she is asleep and pliable, like a baby, but then she finds that she doesn't want to. She wants, instead, to leave her there: cold and damp and unable to help herself, at least for a few minutes.

She can still smell the ferric tang of Elsa's urine hanging in the air. She remembers that blue silk scarf; the pale green French dresser. There she was, her mother-in-law, who had once been so distant, so superior, reduced to this: a shrunken old woman losing her faculties. She walks over to the bucket and she tips it over with her foot, quite deliberately, so that the water gloops and splashes onto the carpet, the soap bubbles popping noiselessly. She glances at Elsa, her face finally peaceful, her mouth agape so that she can see her tongue, the tip of it waxy red. As Caroline watches, a faint spray of goosebumps appears across the top of Elsa's thighs. She jiggles Elsa's arm brusquely, saying her name loudly to rouse her.

Elsa wakes, uncomprehending. And then she sees it is Caroline and Elsa's face is infused with unsurprised, semi-distant recognition, as though she has rung a bell and a maid has appeared.

'You wet yourself, Elsa,' she says. 'You slapped me when I was trying to clean you up.' And then Caroline walks out of the room, leaving Elsa half-naked and shivering in the armchair, unable to do anything but wait for her return.

Elsa

WHEN ELSA WAKES, HER first feeling is one of panic. Small circles of brightness float in front of her eyes, as if cells are being pressed underneath a microscope slide. She cannot see properly and she cries out with the confusion of it. After a while, the dots begin to clear and Elsa breathes more calmly, feeling the reassuring rise and fall of her chest.

She is sitting in an armchair and she is cold, very cold. Her head feels too heavy for her neck and she cannot, for the moment, lift it up to take a look at her surroundings, to attempt to work out what has happened to her.

Her thoughts judder into place, unsure of themselves, jostling for position. They slide around, looping from the present to the past and back again, like skaters on ice painting figures of eight with sharpened blades. Her mind flicks through various disjointed images: herself as a child, reading a book; a flash of her wedding day, dressed in organza silk; her young son, handing over a pine cone he has found, the gum of it sticky on her fingers; lying in bed with her husband, awake, feeling hurt over some unintended slight; Mrs Carswell, smiling broadly, cutting the crusts of sandwiches; falling down the stairs, the pain slicing into her hip, the hospital, with its disinfectant smell and the slick of baked beans on each plate . . . And then? Then what had happened?

Vast, grey clouds pass through her imaginings, colliding and shattering and exploding into a thousand tiny pieces of float-away ash before coalescing again. Slowly, painfully, her mind shifts into focus. That's right, she thinks, then she came here, to Andrew's house. This is where she is being looked after.

As the fogginess of sleep starts to scatter, she finds that she is thinking of that woman, the one with the pale blue eyes that seem to look without seeing. She is wondering why the woman wants to hurt her and, at the same time, she is consumed by the familiar unexplained certainty that she has done something wrong. She must have done something wrong to be punished. It must be her fault.

What is that woman's name? She shakes her head, like a cat trying to shake a flea from it's ear. That woman. Elsa does not like her. She never has, she thinks to herself, strangely satisfied by this scrap of remembered feeling. She has never trusted her, never believed that the woman is capable of telling the truth about herself.

Who *was* she?

And why does Elsa feel so cold?

She looks down then, moving her eyes from her chest down towards her waist and she sees she is not wearing a skirt. Shame subsumes her. Elsa is shocked and tries to cover herself with her hands. Her thighs feel moist and clammy to the touch. Why is she wet? Did she forget to dry herself when she got out of the bath? she wonders. Has she got caught in a rainstorm on her daily walk around the Grantchester fields? Is she waiting for her clothes to dry on the radiator until she puts them on again, feeling the stiff crinkle of the fabric against her skin?

And as she is asking herself these endless, pointless questions, the image of the woman with the blue eyes becomes confused. She sees her father instead. She feels she has angered both the woman and her father in some way, that she is at fault without knowing why. What can she do to make it better?

Elsa extends her fingers, flexing them as far as she can. She tries, once more, to lift her head but her muscles feel numb and tingly and she cannot find the energy to do it. She will not show she is scared. All her life, she has prided herself on being able to keep her feelings in check, on being able to hide what was really going on inside underneath the smooth, elegant surface she presented to the world. She had become hard. Her feelings were her own. She did not even reveal them to Oliver, not really, in spite of the fact that she had loved him so much. There was always a darkness, deep down. It made her feel safe to keep it there.

The door to the room swings ajar. The woman, the one whose name she cannot remember, comes over to Elsa and she is carrying a bucket of water in one hand. The woman's face is sharp and pale apart from two distinct patches of pink in each cheek. Her mouth is set in a firm line, the corners twisting ever so slightly downwards.

'Right, Elsa, let's get you cleaned up,' she says, and she kneels down on the carpet and dips a sponge into the bucket, squeezing out the excess water with rapid, edgy movements. She seems impatient, Elsa thinks. Impatient and slightly frenzied, as though something has gone badly wrong that she is not admitting to herself.

The woman reaches forward and starts to wash down Elsa's legs but she moves too briskly and presses down so hard that the sponge prickles against Elsa's skin, leaving behind a tracery of red marks. The woman returns the sponge to the bucket, wringing it out, and then tries to shift Elsa on to one side so that she can reach behind. Elsa does not help. She makes every muscle and every bone in her body as heavy as she can and she sees the woman struggling with the weight and for a moment, Elsa feels triumphant.

'Oh for goodness' sake, Elsa, can't you bloody well move?' the woman says through gritted teeth. Let her struggle, Elsa thinks. Let her see what it feels like.

'Fine, have it your way,' the woman says, giving up the fight. Dropping her voice, she adds in a half-whisper: 'You always have.'

And then Elsa remembers. It is Caroline. It is her daughter-in-law. She gives a crooked smile, glad to have made a nuisance of herself. She watches through narrowed eyes as Caroline walks over to the wardrobe and, after jangling the coat hangers, takes out a fresh skirt. Without speaking, Caroline bends down to put the skirt on the floor, lifting Elsa's feet up, one by one, to place them through the waistband. She slides the skirt up Elsa's legs, grappling a bit when she gets to the thighs, still stuck clammily to the chair seat, but she manages it after a few seconds.

And then, as she turns to go, Caroline notices Elsa's smile. Elsa can see her register it. She can see Caroline's lower lip tremble; she can see her expression go blurry and distant; she can see her hands begin to shake with the heaviness of the bucket.

After she leaves, Elsa chuckles to herself.

Coward, she thinks. She mouths the word over and over, then whispers it out loud, and the two slinky syllables of it sound familiar and well worn. She's a coward. Just like Horace. Just like her mother. Just like all of them.

Elsa shifts in her seat, attempting to get more comfortable. On the wall, a clock tick-tocks noisily. She gazes at it, remembering the clock on the kitchen wall in Grantchester which sounded a different bird call on the hour. She had bought it from the RSPB catalogue a few years ago. It cheered her up when it got to one o'clock and it was the woodpecker, her favourite.

When Max came to stay, he always joked about how awful the clock was, how he couldn't relax because he was always on the edge of his seat waiting for a pigeon to coo or a parrot to squawk. The way he said it made her laugh. Elsa is warmed by the memory. She sees Max quite clearly in her mind's eye: standing at the sink with a dishcloth in his hand, drying plates as she passed them to him, his hands too big for the task, his hair flopping forwards so that he had to keep blowing it out of his face and the bird clock on the wall about to sound its hourly call.

Max had not been a coward, she thinks. He had fought for what he believed in. She was proud of that, proud of the fact that her grandson had righted the wrongs of her father's moral failure. Max was a good man, she thinks. He would have been a good father.

Her thoughts slide and dissolve, the memories once again become grey and indistinct. She senses the wave crest over her, tugging her down, pounding against her limbs until they are woollen and useless and she must surrender herself. She feels herself go under, the water lapping over her head, pushing away all her former certainties, the tide crashing against her thoughts and grinding them up like sand, carried off by the sea until the salty wetness on her cheeks is all that is left and she does not know why she is crying.

She cannot remember where she is or what she is doing here or how long she has been sitting in this chair.

And that woman, the one with the blue eyes, what was her name?

Caroline

WEEKS HAVE PASSED. CAROLINE is watching the television news when the postman rings the doorbell with a package that will not fit through the letterbox. Although it is past 11.00, she has not yet managed to get dressed, so she answers while still in her dressing gown, her hair in disarray.

'Late night?' asks the postman with a leer. He is barely more than a teenager, with a shaven head and a gold stud in one ear. She notices that his right eyebrow has been sliced through three times with a razor. The skin beneath is gleaming and untouched.

She doesn't answer and he, sensing coolness, scowls as he hands her the electronic pad.

'Just need your signature,' he says, looking her up and down with casual interest. She draws the dressing gown more tightly around her and signs on the screen with the plastic stylus. He passes her a wide padded envelope, holding on to it a second too long as Caroline tries to take it from him. He laughs before letting go. His swagger makes her feel scared and she shuts the door quickly so that she is safe again, contained within the familiar four walls.

In the kitchen, she turns the package over in her hands, squinting in an attempt to make out the postmark. It had been franked and the address typed across the front. She slides her finger underneath the envelope flap, feeling the stickiness give way as it opens. Inside is a bulky square of bubble wrap, wound round with strips of Sellotape. There is an accompanying letter but she is so intrigued by the contents of the package that she ignores it. The package is light and she finds herself thinking that it would not have required any extra postage to send.

She sits down at the table and places the bundle in front of her. The Sellotape is overlapped in several places as though the person wrapping it had been in a hurry. She takes a pair of scissors from the knife holder and cuts into the plastic, the air bubbles flattening, the layers of tape parting smoothly to reveal what was inside.

At first, Caroline does not understand what she is looking at. She can see that it is something metallic. For several seconds, she simply stares, feeling herself disappear into one of those somnolent dazes. Then Caroline reaches out and touches the dull grey circle of metal, picking it up and holding it to the light. A chain unravels, making a slippery sound against the slickness of the plastic and she realises, all at once, what she is holding. Max's identity tags. There are two slim discs attached to the chain, each one dented and dimpled so that the thin engraved lines that spell out his name and blood type are obscured.

The upper half of one of the discs seems to have been corroded by rust. She looks at it more closely, bringing it up to eye level, and then, with the edge of one fingernail, she scratches at it to see if it will flake off. The stain doesn't shift. A speck of it lodges in the tip of her nail and she understands, all at once, that the irregular patch of orangey brown sticking along the edge of Max's dog-tag is not, in fact, rust. It is blood.

Her insides contract. She drops the tags to the floor, sending them skittering across the linoleum. She rushes to the sink and vomits, the bile stinging against the back of her throat. She has not eaten so there is not much to show for her retching. When she looks down, there is only a thin plume of yellowish liquid that sits, gelatinous, around the plughole. She turns on the tap, washes it down and then fills a glass with water. She takes small sips, leaning her weight against the sink until the nausea subsides.

She looks at the dog-tags by her feet. She cannot bring herself to touch them again. Caroline slides down on to the floor and sits with her back against the kitchen cupboard. She can feel the coolness of the linoleum against her shins. She does not cry. Instead, she retrieves the dog-tags, wraps them back up, slides them into the envelope and leaves it on the table for Andrew. Then she goes back to the sitting room, turns up the volume on the television and watches as a hearse rolls across the screen.

She turns up the volume as loud as it will go and the sound swells up, pumping and pressing against the walls, and she imagines the force of the noise making the bricks and beams buckle out of shape. Another two servicemen dead, this time marines. The news reporter says that one of them, a boy called Ted with a heart-shaped face, was known as 'Boss' by his men. Boss, Caroline thinks, even though he looked so young.

A woman in the crowd is being interviewed now, talking about what a tragedy it was that two mothers had 'lost' their sons. Caroline had always disliked that phrase, the idea that she had lost Max, that she had put her child somewhere, then forgotten where he was. As if she had mislaid him, left him behind so that she could no longer find him. As if she had been negligent. A bad mother.

She chews her lip.

She imagines her own mother then, sitting across the room from her, swinging backwards and forwards in the rocking chair that had stood in their kitchen for years, the wood dark and mottled with age.

'Never were much good at anything, were you?' her mother says. She would be in her eighties now, Caroline thinks, but still her shoulders are erect, her mouth fierce. There is a packet of cigarettes on her knees, a lighter gripped in her left hand.

'Please don't smoke in my house,' Caroline hears herself saying, even though she knows her mother is not there; that this is a hallucination.

Her mother glares at her. 'Ooh, all hoity toity now, aren't we?' Her mouth is set in a defiant line and she fumbles with the pack of cigarettes and takes one out, slipping it between her lips. 'I'll have a smoke when I want one, thank you very much. You can't tell me what to do, young lady.' She flicks the lighter, the flame shooting up to the tip of the cigarette and she sucks in loudly, watching the ash blacken, inhaling a lungful. Then her mother meets Caroline's eye. 'Look at the bloody state of you,' she says and she starts to laugh, a spluttering sound that turns into a cough.

The coil of fear that has been in Caroline's stomach unspools. She lunges forward, wanting to grip her mother by the throat and squeeze out the breath in her veins, but the movement propels her into space and her fingers grasp wildly at nothing, and she collapses on to the floor, catching her knee on the edge of the coffee table as she loses balance.

She stays on the floor for several minutes, listening to the television. She digs her fingernails into the palm of each hand.

She misses Andrew.

She is alone.

Day after day, the same loneliness.

She feels in her dressing-gown pocket, tracing the brushed cotton lining with the tip of her finger until it pushes against a small, hard circle.

A pill. Relief.

She takes it out, cups it in the palm of her hand. She realises she has nothing to wash it down with and although she is capable of swallowing it dry, she remembers the drinks shelf in the corner of the room. Easing herself up on to all fours, Caroline crawls across and takes down a bottle of gin, the green glass muddied by dinner party thumbprints. She unscrews the cap, lifts the lip of the neck up to her mouth and knocks it back. A pleasurable light-headedness envelops her.

There is a crashing sound from down the corridor. She is so dazed that for a brief second she wonders if she has imagined it. But then there is another noise, a kind of shouted whimper, and she remembers that she is not alone in the house after all. There is Elsa. Always Elsa. She had forgotten, momentarily, that the carer had called in sick this morning. Andrew is coming back at lunch. Until then, Caroline is in charge.

She puts the bottle back and stands up. She finds her way along the hallway to Elsa's bedroom, keeping the palm of one hand flat against the wall to steady herself.

She pushes open the door. The table lamp that normally stands on the bedside table is lying on the floor, its wire tangled around the shattered base. Shards of turquoise-patterned china are scattered across the carpet and the shade is lying at an odd angle against the skirting board, where it must have made the first impact as it fell.

It is a lamp that Max gave Caroline for her fiftieth birthday two years ago. He had asked her what she wanted over email and Caroline had sent him the link for this lamp from an online furniture shop. She had loved the colour of it: the delicate swirls of lace-white against the vivid hues of greenish blue. She had initially given it pride of place in the sitting room, on the table where she kept all the silver-framed family photos. But then Andrew had moved it into Elsa's room so that she could see better at night and Caroline had not thought to protest. Looking at the lamp, now broken, irretrievable, Caroline feels a pain in her. Nothing more can happen, she thinks to herself. Nothing.

She looks up from the broken china to see Elsa, propped up in bed, her shoulders sagging forward because the pillows that Andrew plumped up behind her this morning are now bunched in a bundle in the small of her back. Elsa moves her eyes when she hears Caroline approach but does not lift her head. Caroline is left with the curious impression that she is pleased with herself, that she is hiding her face like an unrepentant child.

Some force presses against the inside of Caroline's cheeks, pushing the capillaries to the surface so that she can feel her face burning. She senses that time has been brought to a temporary standstill. She feels, in this second, a strange kind of detachment. Her sensations seem to untether themselves, one by one. She takes a deep breath. It feels good to hear the air being drawn into her.

And then, as Caroline exhales, there is a sound in her ears, a sucking noise as though a stretched piece of cling-film has been pierced. She glances at Elsa and she sees that the old woman is laughing. At first, Caroline cannot believe it. She stands stock-still. Elsa's face is immobile, her lips open only by a millimetre but she is smiling, making a mumbling-grunting sound, her shoulders shaking with unexplained mirth. She is laughing, Caroline thinks to herself. She is laughing at me.

She takes two steps forward and raises her arm high above her head, bringing her hand down swiftly, sharply against Elsa's cheek. The swipe across Elsa's face knocks her skull to one side, the sound of the slap reverberating across the room. Caroline is panting, her breaths crowding in on each other.

Elsa shrieks. A red patch spreads across her cheek. She looks at Caroline wildly, her pupils bullet-hole black. But instead of fear and apology, Caroline sees nothing but indignation in Elsa's expression. She brings her face right up close to Elsa's so that she can feel the warmth of the old lady's breath on her cheek.

'Don't . . .' Caroline starts, hoarsely. 'Don't you dare laugh at me.'

Elsa shifts her head to one side, refusing to look. Gently, Caroline places her thumb and forefinger in a V shape on Elsa's chin and turns her head back to face her. She pushes down with the tips of her fingers, feeling Elsa's puckered flesh smooth out underneath the pressure of her grip. Her mother-in-law blinks. A thin string of saliva is trickling down from one corner of her mouth.

Caroline takes her hand away, letting Elsa's head loll back on the pillow. There is a shadow of a fingered mark just above the ridge of her jawline. For a few seconds, Caroline stays there, inches away from Elsa's face, resting her head next to hers and she has a sense of perfect calm, of having taken control. The rage she had felt moments earlier begins to subside. She doesn't even feel surprised by what she has done.

Elsa closes her eyes. After several minutes, her breathing becomes slower, more wheezy. Asleep, she looks so harmless and fragile, her face small and soft, her eyelids quivering like the wings of pale moths.

As Elsa dozes, Caroline begins to shiver, each tiny muscle and synapse twitching and trembling from her toes right up to her temples. Her teeth start to chatter. All at once, the horror of what just happened sweeps over her, swift and cold.

Had it really happened? She feels her head spin with the weight of her calculations.

Is she drunk?

Has she taken too many pills?

She is scared of the answers. She forces herself to close off her thoughts. She concentrates solely on practicalities: on placing one hand on the top of the bedside table to steady herself as she stands;

on walking out of the room and closing the door behind her; on finding her way to the cupboard underneath the stairs; on reaching for the dustpan and brush amid the bottles of bleach and the packets of vacuum cleaner bags. She steels herself to go back into Elsa's room, because she does not want to face her again, because she is afraid of what she will find.

She bends down to brush away the broken china, sliding the dustpan underneath the scattered fragments. The smaller ones get caught in the brush, bright turquoise specks against the dull green bristles. She wraps the detritus in an old newspaper, scrunching it up into a bundle and then flipping open the kitchen bin and letting it fall, removing her foot from the pedal as quickly as possible so that the lid slams down and she does not have to think about it any more. She can pretend it never happened.

Automatically, she fills the kettle and puts it on to boil.

In the midst of this strangeness, Caroline finds she is thinking about what she can cook Andrew for dinner. She walks across to the pile of recipe books and takes out a dog-eared favourite, a long-ago Christmas present with the smiling features of a glamorous female celebrity chef on the cover. It falls open at the page for a spinach and feta frittata. She is seized by an unfamiliar enthusiasm. As she skims through the ingredients, she can taste the saltiness of the cheese, the richness of the spinach, the melting warmth of the eggs. She realises she is hungry; hungrier than she has been for months. She tears a scrap of paper from the calendar on the wall and starts jotting down a shopping list. Yes, Caroline thinks to herself, why not? I can go out and get in the car and put the key in the ignition and drive myself to the supermarket. I can buy all these things and I can follow the recipe and I can make something for supper that Andrew will like. Adrenalin surges through her and then, once the curious excitement has subsided, she feels calm, as if order has been restored. It is as though, after a period of absence, she has woken to find that she still exists, as though she has opened a window and let the breeze into a stuffy room.

The rest of it – the unanswered questions; the greyness around the edges – she pushes away, parcelling up the unpleasantness so that she does not have to look at it. It does not exist. Not if she chooses to ignore it. Not if she chooses to carry on as if nothing had happened. Not if she tries hard – very, very hard – to believe that she can be a good person after all.

She goes upstairs to get dressed and, as she passes Elsa's door, she pulls it firmly to, hearing the lip of the lock click into place. When she comes back down, wearing a pale pink T-shirt and jeans, she sees the package containing Max's tags still on the kitchen table. She looks at it and remembers the letters Max's army colleagues had written to her – the Dans, the Robbies, the Johnnos, the Eds – their names always shortened, their emotions concealed on the page, the rawness of them masked by the expression of careful, decent thoughts. She remembers they had tried, some of them, to tell her what had happened that day.

Did they know, when they got to him, that Max was going to die?

Would Max have known?

She hears the thrumming of rotary blades, the sound of it so clear she can, for a moment, believe a helicopter is landing right next door.

She stops. The supermarket, she thinks, let me just concentrate on that. And before she has a chance to change her mind, Caroline walks out of the door to the car, pressing down on the key fob so that it unlocks with a beep and a flash of its lights. She starts the engine, turns on the radio and rotates the volume dial as far as it will go.

Max

HARD-BAKED BY THE SUN, the earth crackles underfoot like tinder. The rainy season has long passed. The riverbeds have receded, the muddied tracks have dried out and the earth has formed itself into strange eddying patterns so that the ground rises and falls in whipped peaks like freshly baked meringues. As he trudges forward, his boots crunch against the parched brown soil.

The strap of Max's helmet scratches the roughness of his stubble. Sweat drenches his hair. Rivulets of it trickle down his forehead, into the corner of his eye sockets, down the side of his nose and then slip across the cleft of his lip into the corner of his mouth.

Johnno, the 'Vallon Man', is way out at the front of the patrol, sliding his metal detector left and right and left and right over the ground. Vallon is the name of the metal detector used to sweep for bombs. So Johnno, inevitably, is known as the Vallon Man. The army isn't, after all, to be congratulated for its originality with nicknames.

It is just after 10am in Upper Nile State, South Sudan and here he is, an insignificant stick man in uniform in the middle of Africa, part of an eleven-strong search team, criss-crossing back and forth to clear a strategic mound of mines left scattered across the barren fields by insurgents. Every step they take is a step closer to getting it over with.

There is an abandoned village to the left of them, the ground blackened with the remnants of a recent fire. The huts are in varying states of collapse: one of them has lost its roof and half its external wall. The tightly padded clumps of straw and mud have started to disintegrate, leaving the half-formed hut standing like a rotten tooth against the low horizon. A goat lies dead underneath a mango tree, its scrawny neck still tethered to the trunk. A cloud of flies has formed around the animal's stomach. There is an unmistakable stench of putrid flesh.

There are no children. No shouts or giggles or scamperings to alleviate the density of the silence, the thickness of the air around them. Normally, when they come to a village like this one, the wheels of their armoured vehicles throwing up clouds of dust as they approach, the children run out to meet them. They come with big smiles and pipe-cleaner legs, their feet bare, their bodies swathed in a raggedy array of clothes donated by faraway Western families: football strips torn and dirtied with age; a too-small T-shirt emblazoned with an image of SpongeBob SquarePants. They run up to the soldiers in a sudden swarm and ask for pens or chewing gum or packets of cigarettes they are too young to smoke. Usually, Max will drop to his haunches and laugh. He allows them to try on his helmet and gives them a few biros he has stashed in his pockets for just such an eventuality.

He is good with children. They like him; gravitate naturally towards him.

Hearts and minds, the army calls it. As though the two could be distinctly separated.

The children have no mistrust in their eyes. It is the adults who are wary: the village elders who hang back in the shadows with scowling faces and shifting gazes, attempting to work out what these foreigners want from them.

The insurgents are everywhere, hiding beneath the most unlikely carapace: the elderly man with the stooped shoulders and the baggy, wrinkled face or the young woman in the bright pink sarong with the high cheekbones and elegant neck. Max cannot trust anyone. Even the landscape, with its rugged beauty, once the preserve of adventurous back-packers and NGO volunteers, conceals deadly secrets.

It can be the most insignificant thing that gives a bomb away: the thin sliver of glinting yellow from the cooking oil container packed full of farming fertiliser, or the snaking length of electrical wire waiting to be pressed underneath a soldier's boot or the tread of a vehicle wheel. You have to be alert, even when the heat saps your energy and your concentration. You have to remind yourself of the danger, just to keep your heart rate up, to keep the adrenalin flowing.

The Vallon Man stops. The search-team halts, momentarily. Max waits, his pulse rate quickening, his muscles tensed in readiness. The ten men around him do the same, their nerves stretched tight as trip-wires.

But it is a false alarm and, after a few minutes, they move on and resume the familiar shuffling movement forwards: one foot in front of the other, eyes scanning each peak and dip of the ragged ground.

After what feels like hours but is probably only a matter of minutes, they come to the edge of a dried-up river, the banks falling steeply on either side of the gulley. Johnno scrambles down first, clumps of soil breaking off in his hands as he manoeuvres himself gingerly towards the bottom of the natural trench. Again, he sweeps the metal detector over the surface, the movement of his hands rhythmic and steady. Johnno signals to let them know the way is clear.

Max steps forward. The tip of his boot makes contact with a piece of rock, about the size of a child's clenched fist. As he shifts his weight on to his foot, the rock splinters into quarters. A blast rips through his body.

He is thrown back several metres, his body thumping to the ground, his neck twisted slackly. His helmet rolls to one side, the strap sliced through. It happens so quickly.

Cracked mud. Redness. Voices all around him, shouted orders and screams for help, each one registering at a different decibel, each one with its own jarring note of discord, a miasmic babble of noise.

'Come on, Max, come on, you fucker, don't you dare leave us now, don't you fucking dare.'

Someone is kneeling beside him, sleeves rolled up, pushing down on his ribcage. Their bare hands pump up and down, blood spitting on to skin.

His eyelids flicker shut.

His heart beats frantically, trying to keep up, but soon there is too much blood and his heart seems to be drowning in fluid, like a rock sucked into the quicksand, and although they are trying, all of them, trying so, so hard to keep him alive, it is too much effort to take another breath. There is too much blood.

His heart stutters. Then it stops.

Was that how it happened? she wonders. Or was it another way?

Maybe he woke up that morning with an intimation of what lay ahead, a bad feeling, a sense of what fate had in store for him.

Maybe, in the moments just before the bomb exploded, he had been laughing, sharing a joke with his mates and not paying enough attention to where his feet were falling.

Maybe the blow was instant and there was no time to feel pain or hurt or sadness or panic or any of it – any of it at all. Maybe there was no time to think.

Maybe he was calm.

Or panicked.

Or resolute.

Was he convinced he was going to make it through?

Maybe he thought of her just before he died. Because isn't your life meant to flash before your eyes? Isn't death meant to bring you back to the moment of your birth?

Or maybe, instead of his mother, he thought of Andrew.

Or of Elsa.

Or even of Angelique.

But then again, maybe he didn't.

Maybe he didn't.

And maybe none of it happened quite the way she imagines, she thinks, shifting the car into gear, trying to remember the quickest way to the supermarket. Because how could it?

Because how could she possibly know?

Andrew

ANDREW WAKES AT 6.38 in the morning, exactly seven minutes before his alarm is due to go off. He is always roused at exactly this moment, his mind jolted into consciousness by some automatic reflex. He once experimented by falling asleep without setting the alarm clock and found that he overslept. Andrew was tickled by the idea that his subconscious mind reacts to the idea of regulation rather than the practical exercise of it. He is, generally speaking, a creature of habit.

He pushes the flat black button on top of the clock-radio to mute the beeps before they sound and then slides out of bed as carefully as he can so as not to wake Caroline, although he knows her sleep has been twitchy and disturbed of late. There is an uncomfortable pressure on his bladder and he walks over to the lavatory to relieve himself, noticing as he does so that the bathroom needs to be regrouted. Patches of black mould are dotted along the white tiles. The bath is ringed with a pale brown water line and the whole room smells damp and mildewy.

They had only put this bathroom in a few years ago but already it needs an overhaul. Andrew groans at the thought of it. There was a time when he would have done it himself, rolled up his sleeves and got out his toolbox and fixed whatever needed to be done. He used to like DIY even though the results, admittedly, were somewhat mixed. But there was something about the simple practicality of a manual task that appealed to him: he did not have to think while he was painting a wall or drilling a hole or scraping flat a patch of Polyfilla, he simply had to follow the rules. And then there was always the sense of satisfaction, how-ever slight, that you got when a task had been completed, when a problem had been rectified, when things were straight and ordered once more. Was it absurd to say that it made him feel more like a man? Possibly.

But increasingly he found he was too busy for DIY. He began to realise that his tinkering with screwdrivers had only ever been an indulgence, a hobby he could pursue because he possessed the luxury of time and because he also knew that professionals could be called in whenever something went seriously wrong. With Elsa living under the same roof, he found that he had less and less free time at his disposal. He was working long hours at the office – a tricky new corporate client needed mollifying on a regular basis – and Caroline was still not herself, so Andrew found he had to pick up the slack more and more. It had been agreed before his mother moved in that Andrew would take on the bulk of the care but he had not realised then quite how much he would need to do. Elsa was in rapid and apparently irreversible decline – where once he could have relied on Caroline to keep an eye on her during the day, now he was forced to rush to and from the office to help the carer lift and change his mother's incontinence nappy.

The main carer was a cheery-faced Kenyan woman called Sana-pei – 'but you can call me Snappy,' she had said on her first day with a giant smile. Andrew had managed to arrange with a local care agency for her to come four times a day to change and wash his mother. It was a laborious task that required two people and although normally he could have relied on Caroline to help Sana-pei, he thought it was safer to arrange someone else to be there. But the other carer, a quietly spoken Ukrainian woman he'd found in the Classifieds section of the *Malvern Gazette*, could only come twice a day – once in the morning and once in the afternoon – so Andrew had to rush back from work to cover the other two slots with Snappy, at lunchtime and in the early evening.

Even in the short time that Elsa had been with them, the change had been dramatic. She could barely talk at all now and her mental acuity was slipping away from her. Andrew was no longer sure what went in and what didn't. The other day, he had walked into the room to see an expression of intense anxiety on her face and he had to remind her who he was, reaching out to give her a reassuring touch on the shoulder.

It was, Andrew found, difficult to readjust. His mother had always been the one in control. Growing up, Elsa had been easier to admire than to love. He remembers with perfect clarity the party she threw for his fifth birthday. He had invited three friends, all of whom lived nearby, and Elsa had bought a cake from the Fitzbillies bun shop. She lit five candles and brought it into the kitchen where the four boys were seated round the table in paper crowns. They sang Happy Birthday, with his father providing the only baritone voice, and then Andrew blew out the candles in one go, which gave him an immense feeling of pride. He looked up to his father for confirmation that he had done well and Oliver broke off from patting tobacco into the bowl of his pipe to smile at him and raise his eyebrows to show he was impressed. Andrew's cheeks burned with happiness.

Elsa took a long shiny knife out of the cutlery drawer to cut the cake. It was the biggest chocolate cake Andrew had ever seen and his stomach had rumbled in anticipation of eating it. There was a thick layer of icing that dripped down over the sides and Andrew, overcome by greed and excitement, reached out to pick off a small piece of it with the tip of his index finger. Elsa did not notice Andrew's finger as she started to cut. He felt a sharp stab of pain in his hand. He cried out with a yowl. There was blood on the yellow tablecloth, mixed in with a muddy stain of chocolate. The other boys were shrieking with shock. Elsa, at first unaware of what all the fuss was about, quickly realised what had happened. And what Andrew remembered most vividly about that day was not the pain of the cut but rather what his mother had said next.

'Oh Andrew, stop being such a baby,' she said, putting down the knife and turning away. 'It's only a scratch.' She did not comfort him or put her arms around him. It was left to Oliver to scoop him up and take him to the bathroom, where he ran Andrew's finger under the tap and put a plaster on it. 'All right, old chap?' Oliver said, and his breath smelled of tobacco. Andrew nodded his head and the movement caused a single tear to spill out on to his cheek. Oliver, embarrassed, took his hand roughly. 'Come on then.'

The cake, when he ate it, did not taste as good as he had imagined it would.

Years later, Andrew had asked his father about this, about whether he thought it unusual that Elsa appeared so detached from her own child. By that time, Andrew was married himself and Oliver, always gentle, had mellowed to the point that he could quite easily be moved to tears by a heart-wrenching story on the evening television news. He hadn't been surprised by Andrew's question. In fact, it was almost as though he had been expecting it.

They were sitting in the living room of the house in Grantchester, where Andrew and Caroline had come to stay for the weekend. They were reading the papers while Sunday lunch was being prepared in the kitchen down the hallway and occasionally there would be the reassuring sound of jostled cutlery or an oven door being opened and shut. The buttery smell of roasting potatoes thickened the air around them. Caroline had gone upstairs to change, even though Andrew kept telling her she didn't need to.

'I think I should open a few bottles of that red,' said Oliver, folding up his section of newspaper and putting it on to the nest of tables to his side.

And Andrew asked him, the question coming out of the blue. He hadn't even been aware he was thinking of it but then it popped out of his mouth.

'Do you think Mummy ever really loved me?' he asked. 'As a child, I mean.'

Oliver looked at him over his reading glasses, his chin tucked into his neck. He considered the question for a few seconds and then, taking off his glasses, he said: 'Of course she did, Andrew.' His voice was straightforward, not unkind, but not especially comforting either. Oliver sighed, rubbing the back of his neck. 'Elsa has always found it difficult to show her love. I suspect she thinks it would be a weakness to do so.'

There was a pause.

'Listen, she loves you a great deal, Andrew, as you well know, but there are things about her . . . her upbringing that make it hard for her to admit it. She'd hate me talking about her like this,' Oliver shook his head, 'but it's probably a lot to do with her own parents. She had been very close to her mother but then, when her father came back from the war.' He stopped. When he spoke again, his voice was tight. 'He was an absolute brute.' Andrew glanced at him. His father's face had grown mottled and red. 'It was bloody lucky, all things considered, that I didn't serve.' When Oliver had volunteered to fight in the Second World War, so Andrew recalled, the doctors had discovered a heart murmur at his medical check-up. He spent the rest of the war doing something rather secretive and unexplained in intelligence. 'I think it would have undone her,' Oliver continued, fixing his gaze at a midpoint on the wall. He seemed to be struggling with something, uncomfortable at what he was about to say. 'There are things we never told you, Andrew, things you shouldn't ever have to hear about your own grandfather. Elsa couldn't even speak about him. Couldn't mention him by name.' Oliver stood up and smoothed down his chinos, scattering the crumbs from a messily eaten handful of Twiglets on to the Afghan rug. 'Now I really must get on with that wine or I'll be for it.' He walked past Andrew's chair towards the drinks cabinet, pausing briefly to pat his son on the shoulder.

'Try not to worry so much,' Oliver said and then he left the room.

When, some time later, Andrew had become a father himself, he had tried very hard to show his love. He can vividly remember the first time he saw Max in the hospital: a tiny baby with a scrunched up face and a pot-belly and he remembers, too, how moved he had been by the sight. And yet, he found it almost impossible to put the profundity of his feeling on public display.

'Do you want to hold him?' Caroline had asked, moving the baby's head away from her breast. Andrew had shaken his head, had not been able to risk taking this fragile, perfect package in his clumsy arms in case he did something wrong, in case he ruined it somehow. Caroline had looked at him and he hadn't been able to find the words to explain what he felt, either then or at any time since.

*   *   *

After he has shaved, he goes downstairs to prepare Elsa's breakfast. He unpeels a banana and mashes it with a fork on to a small plate with some full-fat milk and a squeeze of lemon. His mother had never had a big appetite, even when she was well, but now it has dwindled dramatically. When she first arrived, Andrew used to go through to her room in the mornings with a full tray containing a bowl of muesli, a pot of freshly made coffee, two slices of toast and marmalade and half of a chopped Cox's apple. These days, she often struggles to finish the banana.

He shoves a slice of bread in the toaster for himself and then takes Elsa's breakfast through.

She is already awake, lying flat on her back with the duvet drawn right up to her neck so that the only thing he can see in the dusky half-light is her delicate face, the cheeks sunken beneath the bone. Her eyes turn towards him as he enters.

'Morning, Mummy,' he says, as cheerfully as he can. He glances at the clock on her bedside and sees that it is already 7.15. He needs to leave in a quarter of an hour.

But of course, everything takes much longer than it should – hoisting Elsa up into a sitting position, making sure she is warm enough, passing her a beaker of warmed water to sip on, feeding her the banana so that she does not spill it on to the bedsheets and then brushing her hair so that she looks presentable for the carer. He opens the curtains. The sky is the grey-white of a seagull's wing, blurry at the edges with threatening clouds of rain.

'All right, Mummy, I'll see you later,' he says, walking back to the bed and bending down to give her a peck on the cheek. Her skin is cool against the brush of his lips. She stares up at him. Andrew feels a stab of guilt. He turns on the battery-operated radio, tuning it to the soothing tones of a cello concerto on Classic FM. It is the kind of populist radio station she would normally have hated but recently, he has found that she reacts better to more familiar music. As he fiddles with the antenna to get rid of the static, he thinks he sees Elsa smile. When he looks at her again, her eyelids are almost shut, droplets of moisture gathering in the ducts.

He gathers up the breakfast stuff. Just as he is about to leave, he notices that the pink bed jacket he has put around his mother's shoulders has slipped off. He puts the tray on the floor and reaches across Elsa to gather it up, coaxing her into leaning forwards so that he can slide the fleecy material behind her. She flops towards him, her muscles slack.

He notices there is a small but livid bruise just below her right cheekbone. It is the size of a five-pence piece and the colour of a ripening plum. The bruise looks unnatural against the scraggy pallor of her skin. Andrew leans in to peer at it more closely and then gently eases Elsa back against her pillows. He wonders how she got the bruise and makes a mental note to tell the carers they must be more careful when they handle her. But the thought of it does not trouble him unduly. Probably just one of those things that happened as one got older, he thinks, and it does not appear to be causing Elsa any pain – in fact, she didn't seem to be aware of it at all.

He clears away the plate and the fork. Then he retrieves his car keys from the bowl by the fridge and walks outside, pushing the door carefully behind him so that it does not slam and wake Caroline.

He sees the envelope containing Max's dog-tags on the kitchen table and hesitates. Ridiculously, he does not want to leave the package on its own. He picks it up and slips it into his jacket pocket.

By the time he gets into the office, half an hour later than he should have done, Andrew has forgotten about the bruise entirely. The first thing he does is open the top right drawer of his desk and place the dog-tags there, nestled among the paperclips and rubber bands. He rests his hand on the envelope, as if to shelter the contents.

The back of his head seems to tighten and he wonders if that marks the onset of a migraine. He has been suffering from them with increasing frequency and knows the signs: a sense of hyper-reality, the colours bleached from his vision, the world too sharply defined to be trusted and then, as the voices of those around him disappear down a tunnel of noise, there is a staggering pain that will last for hours. He fumbles around for a packet of 500mg para-cetamol, pressing out two from the foil and washing them down with his mug of cooling tea.

He slides the drawer shut, obscuring the dog-tags from view. On his computer screen, the unanswered emails are piling up and he knows he has a small mountain of paperwork to get through by the end of the day but still he cannot seem to motivate himself. He finds his mind wandering, thinking of Caroline and the dinner she had cooked him last night. He should be happy that she was making the effort, that she seemed to be returning to some semblance of stability but instead he felt uneasy. He could not quite put his finger on it. There had been something about her manner – contained but with an undercurrent of panic, as though she was going through the motions, imitating what she thought of as normal behaviour in order to divert his attention from what was actually going on beneath the surface.

The spinach and feta frittata, once a dish that Caroline could have prepared blindfold, had been undercooked: the egg albumen still slippery and raw, the cheese unmelted in big, salty lumps. She had tried to do everything too quickly: laying the table with such haste that she had given him a spoon instead of a knife and spilled the water as she poured it. She had laughed, too shrilly, when he pointed this out. And then she had looked at him with such hopeful expectancy when he ate his first mouthful, her eyes sharp, her mouth drawn in a tight little smile, that he had been forced to lie and tell her it was wonderful.

'I'm glad,' she had said, tentatively reaching out to take his hand. He gave it to her but he felt nothing as he did so; none of the familiar intimacy he had once so valued. 'I want to try . . .' Caroline looked away. 'I want to try and be better.'

She sounded so desperate to please. 'You mustn't force yourself,' he said. And then, neither of them could think of anything else to fill the gap and they had lapsed into a long, shapeless silence until they went to bed. Andrew knew she was disappointed in him. He had tried to touch her under the sheets, to scoop her into the concave curve of his body, but she had shifted away to the edge of the mattress.

He slips out of his reverie and notices that his computer screen-saver has clicked into a shifting kaleidoscope of geometric shapes. The phone rings.

'Hello,' he says, picking up the receiver.

'Andrew, it's me.'

'Caroline. How curious. I was just thinking about you.'

'Nothing bad, I hope.' That shrill laugh again. It set his teeth on edge to hear it.

'No, no.' He drums his fingers on the desk. He glances at the clock on the wall and wonders why she is calling him. 'Are you all right?'

'Yes, more than all right. Derek Lester's office called.' She pauses, waiting for his reaction. 'We've got an appointment to see him.' Her voice is thrilled. He can imagine her standing in the hall-way, shoulders tensed, one hand playing with the phone cable, fiddling with one ear lobe as she always does when she is nervous.

'That's good,' he says, evenly.

'Good?' She laughs again. 'I'd say it's more than good, Andrew. It's what we've been waiting for, isn't it?'

How should he best respond? In truth, he does not think Derek Lester will be able to provide his wife with the answers she so craves. He is worried that she has spent so much time on this and concerned, too, that her mind seems to have been twisted out of shape by its obsession with conspiracy.

'I just don't want you getting your hopes up,' he says.

Andrew can sense her frustration radiating towards him. 'Right,' she replies, clipping the word short. 'Well, I just thought I should let you know. In case you can be bothered to come.'

He exhales to the count of three. 'Of course I want to come. I just . . .'

'I thought you'd be pleased.' There is a catch in her voice. 'Don't bother coming back at lunch. I can deal with Elsa.' Caroline hangs up.

He puts the receiver back carefully, resting his hand there for several seconds and then he takes a sheet of paper from his in-tray and tries to concentrate on what the typed letters and numbers are telling him. After a few minutes, there is a knock on his door.

'Yes,' he says, glancing up over the rim of his glasses.

Kate puts her head round the door. Her blonde hair is tied back in a loose ponytail. She is wearing fashionably square black-rimmed spectacles that he has never seen before. Andrew finds himself thinking that she looks better with her hair down, that it suits the softness of her face more.

'Hi, Andrew,' she says, smiling, her lips shiny with some kind of gloss. 'I was just wondering if you fancied some lunch?' Her hand is still on the door handle, as though she is prepared for him to say no, as he usually would. But today he finds that he wants to do something out of character. He wants to be someone else for a bit.

'Yes,' he says. 'Why not?'

They go to an Italian place that has just opened round the corner, situated on a pedestrianised stretch of shops that is dingily lit and unprepossessing. The restaurant itself is all faux leather and cleverly angled mirrors. The other tables are empty apart from one elderly couple, both still in their overcoats. The woman is eating a bowl of soup but her hand is shaking and some of it has spilled off the spoon, leaving a splodge of green on the lapel of her mackintosh.

Seeing this, Andrew feels a clutching at his insides. He thinks of Elsa, back at home, trapped in bed, waiting. Always waiting.

'Follow me, please,' says the waiter, leading them to a squashed-away table right next to the lavatories.

'Will you be OK here?' asks Andrew once the waiter has left them with the laminated menu card.

'Yes,' says Kate, bemused. 'Why on earth not?'

He feels caught out without knowing why. 'I just thought . . .' he is stumbling. 'If there's a draught . . .' he gestures vaguely towards the door.

'I'm sure I'll cope,' she says and then she leans across the table so that her blouse dips forward and he can see an exposed triangle of flesh and there, just beneath, a glimpse of black lace. She reaches her hand across the napkins and the wine glasses and the single wilting carnation in a vase and she touches the top of his wrist lightly. 'Thanks for asking.'

The food, when it comes, is good. Kate eats precisely half of her spaghetti vongole and drinks two large glasses of a rosé wine that Andrew learns, for the first time, is called Pinot Blush. He has little appetite but eats most of his veal escalope without too much effort.

He pushes the leftovers around his plate restlessly, so as not to make eye contact. The conversation is fluent, not stilted at all, but for some reason he cannot look at her. He feels that to look at her would be fatal. It would unravel him.

'Are you sure you don't want a drink?' Kate is asking him, a teasing note to her voice. 'Is your afternoon really so jam-packed with Important Business?'

'No, no . . .' he starts. Then the waiter interrupts him to take their plates away, which seems to take much longer than it should, and by the time the table has been cleared, he finds he has changed his mind. Bugger it, he thinks to himself. Why not?

So he orders a small glass of Burgundy and a tiramisu. Kate shakes her head when he passes the dessert menu to her.

'No, I'm kind of watching what I eat,' she says. 'I've put on so much weight since sitting around that office. I look like such a blob these days.'

'Nonsense,' he says. 'You look pretty good to me.' He wishes as soon as the words are out of his mouth that he could reel them back in.

Kate flicks her eyes up quickly. 'Do I?' she says, leaning forwards in that distracting way again.

He fiddles with the edge of the tablecloth. 'That thing you were saying about the Kilner account . . .'

Kate laughs, lightly. 'Yes, let's talk about work.' A pause. 'Much safer.' She sits back in her chair, lifts her handbag on to her lap, takes out a small compact and applies a fresh coat of lip gloss to her mouth. He is shocked that she does this in front of him. It seems so intimate, somehow, and also a touch slatternly. He realises he has never seen Caroline in lip gloss.

The image of his wife burns a hole through his thoughts. His eyes moisten, briefly. Disgusted, he bows his head so that Kate will not see.

'Shall we get the bill?' she asks.

They go to her flat. Kate tells him she has forgotten a crucial piece of paperwork that she needs to take back to the office but they both know this is a lie. She lives above a travel agent and the entrance is to one side of a multi-coloured display advertising the latest winter sun deals to Egypt and Florida. Kate unlocks the door and walks ahead of him into the shared hallway. The sight of her bending to pick up the letters that have collected on the carpet is enough to make him feel the nudge of an erection through his trousers.

Quickly, so that he does not have time to think, he grabs her from behind and pulls her to him. She turns round and kisses him, violently so that their teeth clash and then her tongue, loose and wet, is in his mouth and he is shocked, again, that she is so forward with him. The kiss stops as quickly as it started. She reaches down with one hand and before he knows what is happening, she has taken his cock in her hand, is grabbing at it through his trousers.

He draws back, stung by the audacity of it. Kate looks at him, surprised. She wipes her mouth with the back of her hand leaving a shiny smear of pink across her skin.

'I'm sorry,' he says, foolishly. 'I'm not used to this.'

'Let's go upstairs. I'm sure I can make you comfortable if I try hard enough.'

He follows her, mutely. His erection has gone. The brief excitement of the moment has dissipated into embarrassment and horror that he has got himself into this situation. He knows that he does not want this any more, that he never really has. He wanted to show it could be done, that he had it in him, but now it seems pointless. And yet, stupidly, he is too polite to back out. He knows he will go through with it.

Kate's flat is modern and serviceable and almost entirely devoid of personality. There is a corner sofa in the small living room that doubles up as a kitchen. A white-framed photograph on one wall shows Kate and three other girls in summer dresses, all of them shiny and smiling.

She leaves her handbag on the kitchen counter and then takes his hand, leading him to the bedroom. 'Come on,' she says and he sees that with her other hand, she is already unbuttoning her blouse. She releases the blind so that it falls against the single window with a clattering sound and the light becomes fudged. She sits down on the edge of the bed in her underwear and starts undoing his trousers. He stops her, gently, then undresses himself. She watches him as he does so and this makes him uncomfortable. He feels the energy drain out of him.

Naked, he goes to her. She grasps him round the waist and pulls him down on top of her, kissing him again with that curious fierceness. He tries to kiss her back in the same way but it seems so wrong, so lacking in tenderness. She shifts up the mattress and tilts her head back, pushing her chest out so that her breasts graze his lips and he can do little else but circle his tongue dutifully round each nipple, as seems to be required of him. She starts to moan and then to whisper in his ear what she wants him to do to her but the words sound harsh and rasping and wrong.

Where did she learn to be like this? he wonders. He is taken aback by how mechanical her movements seem, as though she is watching a film of herself, as though she has a mental checklist of erogenous zones that must be ticked off before either of them can be truly satisfied. She flips herself on to her front and so she is on all fours in front of him. He finds it easier without seeing her face and, when he finally pushes himself inside, she screams out his name and he is instantly worried that the neighbours might hear. He feels no release.

Afterwards, he disengages himself almost immediately and sits up on the side of the bed, clicking the strap of his watch back into place. 'Don't go,' murmurs Kate, her head half-buried in a crumpled pillow.

Even this sounds like something she thinks she should say.

'I'm afraid I have to. Things to do back in the office.'

She turns to look at him, hurt.

'I'm sorry, Kate,' he says, dully. 'I don't know what I was thinking. It shouldn't have happened.' He realises, as he speaks these hollow words, that for the first time in weeks he feels nothing. He has slipped into a void, a vacuum, an empty hole of space. He is not thinking of Caroline or Max or Elsa. For this moment in time, he is rid of them all. It is a sensation of pure relief.

He bends down to kiss Kate chastely on the mouth. She senses something has changed and narrows her gaze. 'Sure,' she says, feigning nonchalance. 'Whatever.' He can see her weighing up whether to say something cruel but for some reason, she decides against it. 'I'll see you back in the office.' She turns over on the bed so that her naked back faces him. He looks at her skin: smooth, unblemished, young. And then, because he cannot help himself, he thinks of Max.

He nods, just the once. Then he walks out of the flat, letting the door slide shut behind him.

He does not go back to the office straight away but instead heads towards the Priory and sits on a bench overlooking a patch of grass and gravestones. He expects to feel sickened or anxious or guilty but in fact, he is calm and his heart seems to be beating more slowly than usual. His head is clear.

He leans back against the wooden slats of the bench and loosely crosses his legs. Two pigeons cautiously strut towards him, giving exploratory pecks at the leftover crumbs of someone else's lunch-time sandwich on the ground by his feet. He watches them. He takes in the names on the gravestones around him: Isabelle, beloved wife of; Alice, passed away in the year of our Lord; Enid, with the angels; Alfred, much-missed father; George, younger brother; William, killed in action; Horace . . .

Horace. The name brings him up short. It is his grandfather's name, a man whom Andrew knows so little about and yet, in recent weeks, he has been thinking of him more than ever. From what his parents had told him, Horace had been irrevocably changed by the First World War. When, as a young child, he had asked why he never saw his grandparents, the answer had been evasive. As he grew older, and the questions remained, Oliver became more blunt in his replies. Before he went to university, Andrew had tried to raise the issue again with his father over a pint in a pub – he knew, without being told, never to speak of it to Elsa.

'He was abusive,' Oliver said, removing his pipe from the corner of his mouth. 'Treated your mother like dirt. And if you want my advice, Andrew, you'll not pursue this any further.'

'But what if . . .'

'There's no bloody what if,' Oliver cut in, his voice quiet. 'Horace was a violent bastard. I didn't want any child of mine having anything to do with him. Neither of us did.'

Andrew, taken aback by Oliver's strength of feeling, stayed silent. Oliver looked at him. 'I absolutely won't have your mother upset by this, do you understand? She's been through enough.'

'Yes, fine, fine. I just wondered –'

Oliver patted him on the arm. 'I know – natural curiosity. But I'm asking you to let it rest.'

And he had. Andrew had never spoken of Horace again – at least, not until Caroline had started believing in conspiracies that didn't exist. Then, choosing his moment carefully one evening after she'd finished watching the 10 o'clock news, he told her what he knew of Horace's story, about how the war had scarred him – if not physically, then mentally – and how a lot of Elsa's subsequent behaviour – her distance, her self-reliance, her vulnerability disguised as *froideur* – could be explained by this.

'I don't see what this has to do with us,' Caroline said.

'I suppose what I'm getting at is that sometimes –' and he could feel himself slipping into a place he would not be able to return from, even as he spoke '– sometimes, it might be better to die a hero rather than coming back a broken man.'

The words, when they came out, sounded stilted and pathetic. Caroline looked at him, uncomprehending. 'I can't believe what you've just said. You – you think it's better that Max –'

'I'm not talking about Max,' he protested, although in a way, of course, he had been.

'Why are you telling me this?' she cried. 'I'd do anything – *anything* – to have Max back, you know that.'

'Of course I do.'

'I wouldn't care what state he was in. I wouldn't –' She was crying now and he, as usual, felt dreadful for having prompted her tears. He offered her a handkerchief, put his arms around her, but he knew, without anything further being said, that one more silent inch had slotted into the widening space between them.

On the bench, he uncrosses his legs, aware of a stiffness in his limbs. The pigeons scatter. He imagines Kate, sprawled across the messy tangle of sheets in her soulless flat, and he is shocked, for the first time, by what he has done. She is young enough to be his daughter, he thinks, and then, the half-occluded thought that has been crouching in the corner of his brain for the last few hours clicks glaringly into focus.

Young enough to be his daughter.

Had that been part of the attraction?

Had he wanted, just for a moment, to be more like Max?

For a moment he considers this. And then he forces himself to laugh. Ludicrous notion, he thinks. Cod-psychology at its worst.

A woman in a baggy tweed overcoat walks across his sightline, carrying a small bunch of pink flowers. He watches her as she wends her way towards a medium-sized gravestone, on the far side of the church. She bends over, placing the flowers carefully on the ground, and then she stands for a few seconds with her head bowed. He can see her lips moving. Before turning to leave, she touches the top of the headstone with her gloved hand. As she walks past Andrew on her way back out of the churchyard, she smiles at him. He notices that the corners of her eyes droop down as she does so.

Will he tell Caroline about what he has done? He is in two minds about this. There is part of him – the noble part – that feels he should, that he must, that he would expect the same of her, that their marriage will flounder if such dishonesty is allowed to flourish. But then there is another part of him that realises the knowledge of it would destroy her. It is not as if he intends to repeat the mistake, he reasons with himself. The episode with Kate had been a ghastly aberration, little more than that. He still loves his wife. He does not want to hurt her – not now that her sense of self is so fragile.

Sitting in the graveyard, with the pigeons at his feet, and without even feeling he is making an excuse, Andrew decides he will not tell her. It wouldn't be fair, he thinks. Having come to this conclusion, he stands up, shakes out his raincoat, and walks back to the office, certain – as he always has been – that he has her best interests at heart.

Elsa, 1936

S HE MEETS HIM AT a party in Fitzroy Square. Her first glimpse is of him standing on the stairs, dressed incongruously in a white tie and tails while everyone around him is a swirling mass of sailor's trousers, velvet jackets, backless dresses and garnet-red jewels. He looks so formal, with one hand in his pocket, his body curving forwards so that he can hear what the girl next to him is saying. In his free hand, he is holding a tumbler of clear liquid without ice cubes. His bearing is sharp, angular, as though his body has been reduced only to its essential parts. But his face is softer than the rest of him. He has cheeks like small pillows. When he smiles, the pillows are pressed upwards, as if the feathers are being plumped to the corners by some unknown hand.

She looks at him for several seconds, unobserved in the shadows of the entrance hall, and it is only when someone tugs on her sleeve that she realises she is still wearing her coat.

'Elsa, why have you got this on, you must be boiling!' It is Rosa, her friend from the dark little office in Bloomsbury where they are both secretaries. 'Come on,' Rosa shouts. 'You're missing all the fun.' And then Rosa disappears with a short, balding man into a room full of dancing couples and a loud swell of gramophone music.

Elsa shrugs herself out of the coat – it has blue and black che-nille flowers on it and is her favourite item of clothing. She wears it every day, as a suit of armour. Now, without it around her shoulders, she can feel the coolness of the evening breeze on the back of her neck, mingling with the dense cloud of other people's heat emanating from the drawing room. She experiences a tingle of nervousness, the anxious expectation that sweeps over you at the beginning of a party when you don't know how it is going to turn out. She makes herself smile, mouths the word 'brush' under her breath and then she walks up the stairs, following the strains of the saxophone and the big band and the occasional scratchiness of the gramophone needle, stuttering over the loosening ridges of sound.

She brushes against him as she passes and feels the lip of his glass against her upper arm.

'Sorry,' Elsa says, brightly, as though she hasn't given him a second thought. Close up, she can see that he has dark brown eyes and his hair smells of pipe smoke. His bow tie is slightly skewed. She glances quickly at his companion: a plump, pretty girl with a string of coloured beads tied tightly round her neck. Elsa starts to carry on up the stairs but he stops her, taking his hand out of his pocket and lightly grazing her wrist with the tips of his fingers.

'So who are you?' he says, amiably, his eyebrows fractionally raised.

'Oh, I'm . . . I'm Elsa.'

He smiles, the corners of his lips curling upwards and then staying like that, even when the smile begins to fade, so that the amusement lingers just below the surface of his features. They stare at each other. A heat passes through her.

'Delighted to meet you, Elsa. I'm Oliver. And this –' he turns towards the plump girl but she has gone. 'Ah,' he starts to laugh. 'I must have been terribly boring company.' He looks at her. 'I'd make your escape while you can.'

But, of course, she does not want to be anywhere else and, without having to say anything more, she knows that he can sense this, that he knows immediately how she feels.

'I'll take my chances,' she says, placing her hand on the banister and leaning fractionally backwards so that her cheekbones catch the light.

He nods, then takes a sip from the tumbler. 'Oh, I say, you don't have anything to drink.' He starts to dash up the stairs, taking two at a time. 'Wait there. I'll be back.'

'No – really – I – I –' Oliver stops. 'I don't need a drink. I can talk to you.' She smiles and she can taste the creaminess of her lipstick against the edge of her teeth.

He comes back to her. 'Well, at least have a cigarette.' He slips out a silver case from his inside pocket and clicks it open with his thumb. She takes one and he lights it for her, bending his head towards hers so that they are almost overlapping. She breathes him in.

'So what brings you to this particular den of iniquity?' he asks, standing closer than he needs to so that, if she wanted, she could reach out and touch him, letting her hand rest on his waist, on the imagined slant of his hip bone.

'I work with Rosa. We're secretaries. It's not very interesting,' she adds apologetically.

'So why do you do it? A girl like you –' He lets the thought hang, unfinished, between them. Every silence they share seems to crackle.

'I'm afraid a girl like me isn't qualified to do much else.' She gives another tight smile, looks up to meet his eye and then drops her head, too nervous to hold his gaze. 'What about you?'

'Oh, I'm a friend of Rollo's.'

'Rosa's brother?'

'Yes. We were at Cambridge together.'

There is a pause. Elsa sucks on her cigarette, inhaling then breathing out the smoke and noticing the stencilled red shape of her lips on the paper. Emboldened, she asks: 'Did your father go there?'

He guffaws. 'No. I got in on a scholarship programme for people without connections.'

She laughs. 'I see.'

'As luck would have it, they've allowed me to stay on to do a PhD so . . .'

He knocks back the remainder of his gin. Neither of them says anything for a while. She is aware of Oliver looking at her, trying to work her out. She thinks he is probably the kind of man who is used to being asked questions, to having conversation made with him by girls wanting to impress and this suspicion makes her want to be different, to stand out from the others. So, quite deliberately, she says nothing. She blinks, slowly, and keeps smoking her cigarette.

'So, Elsa –' he says, drawing out each syllable of her name. 'Did you grow up in the countryside like Rosa?'

She shakes her head. Her pearl-drop earrings dangle against her jawbone.

'No, Richmond.'

'I sometimes go riding there,' he says. 'In the park.'

'I don't go back much,' she says. In fact, she had left the stagnant atmosphere, the unacknowledged tensions of her childhood home as soon as she was able. She had trained as a secretary in one of those colleges that had sprung up after the war for a new generation of surplus spinsters. 'Baches' they were called. Female bachelors. For five years, Elsa had lived among them, scrimping and saving for new stockings, never eating more than soup and a bun for lunch, spending the evenings pretending she was happy by the gloomy light of the single-bar gas fire. The rest of it – her childhood, her father and mother – she refused to remember. In a way, she had reinvented herself. And now, all she needed was the right man to make her escape complete.

She turns back to gaze at Oliver, eyelids half-closed, mouth seductive, waiting for him to speak. He shakes his head, smiling, and she realises he is nervous. He swallows drily. 'So,' he says, searching for something to say, 'your parents are –'

Her heart skips a beat. She stops him before he goes any further.

'Your glass is empty,' she says brightly, taking it from him. 'Let's get a refill.'

He smiles at her and moves to put his hand on the small of her back. She turns, and walks past him up the stairs, knowing all the time that he will follow.

The next day, she gets into work a shade past 9am and Mr Burns, the insurance broker for whom she types and answers the phone, gives her a disapproving glance from behind the glass screen that separates his office from the rest of the room. Elsa feigns ignorance and flashes him a purposefully friendly smile. Two red spots appear on his cheeks and he scowls, bending his head to disguise his embarrassment. Mr Burns is in his late forties and still lives with his mother. He is easy enough to handle.

Elsa takes off her gloves, folding them carefully into her coat pocket, before hanging the coat and her handbag on the hat-stand opposite her desk. She tries to suppress the depression she can already feel seeping into her and sits down with a sense of purpose, taking out her shorthand notebook and removing the cover from her typewriter in readiness for the first of many dull letters about insurance premiums and end-of-year tax assessments she will have to transcribe.

She tries not to question her life too much, tries not to lift it up to the light and ask herself what she is doing with her time. It is enough, she tells herself, that she is away from her parents, that her fate is in her own hands, that her days are no longer shaped by the unpredictability of other people's moods. She prizes the monotony of her routine: the certain knowledge that each day will be the same as the one before. She values the simplicity of it all because, within this uncomplicated existence, she is safe. No one can get to her. Her parents have no idea of her whereabouts. Thus far, they have made no attempt to get in touch. But still, there is an unmistakable sense that she is wasting herself here, that her life should be more colourful than the drabness of a bed-sittingroom flat and a single hob. She thinks longingly back to last night, to the party, to Oliver. She cannot shake the thought of him, and yet she knows that it is hopeless. There is such a scarcity of young, available men these days that all the good ones tend to get snapped up before you have a chance to say hello. Last night, Oliver had been the centre of so much female attention that, despite the initial promise of their conversation on the staircase, Elsa left the party feeling thoroughly disheartened. She sighs, and then she makes a conscious effort to stop thinking. There is work to be done. Glancing up at the clock, she promises herself she will have eight letters done by lunchtime. She begins to type, her red fingernails click-clacking against the keys. The rhythm of the typewriter lulls her into a semi-somnolent daze. At 1 o'clock on the dot, she gathers up her coat, her handbag and her gloves, and she walks outside.

There, leaning against the bonnet of a grey car at the side of the road, is Oliver. He is holding a pipe in one hand, pressing at the tobacco in the bowl with his thumb. When he sees her, he smiles, and the corners of his eyes crinkle in exactly the way she remembers.

'What are you doing here?' Elsa asks.

He looks at her. 'Waiting for you, of course.'

And the way he says it, it sounds like the most natural thing in the world.

Caroline

THEY CATCH THE 8.22 train from Great Malvern for their meeting with Derek Lester. They are late getting to the station because Elsa's new carer got lost driving to the house. She is a kindly, soft-spoken Nigerian girl called Remy. Andrew says she is studying for an MBA in the evenings and has a degree in linguistics from a university in Lagos. Caroline has no idea how Remy has ended up in a sleepy town in the Midlands, changing soiled bedsheets for the minimum wage, but the girl is reliable and gentle and they are lucky that she agreed to look after Elsa for the day at short notice.

Andrew had been hesitant about coming at first. For five days after she phoned him in the office to let him know that Derek Lester had agreed to meet them, he hadn't mentioned it once. She became increasingly cross at his silence but had not wanted to challenge him until one night in bed, with the lights off and the curtains drawn and the two of them lying next to each other without touching, the anxiety she had been feeling spilled out of her.

'I can't believe you show such minimal interest in finding out what happened to our son,' she said.

Andrew groaned. There was a time when he would have made an effort to disguise his impatience.

'It's not that at all, Caroline, as you well know.' He was whispering, even though there was no one in the house to hear them apart from Elsa. 'I simply don't think it's particularly healthy for you still to be raking over the same old ground.'

She turned away from him to lie on one side.

'And I'm not sure this Lester chap will have the answers you want,' he continued. 'You mustn't get your hopes up.'

'My hopes?' The words stuck in her throat like melting caramel. 'I don't have any hopes, Andrew. I lost *hope* a long time ago.'

He didn't say anything and, after several minutes, she realised his breathing had changed and he was asleep. She wondered, lying there, waiting for morning to come, whether he was falling out of love with her and yet she did not have the energy to think of anything other than Max. For the last few weeks, the thought of her son had expanded to fill her mind like a pumped-up balloon, the rubber stretching incrementally with each jet of air until it could be pushed no further and the balloon simply sat there, trapped and bulging and pushing out everything else, squeezing against the edges of her skull so that even the smallest movement reminded Caroline of its presence.

But the next morning, Andrew had leaned across the breakfast table and squeezed her hand. 'Of course I'll come with you,' he said. And she had smiled, relieved.

The train draws into the station, with the clattering sound of screeching metal. Andrew waits in the aisle for Caroline to slide into the window seat – it is an unspoken agreement between them that she, being smaller and female, will always sit in the more restricted space – and then gets in himself, unfolding a copy of the *Telegraph* that he bought at the newsstand before boarding. She is glad to see him do this because it means she does not have to talk.

Her mind is too full, her thoughts too jangling to make conversation.

Instead, she spends most of the three-hour journey gazing out of the window, watching the countryside slip past: fields and barns and cows and women with prams waiting at level crossings and trees with blurred branches skidding by.

She thinks of Elsa and feels sick remembering what she has done. She does not know how to be around her mother-in-law any more, has been scared – almost – that the truth will be visible, that anyone looking at the guilt in her face will know without having to ask.

But no one has noticed. Snappy has continued to treat Caroline with the same professional cheerfulness she has always done. Andrew hasn't mentioned anything. Elsa's eyes have shown no emotion other than confusion. And although Caroline told herself she was going to say something, soon the days were passing and enough time had elapsed to make her think it hadn't happened at all. Not really.

If only actions could be cancelled out by penitence, she thinks now. Her penitence is genuine and deep and awful. She cannot look herself in the eye any more, for fear of what it might reveal. She prefers to block the idea of the slap from her mind. It is the only way she can carry on, the only way to convince herself she is who she once thought she was.

She tries to brush the thought of Elsa to one side and concentrates instead on the view beyond the train window. The trick is not to think. She watches the landscape slide and change. After a while, her mind turns silent and she dozes off.

'Coffee?' Andrew asks, a few minutes later. She looks up at him hazily and sees there is a refreshments trolley in the aisle, pushed by a young man with pale skin covered in small red pustules that look like eczema. His hair has been styled improbably into a 1950s-style quiff that sits oddly with his uniform of nylon trousers and burgundy tie.

She shakes her head. Andrew orders himself a cup of tea and returns to the *Daily Telegraph*, the pages making a crinkling sound as he turns them. Caroline can smell the newsprint, sweetly acrid. She takes a deep breath and the nausea passes.

The train gets in just before 11.30 and they get a taxi to the Ministry of Defence so as not to be late for their midday appointment. The building is rather impressive when they get there and Caroline is surprised by this. She had expected an anonymous modern office block, but the Ministry is built out of a white-grey stone, the colour and smoothness of an opened oyster shell. They walk through revolving doors to the reception area, which is guarded by several police with bullet-proof vests and large machine-guns held in a possessive diagonal across their chests.

The security guard gives them two paper name-tags, each one dangling from black lariats. Andrew immediately puts his round his neck. Caroline leaves hers hanging from her hand. They sit on a squashy black leather sofa for several minutes, staring at a large clock with roman numerals hanging high up on one wall and Caroline makes an effort to calm herself. At almost ten past, a statuesque blonde woman wearing shiny black high heels clip-clops to the security barrier. Caroline senses immediately that this is Camilla. She is wearing a dark grey pencil skirt that is a shade too tight, a tailored pin-stripe shirt and a waistcoat nipped in pro-vocatively at the waist. The policemen look her up and down appreciatively and it is clear that Camilla is aware of this, that she revels in it, and yet her facial expression is one of disdain as she extends a limp hand in greeting.

'Mr and Mrs Weston?'

Andrew says with incongruous jollity, 'Yes, that's us.'

'Hi, I'm Camilla.' She looks at Caroline appraisingly. She does not smile. 'I think we've spoken on the phone.'

There is something supercilious about her manner. It strikes Caroline that, for all that she and Andrew have been through, they are not particularly important in Camilla's eyes. Camilla does not see what the two of them have lost – she can't. She doesn't know who they were before this happened, before Max died. She sees only a middle-aged couple with tired faces and fraying clothes. A man in a suit that is beginning to wear out at the elbows. A woman in a drab raincoat and not enough lipstick. Two people who have let themselves go, who do not make the effort to keep up appearances.

Camilla takes them through the barriers and presses a button to call the lift, standing with her head tilted upwards, humming softly as she waits. The lift takes them up two floors and the doors open with a shushing sound. Camilla does not speak as she leads them through a long corridor, but she walks at a brisk, unforgiving pace so that by the time they reach Derek Lester's office, Caroline is out of breath and her make-up feels slippery with sweat.

They are led into a room with wide, high windows and pale cream walls. There is a wooden desk at one end, on top of which are a stack of papers and an old-fashioned lamp with a green glass shade. A child's painting has been blu-tacked on to a noticeboard behind the desk, the paper daubed with fingerprints of blue and yellow. Camilla gestures to four chairs placed around a low coffee table piled up with the day's newspapers. Andrew and Caroline sit beside each other, facing the windows. The sky lies bleached and heavy against the treetops, as though supported by the tips of the branches. Andrew takes her hand. This time, she does not resist.

'The minister will be in shortly,' says Camilla, turning to pick up a file of papers from the desk and leaving the room without another word.

'Charming,' murmurs Andrew.

Caroline is unable to speak. She takes out a plastic folder full of documents, printed out from the computer at home and leafs through them, mentally noting the paragraphs marked in yellow highlighter, reminding herself of the arguments she must make, the questions she must get an answer to. It feels as though she is revising for an exam. Her stomach flips in anticipation of what is about to happen.

Derek Lester appears from a side door, followed by a man in a dark suit. Caroline hears his voice before she sees him because he is just finishing off a phone call as he walks through. 'Yep, fine,' he says, his Blackberry pressed to his ear. He notices them, then gives a half-smile and a curt nod of acknowledgement. 'Listen, Jeremy, I've got to go. Yeah. Yeah. No, I've got something on. OK. Speak later.' He taps a button and comes over to the two of them, shrugging his shoulders in a show of rueful embarrassment. 'I'm so sorry about that,' he says, his voice betraying a hint of West Country burr. He shakes their hands – Andrew's first – and then sits down opposite, placing his Blackberry on the coffee table. Caroline can see its red light winking at her as Lester speaks. The man in the suit takes a seat in the corner of the room, balances a pad of paper on his knees and removes a fountain pen from his jacket pocket.

'Thank you for taking the trouble to come all this way,' Lester says. He has round features with small, piggy brown eyes and thin wisps of hair that emphasise his rotundity. The collar on his shirt looks too tight, so that the flesh of his neck spills over the edges like an over-iced cake. When he sits down, he gives a tiny but audible groan with the relief of it.

'Before we get started, I just wanted to say how sorry I am for your loss. I've spoken at length to Max's superiors and, by all accounts, he was a truly exceptional young man.' He pauses and Caroline wonders briefly if he is waiting for some sort of thank you. She notices that his eyes slide towards his Blackberry and then, catching himself, he looks up at them again. 'I hope you don't mind if Tom –' he gestures to the corner of the room – 'sits in on this. Civil Service protocol, you understand.' Tom gives a small nod, then returns to his note-taking. 'Now,' Lester says, 'what can I help you with?'

Andrew clears his throat. 'It's good of you to see us,' he starts and Caroline is taken aback. She had not expected Andrew to speak first and she is, unaccountably, infuriated. He knows nothing about the background, she thinks. He hasn't done any of the work.

Before she can stop herself, Caroline interjects and although she intends to say something fluent and to the point, she manages to utter only two words. 'Body armour,' she says.

Lester twitches his head. 'I'm sorry?'

'So you should be,' Caroline replies and when she speaks it is as though the words are someone else's. Andrew squeezes her hand roughly, warning her to stop. She ignores him. Lester's face betrays no surprise. He leans back in his seat, crossing his legs and contemplatively propping up his face with the thumb and forefinger of his right hand.

'I can understand how difficult this must be for you, Mrs Weston . . .' he says and his voice has a different tone now, no longer deferential, but harder-edged, almost defensive.

'No, you can't, Mr Lester,' Caroline says, gripping hold of the plastic folder so tightly that the tips of her fingers turn yellow-white. 'Trust me. You really can't.' There is an uncomfortable silence. Outside, a police siren screeches in the distance. Beneath the window, a child laughs in the street below and it is a strange, dreamy sound that seems to come from another dimension.

Caroline looks Lester directly in the eye and continues. 'But what you can do is tell me precisely what body armour Max was wearing when he was killed.' There is a lump in her throat that is making it difficult for her to finish. 'I would like to know,' she says, in barely more than a whisper, 'if his battalion – 1 Rifles, 12

Mechanised Brigade – had been provided with the latest kit. If you, *personally*, as Armed Forces Minister, ensured that Max had the best kit available at the time of his death.'

Andrew's face has paled. His lips are pressed together, his jaw-bone locked in position. He has, she thinks, always disliked a public scene. Across the table, Lester gives a dry little cough and then takes out a badly folded handkerchief from his trouser pocket, dabbing at his lips. The skin around his mouth has become red and clammy. Caroline sees a small nick to one side of his flabby chin where he has cut himself shaving. How odd, she finds herself thinking, to imagine this odious man doing something as mundane as shaving. This morning, he must have presented his features to the bathroom mirror as normal, sliding his razor steadily over his ginger-brown stubble, not yet aware of the confrontation that the day would hold for him; blissfully ignorant of the fact that she, Caroline Weston, mother of Lance Corporal Max Weston, killed at the age of 21 by an IED in Upper Nile State, South Sudan, would be asking him, Derek Lester, to tell her why it had happened.

She can feel herself tingling, as though an electric surge is pushing through her veins. She is buoyed by the thought that she is forcing him to look her in the face, to see up close the grief he has caused. Let him suffer, she thinks. Let him squirm and wriggle and sweat with the cost of it.

'Well, Mrs Weston, as it happens I am in a position to answer that.'

For a moment she does not think she has heard him correctly. She had expected him to obfuscate, to duck and dive and weave around the subject like most politicians do when faced with a direct question.

'I'm sorry?' Caroline says.

Andrew sits forward in his chair. 'You mean you can tell us what body armour he was wearing?'

Lester smiles. He actually smiles. 'Both the body armour he was wearing and the body armour he had been provided with,' he says, confident demeanour regained. He reaches across to the desk and picks up a single piece of typed paper. That single sheet of paper –

so insubstantial, so easily blown away – makes Caroline want to cry out. The fact that Max's life could have been condensed to such trivial proportions, that all the reams and reams of paper she had printed off about shortages of equipment, all the letters asking for post-mortem details, all those black-edged condolence cards and sympathetic handwritten notes sent in the aftermath of Max's death – all of it was just words, just meaningless words. It was worthless. Because all that they need to know is now contained on one side of a single sheet of paper held between Derek Lester's thumb and forefinger. One single sheet.

The room appears to shrink around her. Lester holds the paper for a few seconds longer than he needs to and she realises that she hates him, more than she has ever hated anyone, for the power he holds over them. She focuses her attention on an inky spot of dirt trapped under the crescent of his thumbnail. She must not give into the panic.

'Yes,' Lester is saying. 'All the details are right here in front of me. I know you had some concerns, Mrs Weston, and I can tell you that Max was wearing enhanced body combat armour.'

'The old kit?' she asks and, for a brief moment, she feels triumphant.

Lester nods his head, just once. 'In a manner of speaking, yes,' he says. Caroline glances across at Andrew. She can tell he is surprised. It is proof that she has been right all along: Max was wearing the wrong body armour. It did not protect him sufficiently. This is why he died. And Derek Lester is to blame. Her throat grows dry. Lester is still speaking.

'Nonetheless,' he says, 'your son had been supplied with the Osprey body armour several weeks before his unit was deployed.' The words come out of his mouth in an indistinct jumble. It takes Caroline a while to work out what they mean, to put them in the right order. 'We take our responsibilities towards the men who serve our country very, very seriously, Mrs Weston. It would be a failure of duty if we did not provide them with the very best kit available.'

Caroline is too shocked to say anything. Beside her, Andrew speaks. 'So what you're saying, Mr Lester – and correct me if I'm wrong here – but what you're saying is that Max had the Osprey armour but decided, for whatever reason, not to wear it on the day he was killed?'

'Yes, that's about the size of it, I'm afraid.' He uncrosses his legs, leaning forwards with his arms on his legs, hands steepled in front of his face. 'Mrs Weston, Mr Weston,' he says looking at them both in turn. 'What you have been through in the past few months is more than any parent should ever have to bear. I can only say how indebted we are, as a government and as a nation, to your son's heroic sacrifice and I hope you can find it in yourselves to accept my profound and heartfelt cond—'

Caroline stops him mid-sentence. 'Do you have a son, Mr Lester?' He stares at her sharply.

'Yes,' he says, pushing his chair back a few centimetres. 'David.' He reaches inside his jacket and takes out a battered brown wallet which he unfolds and passes to her. 'He's 19.' There is a plastic section on one side of the wallet which contains a laughing family photograph. Lester is in the middle, wearing a linen open-necked shirt, his face red with sunburn and his arms around a woman Caroline takes to be his wife. His wife is taller than him and unexpectedly pretty. There is a teenage girl on one side of Lester, gawky and limp, glowering at the camera. And on the far left, standing next to his mother, is David. He has curly black, boyish hair and a face rippled with pinkish puppy fat. He is wearing a striped red shirt and there is a fat gold signet ring on the fourth finger of his right hand. Caroline slips the photograph out of the wallet and Lester reaches out his hand, as if to stop her, but then seems to reconsider and sits back in his chair.

Caroline holds the photo up to her face. 'David,' she says, drawing out the shape of the name. 'He doesn't look like a soldier.' And she smiles. Lester chuckles uneasily. 'No, he's not terribly sporty.'

'No, I don't suppose you'd want him to be in the army, would you?'

'Well, if it was what he wanted –' Lester starts.

'You'd be worried, wouldn't you?'

'Caroline,' Andrew says, placing a hand on her knee. 'I don't think this is helping.'

213

She brushes him away. And, for the first time in her life, she knows exactly what it is she wants to say. It is as though she has been waiting for this, collecting everything she needed to understand over years and years and years of not feeling good enough: picking up all the necessary words, all the clever turns of phrase, all the outward manifestations of confidence – all of it for this particular point in time.

'Imagine David lying dead on the floor, blood pumping out of him, his jaw hanging off his face, his body parts scattered across the ground,' she says. 'You know what we were told, Mr Lester? The post-mortem said there were bits of Max – unidentified bits of him – that had been flung more than fifty metres away. Do you know what that's like? To know that about your baby, your only child? To have to think of him in the most extreme pain imaginable, crying out for his life?'

Lester is silent.

'Think of David. What if you had to live with the knowledge that your boy was on his own when he died, without you or his mother there? Can you imagine living with that, day in, day out, with the certain knowledge that you . . .' she falters, 'you weren't there? Can you?'

Lester's fat cheeks have drained of colour. A thin blue vein just by his left temple is pulsing gently.

The tears are running down Caroline's face, but still she finds she has more to say. 'And now that you have that image in your mind, look at me again and tell me how sorry you are for my son's death.'

Lester clears his throat and stretches out his hand to take back his wallet. There is a darkness clouding his features.

'I'm sorry you feel this way, Mrs Weston,' he says. 'But I can assure you that we did everything in our power –'

Caroline cuts across him, aware that her emotions are twisting away from her. 'You're telling me that my son was provided with the correct body armour, the very latest and best equipment and that he chose not to wear it?' She looks at him and notices that he is sweating in the pockets of flesh underneath his eyes. 'You're honestly asking me to believe that?'

'Mrs Weston, those are indeed the facts.'

'I know my son. He would never have chosen not to wear that body armour if he'd been given it. Never.' Her nose is running and she fumbles in search of a tissue but cannot find one in her pocket. 'He knew how much I loved him.' Yet as she speaks, she can hear her own desperation. 'He would never have put his life at risk if he'd known . . .'

She trails off and realises that she is crying even more than before and can't stop. Andrew unfolds the fabric handkerchief he carries in his trouser pocket and gives it to her. Caroline presses it to her face, inhaling the scent of washing powder. It has not been ironed so it is crumpled and untidy-looking and she is suddenly, absurdly, ashamed of what Lester might think of them. She scrunches the handkerchief up into the palm of her hand.

Lester falls silent. Andrew pats Caroline's back gently. 'It's been a difficult time for us,' he says, as though he owes an explanation and this bland little comment, spoken for the simple sake of politeness to a man neither of them respects, does more to trigger Caroline's anger than anything Lester has said up to that moment. She stops crying. A fizzing sense of contempt rises up her gullet.

'You're a liar,' she says, calmly raising her head to meet the politician's gaze. Her words are low and level and dangerous and she can see Lester recoiling in shock.

'I'm sorry?'

'You're a liar. I know you didn't give Max that body armour. I just know it.'

'Caroline –' Andrew starts.

'Don't,' she says, looking at her husband blankly. She cannot even recognise him. 'Just don't.'

'Mrs Weston, I can assure you that I'm not lying,' Lester is saying. 'Your son was one of many men who, despite official advice to the contrary, chose not to wear the new kit.' He glances at his Blackberry again, clearly anxious that they are taking up too much of his time. 'A lot of the guys out there are attached to the old body armour because they find it easier to move around in even though it offers less all-round protection.' He coughs again, drily, as if there is a mote of dust lodged in his throat. 'It was a calculated risk and, for whatever reason, I'm afraid to say your son took it.'

Outside, the child's laughs have turned into sobs and Caroline can hear it wailing, almost choking with the effort. Something about that child's cries stabs at her and she feels herself falling, a brick dislodged in a swollen dam.

Her thoughts shrivel to nothing. The sound of the crying child pounds against the plates of her skull. There is a thumping at the crown of her head and Caroline slumps backwards. Her sight fades and blackens and she is dizzy and everything appears too bright: the daylight streaming in from the windows, the translucence of Lester's face, the white paper of the children's drawings and the blazing bulbs of the strip lighting. Her grip is loosening. She is slipping downwards. And then she falls: like a stone in a well, submerged into blackness.

When she comes round, the first thing she sees is Andrew's face bending over hers. He is stroking her hair, sliding each strand off her clammy forehead and she can feel the concern emanating from him in waves.

'There you are,' he says gently. 'I was worried.'

Caroline tries to sit up but the nausea pushes her back down again. She realises she is resting her head on Andrew's lap and that they are sitting on a sofa in a cool, air-conditioned corridor. She is momentarily displaced but then she sees a framed colour photograph of the Queen hanging on the wall opposite and she remembers they are in the Ministry of Defence and why they had come here.

'Where's Lester?' she asks and her throat is parched.

'He's gone,' Andrew says. 'Couldn't get away fast enough after you fainted. Thank goodness for the security guards. They brought us out here and said we can stay for as long as we need. Do you think you should have some water?' He bends down and offers her a chilled bottle of mineral water with one of those teat-shaped lids. Caroline unscrews the top and lifts the open bottle to her lips. She gulps down deep, chilled draughts.

'I don't believe him, Andrew,' she says.

'Mmm?'

'Lester. I don't believe him.'

He takes the bottle from her and says, firmly: 'You have to, Caroline. *We* have to. He's telling the truth.'

She shakes her head. 'You don't understand . . .' but before she can finish the sentence, Andrew stands up and walks away from her, leaning his forehead against the wall opposite, sagging-shoul-dered and weary. He rubs the back of his neck with his hand.

'I can't take this any more, Caroline.' He turns to look at her. She opens her mouth to ask him what he means but he raises his palm to stop her. 'Please, let me speak. I just . . . can't take it. I can't take the conspiracies. I can't take the unpredictable moods or the self-absorption or your total and utter conviction that no one else can possibly understand what you're going through.' He breaks off. She has never heard him like this before. 'It might have escaped your notice, all that time you've been downing pills like they're going out of fashion, but the fact is, I lost a son too.'

He leans back against the wall and as he does so, the nub of his spine knocks against the portrait of the Queen and tilts it to one side. He drops his head, one hand covering his forehead.

She should feel sorry for him. She should go to him and take him in her arms and comfort him as he has comforted her. She should kiss him tenderly and whisper in his ear that she knows; that she alone understands. But for whatever reason, she can't bring herself to do it. Andrew seems so far removed from her that she has nothing left to give. She wishes she could remember what it was to love him. But every time she looks at him now she can see only the shadow of Max, the trace of what she has lost.

She stays seated on the sofa, the water bottle in her hand, and she waits for him to speak. She can feel the condensation on the plastic dampen on her palm. Caroline grips harder on to the bot-tle's ribbed plastic grooves. It crumples and buckles under the pressure of her touch. She relaxes her muscles and lets the bottle inflate and then she squeezes it again, making her hand into a fist. She pushes down as hard as she can. Then she releases. Out and in. Out and in. Like breathing. For several minutes, she surrenders herself to the rhythmic monotony of the action.

After a while, Andrew looks across at her. 'Caroline?'

She can feel herself sinking into a silent lake. No words come. It's not as if there's any point to it, she thinks. He can vent his anger and feel sorry for himself but they both know that in less than an hour they'll be back on the train to Malvern, back to their play-acted life, back to their miscommunications and misfirings, the endless trudge of the days, the things she hides from him, the care she no longer takes, the hurt looks, the misguided attempts to reach out to each other, the half-sighs and the unspoken resentments. Back to Elsa and the carers and the packets of baby-wipes and the smell of muddied disinfectant. Back to the feeling of horror and shame at what she had done. Back to not trusting herself in Elsa's company. Back to the dusty windows and the overgrown garden with its weeds and greenfly. Back to the un-plumped cushions. Back to the kitchen cupboards with their packets of icing sugar and out-of-date basmati rice, carefully clipped by Caroline in the days when she thought such things mattered. Back to the postman and the milkman and the junk mail and the gas meter needing to be read. Back to it all. Back to the pretence of life going on even though, for her, it had stopped way back when Max died.

Since then, she has been kept alive by the single-threaded purpose of needing to find out who was to blame for what happened to her son. And now she has discovered that there is no one. No smug-faced Derek Lester denying the money needed for proper equipment. No mustachioed military general sending his men ill prepared into the battlefield. No terrorist blinded by his fanatical ideology. Because, really, the only person to blame is Max – for abandoning her to join the army and then for being arrogant enough to assume that he could survive wearing an old piece of body armour. It is Max who is at fault. But how can she ever accept this?

'Do you even love me any more?' Andrew says. 'Well, do you?'

'I . . . I . . . don't know.'

Andrew gives a sharp, derisive little laugh. It is so unlike him, she thinks, to show such rancour.

'Too in love with your son, are you?' he asks, and the sarcasm is so unexpected that Caroline shrinks back. Salt water stings at the back of her throat. She gets up, mutely, puts her handbag over her shoulder, leaves the half-empty water bottle in the back crease of the sofa and starts walking away. She does not know where.

'Caroline, I'm sorry,' Andrew calls out behind her. 'Come back. I didn't mean . . .'

He reaches out to touch her arm but she shifts just far enough away that she is out of his range.

She breaks away from him and runs down the corridor, and presses the button for the lift. She has no thoughts other than needing to escape from Andrew and this stuffy, arid building with its synthetic carpet and its stilted, framed photos of uniformed men. She needs to be outdoors, in the air. It feels as if she has not breathed deeply for weeks, months. She needs to fill her lungs. She needs, more than anything, to see the sky.

Caroline rushes through the rotating doors, her handbag banging against her hip bone. She pushes herself outside and the wind slaps against her like a sail snapping taut and she runs and runs and runs until she can't tell whether the dampness on her face is mostly sweat or mostly tears and she keeps on going, left out of the exit, then down Whitehall, not noticing the tightness in her chest. She runs past the black cabs, the tourists unfolding maps that crackle and buckle against the wind, past the men in grey suits carrying slim laptop cases, past the woman who is bending down and checking the sole of her shoe. She runs and runs and runs. Her thoughts whirl and eddy and twist until they are sucked down into nothing, until their meaning is muted and dulled, until all that she feels is reduced to a single point: a small, red dot like the sticker placed next to paintings sold. She is not thinking any more. She is simply moving forwards.

Then, out of the corner of her eye, she sees it.

She stops, letting the breaths come into her lungs, sharp and juddering. She stares at what stands in front of her.

The Cenotaph. It rises out of the ground, white-grey and with a smooth, linear grace. The stone is immovable, solid, monolithic and yet at the same time, it looks intangible, a hologram that Caroline could reach out and touch only to see it crumble into a thousand scraps of ash. It stands apart from the rush and drone of the traffic: an impenetrable block of stillness that seems to rearrange the molecules of air around it so that instead of simply looking at the monument, she is looking at how it changes the quality of the space it occupies. Pure, unencumbered: a silence instead of a noise. There are three words carved darkly into the surface, each letter casting its own small shadow. The inscription reads: 'The Glorious Dead'.

It seems odd to Caroline that she has only ever seen the Cenotaph in reproduction before now, staring out at her from the newspapers. She has seen it pixellated and two-dimensional in television news reports, surrounded by rows and rows of uniformed men, their heads bowed, their medals gleaming in autumnal sunlight to mark each anniversary of the Armistice. She remembers vaguely that, last year, there had been four ancient men in wheelchairs at the front of the Remembrance Day procession, their spines curving inwards. The television commentator had explained that these were the only four surviving First World War veterans.

She recalls that one of the veterans had a wreath of red flowers propped on his lap. His legs were covered in a tartan blanket, the bones of his knees jutting up beneath the material. He was leaning, almost crouching forwards and he was holding on to the wreath with white, trembling hands as though afraid it would get blown away. His face was contoured with deep wrinkles but his skin, instead of hanging loose, was stretched so tightly across his cheek and jawbones it looked almost translucent.

At one point, the veteran attempted to get out of his wheelchair in order to place the wreath at the foot of the monument but he had no strength to do it. Caroline could see him trying. But no matter how much effort he put into the slow movement of his arms, into the painful attempt to push himself up from the seat of the chair, into the minute shake of the head when someone rushed forward to help him, no matter how much he wanted to make that single, last, small gesture, he could not do it.

The television cameras had zoomed into the man's face. His eyes were moist and Caroline found she couldn't watch. She had switched the television off.

Now, with the Cenotaph in front of her, she thinks of that man and she wonders if he is still alive and, if so, whether he wants to die, whether he feels a fraud for having survived when so many other men – men separated from him only by a split-second of fate – lay dead. She thinks about Max and she wonders, for the first time, whether he would believe it was a blessing he died in that explosion rather than survive with a maimed body and mangled limbs. She wonders if he would feel guilty at having made it through the war alive when so many others had been killed.

She walks towards the monument, feeling the cool shadow of it slide over her as she approaches. There are three steps leading up to the base, each level a square smaller than the last, flowing outwards beneath her scuffed high-heeled shoes, like water slowly icing over. Wreaths of paper poppies lie by her feet. Several large flags hang out from the side of the monument, the material draping downwards, red, white and blue against the grey. She reaches out and places her hand flat against the stone. It is rougher to the touch than it looks. She drags her palm along the rubbled surface, leaving white scratches on her hand.

All at once, she is extremely tired. She pitches forward and allows her back to slide down against the stone. She sits there and she is only half-aware of the surrounding traffic, of the concerned, mildly wary glances of strangers as they walk past. Caroline's skirt is bunched up underneath her thighs and she hoists herself up to smooth the fabric underneath her legs. The sky above her seems to be getting brighter, the clouds bled of colour. She squints, trying to filter out the harsh brilliance of the light, feeling the blazing sweep of the sky pushing down on her forehead like a tightening clamp. Her head is so heavy that she wants nothing more than to rest it against the ground. She slides down further so that she is lying on the stone, and she curls her legs up to her chest and allows the exhaustion to claim her, waves of it lapping at her feet, coming up over her hips and waist, rising and rising and rising until she is almost totally covered by the unconsciousness she craves.

She hears a voice she recognises, calling her.

Caroline opens her eyes and at first she cannot make out his face because it is blotted black against a halo of sunlight.

'Max?' she says, and his features clarify and snap into focus: the blond hair shorn close against his scalp, the nose still misshapen from having been broken in a rugby match, the violet-blue of his eyes, the lopsided grin, the stubble that grows no matter how much he shaves. He is wearing camouflage uniform, the sleeves of his jacket rolled up to his elbows so that she can trace the downy hairs on his arm with her fingers.

'I thought you were dead,' she says and she knows, as she utters the words, how absurd this sounds. Max does not reply. He smiles at her and opens his arms and Caroline sees that his chest is covered in dried blood and that there is a pulsing red hole just to the left of his heart and through it she can see a fragment of bone, the sharpened point of it rising through the muscle. She looks up at him and he nods his head, just once, and then Caroline goes to him and he folds her into what is left of his chest and she can hear his heartbeat and feel his ribcage contract and relax against her cheek and she can smell him – that smell of forest moss and tangy sweat and open air – all wrapped up in the lost beauty of her son.

Her son.

'I missed you,' she whispers, in case speaking too loudly will cause him to disappear. He says nothing but he pats the back of Caroline's head and cradles her softly from side to side and after a while, she feels herself dropping off to sleep in a state of bliss. I am safe, Caroline thinks as she goes under, I am safe.

She does not know how long she is out but it is the most complete sleep she has ever experienced. The guilt that she has been carrying around with her ever since Max died shatters into tiny pieces and is blown away in the breeze. She feels it leave her and she feels the intensity of the release.

And then, when Caroline wakes up, she realises it is not Max who has been holding her but Andrew.

He has been there all along.

PART IV

Elsa

THE WOMAN COMES INTO the room and Elsa pretends to be asleep so that she can observe. Through her thin sliver of vision, Elsa can see the woman is moving about quickly, with a careful economy of movement: there is no action that is not precisely intended, no waste or unnecessary gesture that needs to be trimmed around the edges. Elsa approves. She opens her eyes and grunts, satisfied.

'Hello, Elsa,' the woman says in a pretty, melodious voice. 'And how are you this morning?'

The woman approaches the bed and bends over to press something located beneath the mattress that Elsa cannot see. There is a clunking sound and Elsa feels herself being lifted upwards as the bed mechanically angles itself into an upright position.

'Now, what can I tempt you with this morning?'

Elsa looks at her in confusion, taking in the straight brown-black hair, cut severely into a bob. The woman is wearing a starched pink shirt and matching trousers with a pair of bright purple plastic slippers on her feet. Who is she and what is she doing in her bedroom?

'You don't remember me, do you, Elsa?' the woman is saying, but she is asking it nicely, as though it is a joke they share. The woman gives a theatrical sigh. 'I don't know. A more sensitive soul than I am might take offence.' She has a curious rhythm to her voice, an accent of some sort. 'Sure, don't I come in every morning to give you breakfast? You know who I am, you're just teasing, aren't you? A big old tease, that's what you are. You know who it is! You know it's Ashleigh.' The woman laughs and all the time she is speaking, she is busying herself with various tasks: straightening the sheets, smoothing down the pillows, drawing the curtains and opening the window so that a pleasant freshness airs the room. She returns to Elsa's bedside.

'So Elsa, what'll it be now? Your usual?'

Elsa nods her head and slowly, she is infused with a sense of familiarity. She is comforted by this woman. She feels safe in her presence.

'Great stuff,' Ashleigh says, reaching over to a wheeled trolley that Elsa had not previously noticed. 'A delicious banana special, prepared with my own fair hands.'

She draws a chair up to the bed, lifts a small green plate patterned with blue flowers in one hand and starts spooning an indistinct yellow mash into Elsa's mouth with the other. Elsa twists her head away. She does not want this food. She does not want to be treated like a baby.

'Och, now, Elsa, would you stop it with your fussing?' Ashleigh says, resting the plate on her lap. 'You'll be hungry later on if you don't have any breakfast. And this is tasty, so it is. Look –' she lifts a heaped spoonful to her lips and swallows it in one gulp. 'Mmm. You don't know what you're missing out on, sure you don't.'

Elsa still feels the heated glow of a small, leaden irritation in her chest but her stomach is starting to rumble. She takes the spoonful of banana. It tastes delicious. After a few more mouthfuls, she is happy.

That is how her feelings come these days: one after the other with no explanation. First she is sad, then she is joyful and one might last longer than the other but she never knows which. And yet lately, she has noticed a sense of contentment surprising her when she least expects it.

Elsa smiles.

'Now that's better,' Ashleigh says. 'You've got a beautiful smile, Elsa, and don't let anyone tell you different.'

Ashleigh spoons the remainder of the banana into Elsa's mouth and it tastes sweet and satisfying as it slips down her throat. She much prefers it here to that room with the cream walls and the closed windows. She has a memory of that room, of the sun beating down on her scalp as she lay in bed covered in a blanket she did not need. She had been left there by someone, waiting and not knowing why. Who was it who had left her there? She knows she should remember. She has a feeling of familiarity about the recollection and yet she cannot pin it down. It slips and shimmers beneath the muddy-brown waters of her mind like a gleaming coin thrown deep into the tide, a scrap of silver spiralling away from the tips of her outstretched fingers.

Who was it who had left her?

And afterwards, who was it who had come into the room? She can see the shadow of a figure moving towards her, removing the blanket, crouching down to talk to her.

All at once, Elsa feels a surge of agitation. She squirms and writhes underneath her bed sheets, pushing away the spoon from her mouth with such unexpected force that Ashleigh drops it and it skitters across the stripped wooden floorboards.

'Elsa, what is it?' says Ashleigh and she leans forwards, putting her face close. Ashleigh's forehead is furrowed with concern, a pinch of flesh rising up between her pressed-together eyebrows. She puts a calming hand on Elsa's shoulder.

'You're all right now, pet, you're all right.'

But Elsa can't hear. Her gaze films over. Her mind hollows out. Her thoughts hiss and spit furiously. Her hands bat away at something just in front of her face: a dark shadow, lurking, waiting for her, ready to pounce.

The shadow is getting bigger now, broadening outwards and looming over her until it shuts out the light streaming in from the windows. It comes towards her and Elsa tries to move but she is trapped in her bed, her muscles unable to work quickly enough, and then the shadow is crushing down on her breastbone, making it difficult for her to breathe. The darkness gets larger and stronger and heavier until it is smothering her, wrapping itself around her. Elsa shrieks, but still the shadow comes, deep and dense and covering her body. She must get away from it.

There is a voice. 'Elsa, look at me.'

She tries to listen to the voice.

'Elsa. Elsa. You're OK. You're here with me, with Ashleigh.'

The shadow stops expanding. Elsa lies still so as not to provoke it.

'Look at me, Elsa. Open your eyes. Look at me.'

She looks up and she sees Ashleigh's face just a few inches above her own. She meets Ashleigh's calm, level gaze. Her eyes begin to water.

The shadow bursts and trickles away.

Ashleigh has taken her hand and Elsa is reassured by her touch. She is safe with her, she thinks. This woman will not hurt her.

She has not felt that for a long time.

Elsa has good days when the shadow does not come at all. Increasingly, there are more good days than bad. She likes it here. She feels comfortable because the same things happen at the same time each day so there are no unpleasant surprises. Perhaps because of the daily routine, her memory has started to get a bit better. She no longer needs to expend mental effort worrying over what might be happening next and whether she will be able to cope with it. She is less anxious. She begins to trust in the thought that she will not be punished. It is all so much easier now. She knows that Ashleigh will be pleased if she eats all her breakfast. She knows that if she smiles, it will make Ashleigh happy. She knows that if Ashleigh puts the bed into a propped-up seating position, she can just about make out the deep orange tinge of a flowering camellia through the corner of the bay window. These are the things that soothe her.

On a good day, she will be lifted out of her bed on a mechanical piece of apparatus that resembles a livestock winch and she will be deposited in a wheelchair and then someone will wheel her around the house and give her a change of scene. Sometimes, if it is Ashleigh pushing her and if the weather is nice enough, they will go into the garden to see the camellia. Elsa likes to reach out and touch the leaves, to feel the waxiness on her fingers. She giggles when she does this. She cannot help herself. She loves the smell of the outdoors. It is not something she can remember ever appreciating before: the undiluted scent of grass and wind and salt.

She finds that she enjoys watching television, something that Elsa had always previously dismissed as a brain-rotting waste of time. She is drawn to programmes with lots of action: shouted arguments and slaps, grim retributions and promises of revenge played out across the screen. She enjoys the drama of it, secure in the knowledge that it is all happening behind a thick piece of glass, in a box from which it cannot leak out.

The television lounge appears to be the focal point of the house: there are always half a dozen elderly men and women sitting here, watching intently, their viewing pleasure punctuated by the high-pitched hum of hearing aids turned up to maximum volume. Sometimes, Elsa forgets who these people are and she feels a rising spike of panic at the base of her throat when she sees them. She starts to whimper, in an attempt to convey how she is feeling, unable to find the right words. But then Ashleigh will bend down to her level and whisper in her ear to remind her. 'These are the other residents, Elsa. Sure, you know who they are, don't you? Nothing to be scared of.' And although she will never quite remember, although the facts of Elsa's existence will never entirely shift into sharp focus again, she will be reassured and her mind will temporarily rid itself of the last droplets of fear until the next time something sparks a fit of terrified uncertainty. In this way, Elsa's days have become an ebb and flow, a quietly played-out battle between fretfulness and tranquillity.

In her moments of stillness, Elsa finds her thoughts are so clear, so brightly defined that it is as though they have been lit up from behind. The memories come to her in pictures. She can make out every twist, every small gap and curve, every fragile hairline crack. She can hold them in her mind's eye for hours, tracing each tiny delineation.

In her memories, she is always a small girl. She has been told she is a mother, but she cannot see her own child's face, even though Ashleigh has explained to her that she has a son; has, in the past, shown Elsa photographs of this creature who seems to bear so little resemblance to her. When she looks at these pictures, she feels nothing. She blinks hard and her brow becomes corrugated with concentration. She can sense how much Ashleigh wants her to remember but she can't. Her eyes lose focus, the lids become heavy, the indistinct face of her son in the photographs – now a man; now an adolescent; now a baby boy – mesh and blur together in a thick, soupy liquid. She feels no sadness. How can she feel sad over someone she does not know?

Instead, as she sits in front of the tinny-voiced television or underneath the leafy canopy of the oak tree in the garden, she finds herself thinking of her father, of Horace. She remembers, with surprising acuteness, that she used to hate him. It feels as though half her life has been swallowed up by hating him and now, as she looks down at her resting hands, she realises she is too tired to carry on. The animosity seeps out of her like liquid tar, and it is as if a pool of it gathers at the base of her wheelchair, sticking on the wheels, on the metal frame, globules of it hardening in the sunlight with the semi-sweet smell of melting liquorice. She waits until she has nothing more to fear from it, until the fear of him can no longer tug her underground, and then she feels lighter, more able to breathe.

She sees Horace as he was when he first walked into that house in Richmond, when he shook her hand and looked at her through the far-away sharpness of his tired eyes. She sees, now, how she must have seemed to him: a small child he did not know, a girl who was claiming to be his daughter, an alien being from another life altogether. A life of families and love and gentleness. A life of normality and goodness and honour. A life where no one knew what it was like to stand next to a man and watch him get shot. A life where no one could understand that even if you got clean of the dirt – that endless, unforgiving dirt that clung to death and disaster – that even if you burned your uniform in the back garden, that even if you never spoke of it again, no matter how hard you tried, the mud would stick to you still.

She thinks of Horace and of the war and occasionally a flash of something like remembrance comes to her, an image, an idea, a half-woken memory of a thing she can never have experienced. And sometimes she does not know which of her thoughts belongs to her and which to her father.

*　　*　　*

She sees:

Darkness. A man. The whole of his right side is stuck in some kind of clay, a coagulating slowness that seems to be sliding upwards to his waist.

A bird flapping its broken wing against the ground. The bird has gauze-white feathers and black eyes and its head is swivelling from side to side in terror. She knows that she should kill it. She should wring its neck or stamp on the bird's back with her foot to crack its spine into splintered bone. But she cannot bring herself to do it.

A pool stretching several metres away from her, the size of a small lake or a large pond. She is anxious about the water. She knows that it will keep rising as she sinks further and further into the mire. The mud is not like normal mud. It has desperate qualities all of its own: it will latch on to you and drag you under, it will pull you and crush you and it will spread itself endlessly across the landscape until there is no greenness left.

She becomes aware of a smell, a sweetish aroma like the pear-drop fragrance of chlorine gas. But it is not gas, it is something else, a saccharine smell with a fermented undertone, like an over-ripe plum that is beginning to go bad. She recognises it but cannot quite place it. At precisely the same moment as she remembers, she sees a floating corpse on the other side of the water.

It is half-submerged and she can just make out the tips of the other man's boots, the outline of his grossly bloated face. The man's skin has assumed a variety of gruesome shades: green, black, a bluish purple.

She looks over at the body. She can see the scrappy remains of a uniform. The man's flesh has been grossly distended, bloated and pushed to the surface of the tar-tainted water as if it were a child's bath toy. There is a shadow lying across his mouth, furry at the edges. And then, as her gaze adjusts, she realises it is not a shadow but the man's tongue, lolling to one side: a useless slab of muscle.

A sheet of paper, translucent as the skein of an onion. Written there, in black ink, is the line 'I am quite well.' And she knows, as she reads it, that this is a lie. She knows this, because as soon as you tried to explain, you realised the necessary language did not exist.

A woman called Alice who is sitting on a white garden chair, bathed in late evening sunshine, her boots pressing into the daisies and bending their petals to one side. The brim of her hat is obscuring half of her face so that from a distance, you can see only the tantalising curve of her cheekbone, the twist of her shoulder, the elegance of her wrist as she holds a cup and saucer.

She belongs to a different world.

A man lying dead on the ground in a wood. The trees around the corpse are leafless, charred black and broken into unrecognisable shapes. There is no grass. The ground is pitted with holes and bones and chunks of metal, so that the landscape seems to be defined more by absence than presence: a negative of what it should have been.

The man is freshly killed, the blood still trickling out of his mouth, his eyes calcified in surprise. His moustache is caked in crimson spittle. There is a small scattering of violet-blue forget-me-nots, just below the man's right earlobe. The petals are stained red.

A young girl in a hallway, staring at a man in uniform, unsure of what to do. When the man looks down, he notices that the child is holding a bunch of forget-me-nots. She is clenching them so tightly in her fist that the stems are being crushed against her fingers and a dribble of fluid is trickling down her slender wrist. The child releases her grip on the flowers, sending them falling to the ground, and the man sees that blood is pouring out of a wound in the centre of her palm, a hole that goes right the way through her bones to the other side of her small hand, so that he can look through it like a spyhole in a door.

The man starts to cry.

And then, she wonders where she is.

Caroline

IT IS WHEN SHE is vacuuming that she notices it: a glint of silver underneath the bookshelf. At first, she wonders if it is a trick of the light but whatever it is keeps twinkling at her from the shadows.

Caroline turns the hoover off, the silence of it flooding her ears. She gets down on her hands and knees, stretches her arm out beneath the bookcase and taps her hand along the skirting board. The tips of her fingers graze against something cold and smooth. She eases the object out into the light and, even before she looks at it, she knows. It is the cavalryman. She holds it in her open palm, blinking. The red and blue of the uniform has faded. She scratches at a loose chip of paint on the figure's shoulder, watching a dot of pink lodge under her nail. The memory of a nine-year-old Max playing with the tin soldiers comes back to her, the force of it so acute that she closes her eyes, just for a second, just to believe it is still true and that nothing has changed. She can smell Max's hair, freshly washed by her in the bath with Timotei. She can see him squinting up at her, cheeks dimpled by his smile. There he is. Her son. The wholeness of him . . .

No, she thinks, no. Let it go.

She opens her eyes.

Let it go.

Caroline props the cavalryman on the bookshelf and leaves him there, standing sentry while she finishes cleaning the room. She averts her eyes from the doorframe where she knows, without looking, she will find the series of pencilled lines and dates, each one a horizontal marker for Max's yearly growth spurts. The last is from April 2002, when Max was 12. After that, he'd seemed too big to carry on doing it.

With the hoover switched back on, she doesn't hear Andrew come in and so it is only when he taps her on the shoulder that she realises he has been trying to get her attention.

'Sorry,' she says, brushing hair from her forehead with her arm. 'Didn't hear you.'

'No, don't worry.' Andrew stands a few centimetres from her, hands on his hips. 'All done?'

'Almost. I just want to pass a duster over it and then –'

He nods.

'The bags are ready to go,' he says.

She notices he is not looking at her directly.

'OK. Which charity shop were you thinking of taking them to?'

'I hadn't really thought . . . whichever one's closest, I suppose.'

She stares at the back of his neck, then pats his upper arm. She lets her hand rest there. It feels strange to be so awkward with each other but she knows the effort is worth it. Cleo, the bereavement counsellor they have been seeing, says that they have to focus on what they have, on the support they can give each other.

Andrew glances at her, then takes Caroline in his arms. They stand there, embracing, for several seconds.

'It's hard, I know,' he says.

She doesn't answer.

'We'll never forget him, Caro.'

She tenses. For a moment, she feels the old resentments returning: the fizz of anger, the bleak loneliness. Breathe, she thinks. Take a breath. Count to ten. Remember that he is grieving too. 'I know,' she says, finally. 'I know we won't.'

Time has passed, as it always does. The days have accumulated, the distance is greater. Other people would say she is getting better. She is not so sure. It is true that the numbness has gone, that she feels more connected with the world around her. But the sadness remains, overlain by confusion.

She cannot summon up large chunks of the recent past. Her mind has played a trick on her. The day with Derek Lester has disappeared: she has no memory of fainting, no recollection of collapsing by the Cenotaph. When Andrew tells her how strangely she acted, how obsessive she had become, she finds it curious, as though he is talking about someone else.

Glimpses of clarity will occasionally emerge from the mist. Yesterday, while she was brushing her teeth, she remembered with total precision the sensation of Andrew holding her in his arms on the train all the way back to Malvern. This morning, when she was getting the hoover out of the cupboard below the stairs, she remembered coming to the same cupboard to get the bucket and sponge on the day Elsa wet herself. She remembered how panicked she had felt and the same nausea gripped her again, the same knot of dread in her stomach. And then, of course, the thing that she tried never to remember came back to her, shrieking and vivid, and she had to stop herself, she had to get out with the hoover and close the cupboard door and turn to go upstairs.

Elsa's room stands empty now. The bed has been removed, the furniture rearranged. Caroline goes in there sometimes, to stand amidst the industrial-sized tubs of E45 and the half-used packets of incontinence nappies. There are castor marks on the carpet and a musty smell in the air that lingers, no matter how many times she leaves the windows open. She finds, oddly, that she misses her mother-in-law. Not so much the reality of her presence as the knowledge that there was someone else in the house. Now, the vacant room is another absence, another stillness where once there had been life.

But of course, Elsa is better off where she is. She is being cared for in an old people's home – one of the very best, Caroline keeps reminding herself. The brochure had been glossy and discreet, containing pictures of spacious grounds and chintzy armchairs that made it look more like a country house hotel than an institution for the elderly. Rosedale, it was called: one of those made-up names designed to imply a bygone pastoral idyll. The care, according to Andrew, was 'second to none' and Caroline was pleased about this. It made her feel better. As if, in the end, they had not failed her entirely.

That Elsa should go into a residential home was one of the first things Caroline and Andrew had decided when they came back from London. The day after the meeting with Lester, they had sat at opposite ends of the kitchen table and Andrew had told her things needed to change.

The cold outside was starting to bite. Andrew made a pot of coffee and slid a mug across the table. She took it, wrapping her hands around it gratefully.

'You have to let this go, Caro,' he said. 'These conspiracy theories – they're not helping you. They're not helping Max.' He stopped, then added more to himself than to her: 'Let it go. Please let it go.'

For a while, she couldn't answer. It got darker. Neither of them switched the lights on. Andrew waited.

Eventually, she spoke. 'I can't let him down.'

Andrew knew, without asking, who she was talking about.

'You're not.' He paused. 'You were a good mother.'

'I've never been good enough. For you or my parents or Elsa. Or Max.'

'Oh for Christ's sake, Caroline, that's enough. Enough!' He grabbed her hands in his. 'Don't you understand that I love you exactly as you are? That I always have? Don't you get it?' He gave a short, sharp stab of laughter, then released his grip. 'All of this –' he swept an arm in front of him – 'it's just self-pity. You need to wake up. I need you to wake up. I need *you*. I need you to come back to me.'

And she had, in a way. As the seasons had blurred and the weeks had passed, she had come back to him, more herself but not entirely the person she had once been. The grief, she knows, will never go. But she has discovered that you can learn to live with it, that you can still continue to exist, even when everything is shaded in the colour of loss.

Perhaps, she thinks now as she dusts the furniture in Max's bedroom, there will always be something in her that is lacking but, on the surface, a sort of harmony has been restored between them. This gives her, if not complete contentment, then at least a sense of security, a knowledge that she is loved. The old, cherished intimacy with Andrew might return some day. For now, she finds that she does not miss it.

She wipes the yellow duster across the chest of drawers. When she looks at the rag, it is covered in a fine grey webbing of dirt. Max's room hasn't been cleaned since he died, almost a year ago. She opens the top drawer to clean inside and notices a lumpy shape under the patterned lining. She lifts up the loosened corner of waxy paper and finds a small envelope, filled with pills. She is shocked by this, by the cunning it displays. It is one of her secret stashes of Xanax. She had forgotten it was here.

She is almost off the pills now, the self-administered dosage dwindling gradually while she readjusts to everyday life and waits for her frenetic emotions to burn themselves out, for the accusatory images of Derek Lester and Elsa and Max to diminish. Counselling has helped. It is the kind of thing she never would have had time for before but Andrew had insisted they needed it. They go every week, for an hour, to a bland breeze-blocked building in the centre of town. Their therapist is a woman called Cleo, with dyed red hair and a strident Glaswegian accent. She is fairly no-nonsense.

'Guys,' she said in their first session. 'You need to be honest with each other. Let's start with that, shall we? Let's just give it a go.'

And, for the first time she could remember, Caroline had tried to tell the truth about herself. Instead of being disappointed, Andrew had encouraged her. He seemed, if anything, to love her more for her failings. She felt as though the varnish she had spent so many years acquiring was being stripped back, layer by layer. She felt naked in her own vulnerability but, at the same time, there was intense, overwhelming relief that the struggle was over, that she no longer had to pretend.

Caroline takes the envelope and crumples it, stuffing it into her jeans pocket. She'll throw it away later, she thinks. She unplugs the hoover and gathers up the electrical cord. The carpet is lined with its indentations, like a freshly mown lawn. She goes to the door and rests her hand on the handle briefly, glancing back to check that everything is as it should be. Satisfied, Caroline carries the hoover back downstairs.

She leaves the tin soldier on the bookcase, looking outwards.

Caroline, Andrew

T HEY ARE SITTING AT a metal table in the forecourt of a small café, surrounded by the smell of melting cheese and coffee grounds. It is not yet warm enough to dispense with their coats but it feels good to be in the fresh air, breathing in the first fragrances of spring: the catkins and the crocuses, the turned-over soil, rich with promise.

She smiles across at Andrew, sipping her cappuccino but keeping her gaze on his, silently tracing the solidity and familiarity of his features. He leans forward, stroking the inside of her wrist, pushing up the leather of her watch strap as he does so.

'How are you feeling?'

'Fine,' she says. 'Good, actually.' The more she says it, the more she begins to believe it.

He nods; looks at his watch. 'Best get going.' She finishes off the coffee and scoops out the chocolate-flecked foam with her spoon.

He looks over his shoulder to get the attention of the waitress and then, just as she knows he will, he does a mime of signing a bill. He has always done this, ever since the first day they met. Knowing he will do this, she feels the smallest flicker of well-worn love.

They park on a sweep of gravel outside the home. It is a large red-brick building, a Victorian house with several single-storey extensions winding backwards and looping around a well-tended garden. She can hear the swish-click of sprinklers as she approaches. She presses the bell by the front door and is buzzed through. Inside, it smells of floors polished and meals cooked. She is led down a carpeted corridor by a young girl with a plump face and sensibly cut black hair. The girl introduces herself as Ashleigh and speaks with an Irish accent. She is wearing a casual pink uniform: polyester trousers that rustle as she walks and a loose V-neck. There is a plaster on her upper arm, decorated with illustrations of children's cartoon characters.

'You'll find she's a bit frail, so you will,' she says as she holds open a swing door with a small, padded hand. 'But she's still the same old Elsa.'

Ashleigh takes her to a bedroom situated at the end of a short corridor. There is no noise to indicate a physical presence but you can tell the room is occupied. The air seems weighted differently, stilted and heavy.

The blurred half-light of early evening is pooling across the carpet, a brown-black penumbra growing inch by inch. The door shuts, sliding into place with a click.

At first, the bed in the corner seems only to contain a loose tangle of sheets. As she gets closer, Caroline begins to make out the shape of her, she sees the thinness of her bones and the sallowness of her skin. She had forgotten how small Elsa was, how slight and insubstantial.

Elsa is lying flat, surrounded by a low metal bar on either side of the mattress. Her body is covered in a sheet and a neatly tucked-in blanket but her arms lie long and straight over the top. Her hands are curled upwards into fists, the veins in her wrists exposed. There is something sacrificial about her pose. She turns, slowly, to look at Caroline as she walks towards her but Elsa's face shows nothing. Her mouth gapes open, a blank hole. Her breathing makes no sound.

Ashleigh is busying herself with the bed, pushing the bars down and pressing what looks like a remote control so that the pillow end slides upwards into a reclining position. She helps Elsa sit up, all the time maintaining a constant stream of cheerful chatter.

Caroline draws up a chair and begins to speak, self-consciously aware of the other person in the room. 'Hello, Elsa. It's me. I mean, it's Caroline. I – I – wanted to see how you were . . .'

Elsa makes no movement.

Caroline starts to feel nervous. What is she doing here? Why did she ask Andrew to bring her?

'It's normal,' Ashleigh says, brushing down the blankets. 'It takes a while sometimes for things to come to her.' She pats Caroline on the shoulder and her hand smells of chemicals, of anti-bacterial hand-wash. 'I'll leave you to it.'

'Thank you.'

Ashleigh pads briskly to the door and turns back with her hand on the handle. 'I'll be just outside if you need me. Can I get you a cup of tea or a drink of water?'

Caroline shakes her head. Ashleigh smiles, then leaves.

She is unsure of what to do with herself. Her handbag is on her lap so she starts to fiddle with the strap of it because then, at least, her hands have something to do.

Elsa's eyes have closed. Her lashes are so fair that they have almost disappeared. She seems to be fading away at the edges, as though her physical appearance has lost all those small accents of definition that made her an individual, a person in her own right. Her hair is sparse and patches of her scalp, grey and shiny, are pressing through.

There is a beaker, a child's drinking cup, on her bedside table. Someone – Ashleigh, probably – has put a silver-framed photograph of Oliver there, angled towards the window so that the evening sunlight catches on its glass surface. It is a formal portrait: black and white with Oliver in a suit, holding a pipe in one hand. As Caroline sits there, waiting for some sign of what to do, a distant memory flashes before her, of Oliver in the drawing room in the house at Grantchester, patting down the tobacco in the bowl of his pipe, sucking on the stem with a popping sound as he lit it, and then shaking the match to rid it of the flame.

She had liked Oliver, even if she had never understood his deep love for Elsa. He had seemed so gentle, so forthcoming in comparison to his wife's coolness. If Oliver had lived, would Elsa have been different, more tender, perhaps? Would everything have happened quite the way it had?

'Elsa –' She tries, again, to rouse her mother-in-law, to glimpse some note of acknowledgement but there is none. Elsa shifts her head on the pillow. She is awake, thinks Caroline, she can hear what I'm saying.

In the car on the way to the nursing home, Andrew had told her not to expect too much. 'She's barely there most of the time,' he said, shifting gears as he slid into the fast lane of the motorway. 'You can't get much sense out of her.'

Caroline blinked.

'I just feel I need to see her again, I can't explain why.'

He looked at her out of the corner of his eye. 'Closure,' he said, putting on a faux American accent. 'Isn't that what the talk-shows recommend?'

Caroline laughed. 'Well, not exactly but . . .' She paused. 'I suppose there's an element of setting some demons to rest. I was always so scared of Elsa. Ridiculous, really.'

He didn't speak for a few minutes and Caroline thought he would let the comment pass without reply but then, just as he was indicating to turn off at the next junction, he said: 'No, I can understand that. She was pretty formidable.'

She took Andrew's hand in hers, lifting it to her lips and kissing the knuckles softly. 'Thank you.'

'What for?'

'For giving me another chance.'

Caroline's handbag slips to the floor with a thud. The noise causes Elsa to jolt awake, startled. She moans lightly.

'It's all right,' Caroline says. Automatically, she reaches out to calm her but then stops herself. Her hand stays there, suspended between the chair and the bed and Caroline realises she is frightened of touching Elsa, of what she might do.

The idea of what had happened seems to belong to a different time, to a different person, caught in a fog, as though she is standing on a beach, squinting far across the horizon, attempting to make out the shape of something on the other side of the ocean.

She exhales slowly, readying herself for what she needs to say. This, after all, was why she had insisted Andrew bring her here.

Elsa's eyes are fully open now, darting to and fro, taking in her surroundings. There is a yellow speck of dirt in her left tear duct. She twists her head to look at Caroline, the veins in her neck sticking out with the effort. But, still, in her features, there is no sense of recognition. Elsa's gaze is blank, unfocused but polite, as though preparing to welcome a stranger across the threshold.

'Elsa. It's Caroline,' she starts again. 'Your daughter-in-law. I'm Andrew's wife. Your son, Andrew. And I'm the mother of Max, your grandson.'

She hadn't been sure whether to mention Max but now it seems right. 'I know you loved Max a great deal, didn't you?' Elsa's face is static, her chest rising and falling in shallow dips.

'And he loved you, he really did. He loved your cakes,' she adds, trying to smile.

Her voice begins to break. She refuses to give into it. She forces herself to give a jerky laugh.

'And I was so jealous, wasn't I, Elsa? I was so jealous of your closeness because I – I – well, I suppose I wanted Max all to myself.'

Outside, there is the faint sound of a lawnmower starting up. The window is framed by ivy and the leaves tremble in the evening breeze, so that the shimmering light bounces rhythmically against the glass.

'I never felt good enough for you,' she says, more quietly. 'The truth is, Elsa, I never was.'

She remembers all those times she had felt slighted or maligned by Elsa's supercilious manner and casual put-downs. All those times she had done the wrong thing and had it pointed out to her with a raise of an eyebrow, a curve of the lip, a silence laden with meaning. But how much of it had been Elsa and how much of it had been Caroline? She isn't sure any more. She feels as though she has wasted a lifetime trying to live up to expectations that didn't exist outside her own head. Because what had been the point of it?

The lawnmower outside has stopped. A smell of fresh-cut grass lingers.

'Elsa, I came to say I'm sorry.' Caroline waits but still there is nothing but the rattle-whisper of Elsa's breaths catching lightly in her throat. 'I'm so desperately sorry.'

Cautiously, she puts her hand over Elsa's. The old woman's skin is papery to the touch. Caroline can feel the pitter-patter of her pulse at her wrist.

'Can you understand? I don't know what happened – I – I –.' How to find the words? To explain? 'Whatever I felt about you, however jealous I was, I should never, ever have done what I did. I should never have hit you.' She takes a paper tissue out of her handbag and starts kneading it with her fingers. Scraps of it scatter on to the floor like dust. 'I don't know what it was –'

Before she can go any further, there is a shout from further down the corridor. It fades out, replaced by the sound of murmured, pacifying voices.

At the noise, Elsa seems to wake. She turns to Caroline and stares at her with such concentration that her pupils shrivel to small black dots.

'Elsa?'

Elsa grunts and her eyes are wild.

'I'm sorry.'

Does she understand? Caroline has no way of knowing. She watches as Elsa slips back on to the slanted pillows, her hands flailing against the bedsheets. Her pupils dilate and then her face is clouded by an expression of panic. Her hands uncurl, the fingers scratching helplessly at the air. There is a sound coming from her, not a word exactly, but a disjointed series of noises like a baby's gurgle. She starts to twist her face from side to side, slowly at first and then more quickly so that Caroline can see she is shaking her head with as much force as she can muster.

And all at once, Caroline realises that she is saying no; that her response is refusal rather than forgiveness.

She is saying no.

She is shaking her head.

Caroline withdraws her hand. She has no idea what to do. Some part of her, some naive, arrogant part, had cautiously expected Elsa's understanding. Stupid, really.

And now, looking at this frail, grey old woman, all she wants to do is to get out of the room as quickly as possible.

She pushes the chair away and crosses the floor without

looking back. She opens the door and motions to Ashleigh, who is sitting at a desk halfway down the corridor. She is still aware, even in the grip of her agitation, that she must appear calm and in control.

Strains of classical music are coming from a room nearby. Caroline does not recognise the tune. It is something mournful and insistent, with throbbing strings. Elsa would know, she thinks automatically. Elsa would pride herself on knowing.

Caroline stays by the door, with her back against the wall, while Ashleigh goes to check on Elsa, stroking her hair gently, putting the bars back up around the bed and speaking to her in a lilting sing-song. 'You're grand, aren't you, pet? You're just grand.'

Elsa's face becomes peaceful. Her shoulders relax.

Ashleigh turns to Caroline with a kind smile. 'She's tired out with the excitement of your visit, so she is.' The string music is still audible, the orchestra swelling to a gradual crescendo.

'Are you sure you wouldn't like that cup of tea?' Ashleigh asks.

'No, thank you. I'm fine.'

The music stops, abruptly.

'Goodbye, Elsa,' she says. There is no movement from the bed. Elsa has closed her eyes again. In the dusky sunlight, her skin appears bled of colour.

Caroline slips into the corridor without another word. She walks quickly, tracing her way back across the beige carpets, until she reaches the entrance hallway. Andrew is sitting on a sofa, waiting for her. He is not aware of her presence and for a few seconds, she pauses, unobserved, to look at him. He is reading a newspaper, folded back on itself so that it is easier to hold. His fingernails are neatly cut, square and clean. His hair is almost entirely grey. He is thinner than he used to be and his jacket hangs loosely around his shoulders. He is concentrating on the paper, eyes moving across the printed words, brows pressing down, causing the corner of his eyes to crinkle. Just as he begins to turn the page, he looks up and sees her. Without thinking, he smiles and his face is suffused with the simple pleasure of her presence.

Inside, she feels a great wash of calm. She goes to him. He stands and puts his arm around her, squeezing her shoulder. She leans into his chest, pressing into him so that she can feel his warmth. Tears prick against her eyes.

'Let's go home,' he says.

'Yes,' she says. 'Let's.'

Elsa

S HE KNOWS THE WATER is closing in.

She senses the shadow of it creeping towards her, waves of it lapping over her skin, covering first her ankles, then her knees, her thighs, the small of her back, her neck, until her head is the only part of her that is not submerged.

She gasps, spitting and coughing, but with each inhalation, she takes in more liquid than air, so that her throat seems to become clogged with salt and bits of seaweed. She flicks her tongue from side to side, trying to unblock the airway, but it does no good. She can hear herself wheezing, the sound of it magnified by the echoing sea.

Out of the corner of her eye, she sees a shoal of fish.

They are coming for her: slippery, encroaching. There are thousands of them, each one a twisting sliver of black fin and tail.

She kicks her legs and splashes her arms hopelessly against the tide but the water is too strong, the tug of it too powerful, and after a while she realises she cannot fight it any more. Her arms slacken. Her legs turn woollen and waterlogged. She bows her head, the muscles in her neck loosening.

And then she goes: slowly at first, spiralling gently through the whirls and eddies, her hair untwisting in great clouds behind her. She feels herself filling up with liquid, taking the sea in through her nostrils, her throat, her lungs.

There is nothing more she can do. She surrenders herself to the tide. The panic recedes. The fish swim past. The shadow clears.

She hears voices, someone calling her name. 'Elsa, Elsa. Can you hear me, Elsa?' And then there is movement and a buzzing alarm and arms around her, poking and prodding and trying to wrest her free of the waves but they cannot get to her and still she falls, quicker now, weighed down by the saturated mass of her body. Falling, falling, falling.

She opens her eyes. She sees a shaft of sunlight turned turquoise by the refractions of the water. She feels the warmth of it on her face.

She smiles. She remembers a sunlit day from long ago.

She falls.

Not much longer now until she reaches the seabed.

Not much longer.

Acknowledgements

My agent, Jessica Woollard, for believing in what I write and for telling me so at precisely the right moment, even when on a different continent.

My editor, Helen Garnons-Williams, for her superlative insights and her uncanny ability to see what needs to be done.

The whole team at Bloomsbury, including Erica Jarnes, Laura Brooke, Audrey Cotterell, Anya Rosenberg and Cormac Kinsella – friends as well as colleagues. Also Lea Beresford and Kathy Belden at Bloomsbury USA.

Three books I found extremely helpful for background research: Juliet Nicolson's *The Great Silence: 1918–1920 Living in the Shadow of the Great War*, *Testament of Youth* by Vera Brittain and Paul Fussell's *The Great War and Modern Memory*.

My early – and most trusted – readers: my mother, Christine Day, Olivia Laing, Rebecca Spero, Edie Reilly, Melissa Boyes and Elaine Sturman.

Simon Oldfield and Tim Julian, kind and generous friends who allowed me to hole up in St Ives when I was struggling with the second draft.

Emma Reed Turrell and Kirrily de Polnay Jacobs for seeing me through.

My father, Tom, sister, Catherine, and niece, Tabitha.

Special thanks to Sean Rayment who helped me with key military details. Any faults are, of course, my own.

Finally, to Kamal Ahmed, who reads everything I write with honesty, love and unshakeable faith. I trust your judgement – even if you'll always be wrong about *Star Wars*.

A NOTE ON THE TYPE

The text of this book is set in Linotype Sabon, named after
the type founder, Jacques Sabon. It was designed by Jan
Tschichold and jointly developed by Linotype, Monotype and
Stempel, in response to a need for a typeface to be available
in identical form for mechanical hot metal composition and
hand composition using foundry type.

Tschichold based his design for Sabon roman on a font
engraved by Garamond, and Sabon italic on a font by
Granjon. It was first used in 1966 and has proved an
enduring modern classic.